QUEST FOR
MA'AT

Liminal Books

QUEST FOR MA'AT

Lisa Llamrei

This book is dedicated to my children:
Willow, Lorelei, Riley, Ayesha, and Earle
My life is richer for having you in it.

Tutankhaten, Year 2

(ca. 1332 BCE)

Ankhesenpaaten

Ay's feet stop in mid-pace and his head snaps around as I enter the long entrance to my reception room, passing by the guards stationed at the doors. My braided extensions, still streaming water, soak the linen of my dress. I tie my sash as I step to where he stands, moving over the blue floor tiles, and past the alternating bundles of papyrus and lotus flowers painted on the walls. I keep my voice level, careful to betray no disquiet at his unexpected presence here. "I am told there is a matter important enough to interrupt me in my bath chamber," I say.

Ay makes a sound in the back of his throat as he draws near. "There are a great many matters more important than your bath." He softens his stance a little, places a hand on my shoulder and leads me to sit in the concave seat of one of the wooden chairs. He moves another close to me, dragging the carved lion's-feet across the tiles, sits and strokes my cheek. I notice the webs of lines around his eyes have deepened. "Darling granddaughter," he starts.

I stiffen. Ay seldom acknowledges our relationship save to advance his own position. Never has he called me "darling."

"Last night, your mother, her royal highness, Neferneferuaten Nefertiti, passed into the Blessed West."

I look up at him, searching his face. For an instant, I believe Mother has gone to visit the temples on the West Bank. When at once I understand the full meaning of the statement, I am yet more confused. "That is not possible," I say.

1

He smiles, not a pleased smile, but a grim one. "Sadly, it is true. I have seen her myself."

"But ..." I cannot think, cannot draw a full breath. I feel for the ring on my finger, the one she recently gave my that had been hers. Gold, inscribed with the name of Sekhmet, the lion-goddess, and Mother's protector. Its absence alarms me, gives me the impression that it disappeared with her, until I remember I removed it before bathing. "Last night ... she is strong and healthy."

He shakes his head. "Life is nothing if not unpredictable. This you will learn in time."

I stare at him. Does he think I do not already know that? I, who have buried all five of my sisters and a father. And now must I also bury my mother? "I wish to see her."

"That would not be wise."

"I am your Queen. You will take me to see my mother." I do my best to sound imperious, as she would have done, but my voice quavers and I despise it.

"I only hope to spare you," he says. "It is not a pretty sight. It appears she was poisoned."

"Poisoned?" I repeat, for lack of any more intelligent response. I do not understand. Even now, I can see her at the feast last night. Her head was tilted to the side as she laughed at something her companion whispered in her ear. Her laugh was deep and throaty, and I knew from this that she would be leaving soon, and him soon after. The air was heavy with the scent of perfumes —frankincense, juniper and cardamom competing with the more cloying aromas of rose and lily. And there, close by her feet, on the floor in front of the dais where we sit, was the royal taster. A sample of every dish, every drink, passed through his lips before being offered to us.

This is always so, at every meal.

I shake my head. "It cannot be. We have tasters to prevent this very thing."

"The tasters and the cooks have all been rounded up," says Ay. "I promise you, whoever is responsible will confess and will reveal who is behind the plot. They will all be executed for treason." He clears his throat and glances down at the floor.

He is not telling all and I fear I know what he is leaving out. My belly quivers. "I ate from the same platter as Mother, as did Tutankhaten, and you yourself. We all drank from the same jugs. Had the poison come from the banquet, surely, we would all have died." Again, the throat clearing. "I assure you; we are leaving no stone unturned to discover the guilty party."

I must will my hands not to shake. "Am I to be a target?"

He put a hand on mine. "I assure you; we will find those responsible before they strike again."

I do not find myself assured. I need to see her and am about to see her when I am struck by an image of Mother, her body contorted with pain, covered in her own vomit and excrement. Fear outweighs my love for her, and it shames me. Such a reaction is unbecoming of the Great Royal Wife and ...? With Mother gone, am I now Regent as well? Tutankhaten is still too young to rule, but having been born fourteen annual inundations ago, I am near enough to full adulthood. I scrutinize Ay's face. Does he have a different Regent in mind? Perhaps even himself? What should happen to our beautiful land of Kemet in the hands of an unscrupulous Regent? Realization dawns. I am the only one who may be trusted to ensure the transition of power is smooth. It is I who must steer Kemet back to Ma'at, back to divine order.

"Have you told Tutankhaten?" I ask.

Ay squeezes my hand. "I thought it would be best for it to come from you."

I fail to stop my look of dismay before he notices.

"You are his wife."

A woman should be drying the tears of a son, not those of a husband. I focus on my mother arranging my marriage to a child. If I can find reason to hate her, perhaps I will not feel her loss. But I nod and rise. "I shall collect myself," I say, gesturing to my state of semi-undress, "and seek him out in his chambers."

"He is presently in the courtyard with Nebetah," says Ay.

With Nebetah. His mother. I supress a flash of resentment for Tutankhaten for still having a mother.

Tutankhaten

I'm lifting my game piece to block Mother's when she glances over my shoulder. "We are about to be interrupted."

I turn my head. Ankhesenpaaten stands by one of the lotus bud columns on the portico. When she spies me watching, she walks toward me with purpose, skirting the pond ringed with papyrus, her shoulders square, and her face hard, no doubt on her way to reprimand me for some misstep. "Let's keep playing," I say and turn back to Mother, hoping to delay the confrontation. "I'm going to win in another few moves."

Mother's eyebrows shoot up. "Is that so?"

"You don't have to let me win," I say.

She winks at me. "I never 'let' you win."

"Yes, you do. Everyone does." I sag a little.

"That may well be true about some things, but not about Senet. No one has deliberately lost to you at Senet since your seventh inundation. Not even Nefertiti."

I sit back a little. I hadn't considered that possibility. But Ankhesenpaaten arrives at my spot under the sycamores before I can say anything more. She inclines her head, first to me and then to Mother, says, "in peace," and stands by the table. She wrings her hands in front of her, then seems to remember herself and stops. She's upset about something, and I wish she'd just say it so Mother and I can get back to our game.

"I regret to inform you both that," she takes a deep breath and looks toward the leafy canopy above, "her royal highness, Neferneferuaten Nefertiti was called to the West in the night." It comes out in a rush, and she does not look directly at us until it is over.

"No," whispers Mother.

I look from one to the other. The air around me feels like it's disappearing. "Surely, you are mistaken, dearest sister," I say.

Mother relaxes a little and nods. "Yes, that must be it. You mustn't listen to the gossip in the Women's Quarters."

"It is Ay himself who has told me." Ankhesenpaaten looks directly into my eyes.

Mother's eyes widen and her hands shake.

"It isn't true, is it, Mother?" I ask, but I know it is. Nefertiti is dead. My protector is dead, and Mother is afraid. Her fear alarms me, reminds me of my position. King in name, yet dependent on the adults around me. Nefertiti guarded my interests. Who will do so now? My eyes burn and I swipe at them with the back of my hand. At once, Mother is by my side, pulling me into her arms. I sob into her chest. Her own tears fall across my scalp, and snake down the side of my head and behind my ears.

Through the fog of tears, I see Ankhesenpaaten looking to the side, nostrils flaring, and jaw clenched. I push away from Mother, wipe my nose on my arm, and my eyes with the heels of my hands. Crying is behavior unbecoming of a king. Nefertiti herself would have said so and I wait for Ankhesenpaaten to scold me the way her mother would have and then throw an arm around my shoulders and tell me, in a voice too low to be overheard, that she was there to share my sorrows in private, should I have need. But my wife does not do this. Instead, she jerks her head toward the portico, where Ay is waiting with his guards.

I take up my walking stick and shuffle toward the palace. We enter the corridor I call The River, for its painted murals of ducks in the marshes and blue floor tiles. We do not stop. As Ay and Ankhesenpaaten fall into step on either side of me, Mother moves to the back.

"I must escort you both back to your chambers, where you will prepare to address the palace," says Ay. "The people will need reassurance that the passing of the Regent will not upset the divine order that is Ma'at. You will tell them, of course, that all worship of the Aten will be abolished and the worship of Amun as supreme god will be restored. You will stress that any ideas put forth by Her Royal Highness before her death about raising Ptah and Sekhmet to supreme status will not be implemented."

I feel a pang at the thought of banishing the Aten. Until little more than a year ago, he was the only god I knew. Yet, his destruction is a necessary step on the road back to Ma'at, one Nefertiti herself likely would have taken in time. The other gods are all the same to me – strangers I have barely begun to know. But I do know it was concern over the power wielded by Amun's priesthood that prompted my father's break with Kemet's traditional gods, and Nefertiti's decision to choose another as supreme god. Restoring Amun to his former glory is not prudent.

I stop, but Ay and Ankhesenpaaten continue for a few steps before they notice. They both back up so they may stay in line with me. Ay looks down into my eyes. His are dark and brittle as obsidian. His mouth is a thin, straight line. I remember that last night, shortly after Nefertiti left the feast, Ay followed her. Should I fail to do Ay's bidding, will he one day follow me to my chambers? I must grip my walking stick tightly to keep it from rattling against the tiles. Perhaps I am seeing that which is not there. Killing the most powerful woman in Kemet in her own palace would be no small feat. Besides, she was his daughter. Though, her final act was to undermine the very priesthood of Amun that is Ay's strongest ally, whom he now insists I reinstate. I dare not defy him openly, though would be wise to mitigate Ay's influence. I look straight ahead and continue to my chambers.

Tutankhamun, Year 3

(ca. 1331 BCE)

Ankhesenamun

The good ruler, performing benefactions for his father, Amun, and all the gods, for he has made what was ruined to endure as a monument for the ages of eternity and he has expelled deceit throughout the Two Lands and justice was set up so that it might make lying to be an abomination of the land, as in its first time. Now when his majesty appeared as King, the temples of the gods and goddesses from Elephantine down to the marshes of the Delta had fallen into neglect. Their shrines had become desolate, had become mounds overgrown with weeds. Their sanctuaries were as if they had never been. Their halls were a footpath. The land was in chaos and the gods turned their backs upon this land.

These words sit heavy in my chest and yet, there is nothing I can do to erase them. I read the words on the stela erected in Ipet-Iset, the great Temple to Amun across the river from Waset, proclaiming to the gods that Tutankhamun is the one to restore to them their rightful places. That our father persecuted all gods apart from the Aten, and most especially Amun, is not in question. But the great temple with its giant, brightly painted pylons, appears less like a footpath than any sight I have ever seen, with not a weed in sight. I wonder how, if the destruction were so total, Amun's greatest stronghold managed to escape unscathed. But then I supposed accuracy must be secondary to perception.

I grip the handle of the sistrum in my hand, watching the light catch on the jingles hanging from the crossbars. I have a role, and I will play it.

In order to be secure on the throne of Kemet, we must be seen to be its saviors. The first victims of this policy were our names – the despised name of Aten being replaced by that of Amun. And so, I will not only to refer to my husband as Tutankhamun, but I am to forget he ever had any other name.

At the time of my birth, my father had not yet banned all the other gods – the false gods he would have said. Yet, my childhood carries no memory of any god save Aten. His grand temple lay open so that we might feel the warmth of his rays on our skin as we worshipped him. Each morning, we would sing:

But when day breaks you are risen in the horizon,
And you shine as the Aten in the daytime.
When you dispel darkness, and you give forth your rays
The two lands are in festival,
Alert and standing on their feet,
Now that you have raised them up.

Now, we royals must act as priests of a god we do not know and were raised to mistrust, one who skulks about in dark corners, seen by none but the high priest except at times of festival. The King himself is permitted to look upon the face of Amun only moments before the multitudes.

I shake the tinkling sistrum in my hand, wet my lips and repeat the words of Parannefer, Amun's new high priest, lately chosen by Ay.

Thou findest him who transgresses against thee;
Woe to him who assails thee!
The city endures;
But he who assails thee fails.
Fie upon him who transgresses against thee in every land ...

I suppress a shiver, lest Parannefer perceive my disquiet. I cannot but feel Amun's wrath directed at me, for no matter my words and actions, in my heart I cannot love one so remote as he. Are these myriad gods, in their dark temples, all alike in their detachment and their thirst for vengeance? The thought fills me with dread until I realize that would simplify things immensely. I would memorize one set of prayers, switching the names as appropriate. Perhaps there is only one god after all, as my father said. I will not voice this thought out loud, for I am not certain whether it might be blasphemous, even for the Queen.

After practice is over, Parannefer calls me aside. "You learn quickly, Highness."

"You flatter me."

"Not at all. Your mother taught you well," says Parannefer. "She was a woman of great strength and intelligence. I greatly admired her, in spite of our … philosophical differences."

I nod my thanks, though I knew his admiration to be false.

"I also wish to thank you for the appointment," he says, bowing. "You will not regret your choice."

I do not say that I had no part in the choice, though I suspect he knows. This may even be intended as an oblique reminder of my own lack of power.

"At last, the priesthood of Amun and the royal house are reunited in strength," he continues. "May they never be separated again. Should you require anything at all, please know I am at your service, and I do hope the reverse is true as well."

There it is. In my inquiries into Parennefer, I discovered his immense land holdings, with a correspondingly large income. He could, at a whim, fund necessary works of the monarchy. Or withhold funding if he does not receive ever greater power in return.

I keep my face blank. Kemet, and its throne, is now back at the mercy of the Amun priests. The very same situation my father hated and fought against. I admit that is a point in its favor. However paranoid my father may have been, he was perhaps justified in his fear that the priests of Amun meant to wrest control of Kemet away from its rightful rulers. I utter words I hope are sufficiently non-committal. "May we all walk the way of Ma'at, ever keeping Kemet from the forces of chaos."

Tutankhamun

I lean on Ankhesenamun as we enter the banquet hall, and she takes much of my weight. I leave my walking stick behind for such functions because I am told a king must be strong and beautiful and perfect, free from any infirmity. But no one is fooled into thinking I am any of those things because Ankhesenamun must match her pace to mine, and as much as I hold on to her, there is no disguising the lurch in my step.

At our appearance, a group of elegant ladies and gentlemen, redolent with the scents of frankincense, cinnamon and rose, bow to us, and clear the aisle. Among them I recognize ladies of Ankhesenamun's retinue: Meryetre, with a spark of mischief in her eyes belying the solemnity of her expression, with Tuya beside her, her stout figure emanating good humor. There is a third one, younger, tall, and slender as a reed. Ast, I believe her name is. Even while bowing, Ast's eyes never leave mine. I am fascinated by the green and gold flecks in her deep brown irises.

A double row of red-painted palm-leaf columns draws the eye, and our steps, toward the royal dais at the end of the grand room. Halfway there, Ankhesenpaaten no, Ankhesenamun stops and I follow her gaze. Ay is seated at a table on the dais, but he does not have the place of honor next to the King. That has been granted instead to Horemheb, an army general, a commoner rising through the ranks much as Ay himself did in his youth. The two men do not acknowledge each other. I suppress a smile.

Ankhesenamun resumes our walk. "Is this your doing?"

I nod.

"Ay will not be pleased. This will be seen as a sign of his falling out of favor."

"If he were out of favor, he would not be seated with us at all," I say.

"Take care," says Ankhesenamun. "Ay can be a formidable enemy."

I hesitate for half a step, disturbed that she should question me, and perhaps more disturbed that she is right. "I am aware of that."

We reach the dais and I step up, leaning on Ankhesenamun's shoulder as I do so. I nod to Ay and to his wife, Tey. Although I know I shouldn't, when I greet Horemheb, I clap him on the shoulder as I nod to his wife, Amenia.

Our position above the crowd allows us a view of the murals around the walls – scenes of people feasting, musicians playing, dancers performing – a reflection of the live banquet itself, flickering in the lamp light. Once Ankhesenamun and I are seated, the meal can begin. A line of serving girls coils through and around the columns, their oiled skin shining in the rushlights, their breasts swaying with the rhythm of their steps.

Once past the tasters, they offer their delicacies first to me. Pomegranates, dates, cucumbers – all manner of fruits of the Black Land. Reaching for a honeyed fig, the girl holding the platter catches my eye. She looks down quickly, likely hoping I did not notice, for such boldness could be grounds for losing her position. I follow her eyes down. A single drop of honey leaves a trail down one breast, coming to rest in the dark areola of her nipple. A sudden desire to catch that drop with my tongue overwhelms me.

An abrupt sensation below my waist breaks the spell. I drop my eyes, nod my thanks and gesture for her to move on. When she turns to leave, the roundness of her buttocks does nothing to relieve my current predicament.

"Take a bite, Highness," whispers Horemheb.

I lean backward and my head snaps around to look at him.

He nods to indicate the fig, now fallen to the table before me. "Take a bite and concentrate on chewing." He smiles and his eyes twinkle.

I do as he suggests and find it helps somewhat.

Ankhesenamun is staring at me. I try to ignore her by studying the remainder of the fig, but she leans in and whispers, "She will wait in your chamber for you, if you tell her to."

My face feels hot as I turn to her. "She wouldn't want to do that."

Ankhesenamun smiles. "You are King, of course she wants you. Did you not notice her dabbing herself with honey and deliberately drawing your eyes to it?" She studies me a moment. "No, of course you did not."

My face is now burning. I touch my face, and my fingers brush the hair of my sidelock. Most boys would still wear it for a few years yet, but as King I should have shorn it by now.

"I did not expect you to be ready to bed a woman so soon," she says. "That being the case, you must start visiting my chamber so I may give you sons."

My mouth falls open and I gape at her. Unbidden, I imagine the linen of her dress falling away, revealing full curves of her breasts and, farther down, the dark triangle between her thighs. I grip the edges of my table and concentrate to prevent my body from disgracing me in such a way that would be obvious once I stood to leave. When I find my voice, it is thin and high, like a girl's. "I want the serving girl in my chamber."

Ankhesenamun relaxes. I think she is relieved.

"I will make the request. It would be unseemly for you to do so." She summons a servant to deliver the message. Then she turns to me and whispers, "Do you not desire to bed me?"

I gape at her, then quickly close my mouth, ashamed of my obvious reaction. I look away, giving only a cursory glance back. "I think you do not desire it," I say.

"What I desire is irrelevant," she says. "I must do my duty as Queen."

I suspected it, but a suspicion is different than a knowing. Ankhesenamun does not wish to be married to me. My appetite, for both dinner and bedding, shrivels, as does a certain unruly bodily organ. I decide to tell the serving girl not to come after all.

I am about to summon a messenger when Ay crouches by my shoulder. "We must talk, Highness." His eyes shift sideways to where Horemheb is sitting on my other side. "There are certain policy matters that must be addressed."

"Of course," I say. "We shall speak in the morning, after audience."

"It would be best to speak before then."

"In the morning before audience. Will that suit?"

"I'm afraid not, Highness. It is most urgent," says Ay.

Now I understand his meaning. He is not concerned about policy, only about the meaning of Horemheb's presence by my side tonight. I shake my head. "I will not leave in the middle of my own banquet."

He clenches his jaw but says nothing more. He can hardly reprimand the King in a room full of his subjects. I hold his gaze until he breaks eye contact and returns to his own table.

As usual, the banquet is long and dull. Once the food has been served, musicians pick up harps and drums, flutes and clappers. Troupes of dancing girls and acrobats, wearing jewelry and little else, undulate to the rhythms. I force myself to eat and I applaud at the appropriate times, but excuse myself at the earliest possible moment, encouraging all the guests to enjoy themselves in my absence.

Ankhesenamun moves to come with me, but Ay jumps to my side, helping me down from the back side of the dais and allowing me to lean on him as I would on Ankhesenamun.

"You must be more prudent in choosing your companions," says Ay once we are out of the banquet hall and entering my outer chamber.

"If you are referring to Horemheb, I would not describe him as a 'companion'," I say. "He is more of an advisor, as you are."

He sniffs. "Horemheb is not to be trusted. He reaches for whatever power he can grab. He is not concerned with the glory of Kemet, nor of its King."

I think Horemheb is not the only one for whom this is so, but I keep my own counsel. "That does not mean his advice is not valuable."

"Perhaps not," he says, "but it does mean you must always consider who benefits from the advice he gives."

That is true of any advice given by anyone. "Is it not you who told me of Horemheb's skill on the battlefield?"

"Kemet boasts any number of capable soldiers," he says. "Horemheb is far from the greatest."

"I do not refer to his martial skills. That I may see for myself on the training grounds, and while Horemheb is not the greatest, I would not say he is so very far from it. However," I say, "it is his expertise at battle strategy I find most valuable."

"It is valuable when one is at war," says Ay. "There is precious little use for it here at court." His eyes flicker off to the side, which tells me he does not believe it even as he says it.

I nod. "Perhaps not." I lean a hand on the door to my bed chamber.

Ay performs a stiff bow and leaves me. The guards station themselves on either side of my door, and one opens it for me. I walk through my reception room and enter my bedchamber. There is movement in my bed, and I am about to call for the guard, when a figure sits up, half-smiling.

It is the serving girl. I forgot to rescind her order, and so she is waiting for me. I think about asking her to leave, but her cheeks are flushed, and she wriggles her hips.

Ankhesenamun

I slacken the reins, allowing the horses to run. The floor of the chariot vibrates through my feet as the wheels rattle over the ground. As I complete one circuit after another around the lake, I alternately view the river, now much receded from the high flood of last season and sparkling between the palace buildings and the sprawling edifice of our palace, and the vast Red Lands.

Ast and Henutmire ride in a single chariot behind me. Try though they might, they cannot overtake me. I pretend it is because I am the superior driver and not because their chariot carries twice the weight of my own. I face into the wind and revel the feel of it in my closely cropped hair, for a short while freed of crowns and wigs and extensions.

Passing through the stable yard, I lead the horses closer to the fence, take the reins in one hand and hold the other out to clap those of Tuya and Meryetre as I thunder past. After too few such laps, I spy a wiry figure entering the stable yard.

Ay.

He stands ramrod-straight, watching me. I try to ignore him, but the ride has been spoiled.

As soon as I light from the chariot, Tuya and Meryetre unhitch it. Meryetre tells a bawdy joke about a well-endowed peasant and his donkey. Tuya begins to laugh, but at a glance behind my shoulder, lowers her eyes and falls silent.

I turn to see Ay approaching. "I would speak with you alone," he says.

I instruct my ladies to return the chariot and I lead the horses into the stable. Ast dismounts from her chariot and offers a hand to Henutmire. As Henutmire steps down, I notice Ay admiring her bared calf, his eyes wandering up to the curve of her hip, her bosom. She blushes and averts her gaze.

I throw my ladies a smile by way of apology for the curtailed outing., and for my grandfather's unwelcome attention.

Ay follows me in, hands behind his back. "You care for the animals yourself. Excellent."

I tie the horses to posts at opposite ends of the aisle in the stable. "As my mother taught me."

"As I taught her. Your mother was an exceptional driver, thanks to my tutelage."

I do not think he is speaking only of chariots, having been Mother's closest advisor as far back as I can remember.

"I am glad to have caught you outside of the palace," he says.

Ah. I wonder at Nebetah's sudden attack of chills and fever that prevented her accompanying me this day. Did Ay prevail upon her to remain in the palace? He would simply need to phrase the request as a wish to discuss urgent, yet private, matters. The King's mother is, perhaps, too quick to acquiesce at times.

Ay starts brushing one horse. I brush the other. He speaks to the guards, asking them to wait outside the door.

"I am an old man," says Ay when they are gone.

"You have lived through a great many inundations," I say, "but you are yet strong and healthy."

He nods. "True, true. But we cannot predict when the gods will take us. I may have many years left, or I may not wake up tomorrow. When it is my time, I must go to the Field of Reeds knowing that Kemet is prosperous and stable once again.

"Kemet is already stable, and prosperity will soon return to us," I say.

"You are naïve. That is why I must be blunt, now that we are away from the palace, where the very walls can overhear." He stops brushing and places one hand against a post. "The King is nothing more than a crippled boy, weak both in body and mind. It is most unfortunate for Kemet that he is the only remaining male with a claim to the throne. Believe me, had there been any other choice, he would not be sitting on the Horus throne now."

"You are mistaken about Tutankhamun. He is not weak in mind; he is merely young. He can be taught. I believe he will be a strong King when he becomes a man."

Ay shakes his head. "The most dangerous part of your father's legacy is the ignorance of his children. The King's twisted body shows the clear disfavor of the gods. His being on the throne is an insult to Ma'at. See how he shows favor to that general Horemheb. The man makes no attempt to hide his ambition for the throne and the King is the only one who fails to see it."

I look down to avoid his eyes. "Some say the same about you."

"I am an old man," he says. "I am past ambition for myself. What I am offering you is the chance to be more than simply the power behind the throne, but to eventually take the throne for yourself, but instead you refuse power in favor of propping up the weak. You are just like your mother in that regard."

I stop my work, stunned. My mother was co-Regent for my father, and Regent for Tutankhamun when he was first crowned. I didn't know she deliberately declined the leadership role for herself. "It is an honor to be told I am like her."

"Nefertiti was truly unique and special, with a beauty and a mind that could only have been gifts from the gods. You have inherited neither. In fact, you bear a rather unfortunate resemblance to your father, which will do you no favors either with the people of Kemet or with the gods. You're no quick wit, either, but with proper instruction you may manage to keep Kemet from descending further into chaos until the next strong king arrives." He points a finger at me. "If you're smart, that king will be your son and he will be born soon."

The brushing completed to at least minimum standards, I lead the horses back to their stalls to escape that finger and those eyes.

"I know the King has bedded a serving girl." His voice is softer now. "Have you visited his bed chamber yet?"

I start. "I was not aware this was common knowledge."

He shakes his head. "To rule successfully, you must cultivate a network of informers. Did your mother teach you nothing about statecraft? Must I lay the foundation myself?"

I do have informers. I simply did not realize Ay's were equally vigilant. When I heard the girl was boasting, I paid her well to remain silent and sent guards to watch her movements. Should she find herself with child, it would be prudent to cast doubt over its parentage. I approach Ay, intending to head for the door, and the path back to the palace.

He steps in front of me. "The King should have been introduced to manhood by his Great Royal Wife, by you," says Ay, "not some household slave."

I grit my teeth. "I cannot dictate what the King may or may not do with whom in his own bed chamber."

"Never dictate. Persuade. Let him think it's his idea. Did you never watch how your mother controlled your father?"

"She did not ..." my voice is louder, harder, than I intend. I must learn to control my temper. I must always project certainty and control. Mother never explicitly stated this, but she lived it, in how she dealt with her subjects and in how she raised her children. I did not think she was overly fond of any of us until my elder sister died in childbirth. That night, Mother's howls of anguish filled the palace. With each child buried, she howled a little less, either growing inured to the shock or more adept at concealing her grief. I was never sure which it was, until the night my father died, when Mother staggered from her own sick bed to throw herself between him and me. From what I saw, Mother controlled very little.

I take a deep breath. "I rarely saw my father outside of official functions."

"The state of your education is appalling," he says. "Nevertheless, there is one duty you absolutely must succeed at. You must give the King a son, preferably many sons. If your mother had done that instead of bearing girl after girl, Kemet wouldn't be in half the disarray it is now."

I look away. If Mother had succeeded in giving him sons, Father would not have taken his daughters, one after another, to his bed.

Ay Continues. "If he is ready for a serving girl, he is ready for you. You will go to him tonight." He turns and leaves.

I lean against a post and close my eyes. But I cannot block out the sight of my father, lurching into my chambers, stinking of poppy.

Tutankhamun

Entering my bed chamber, I stop short. A figure is sitting on my bed, one knee crossed over the other, bare feet delicately pointed at the floor. At first, I think it is the servant girl back again and my palms grow wet, making it difficult to keep a firm grip on my walking stick. I stop halfway down the long corridor leading to the raised platform, on which rests my bed and the servant girl. I think of calling the guard but then realize how foolish that would appear. Just then, the young woman raises her head. It is Ankhesenamun. She is wearing her Kushite-style wig, with rows of plaits framing her face. Her eyes are lined with kohl and dusted with malachite and gold. She's wearing a robe of linen so fine it hides nothing. My walking stick clatters as it hit the rosette floor tiles. I forgot I was holding it.

I bend to retrieve the walking stick and reach for the wall, so I don't topple. Ankhesenamun rises, steps down from the platform, picks up the stick and holds it out to me.

I straighten and accept the stick. "Sorry. I didn't expect you to be here." I don't want to meet her eyes, but when I look down, I'm confronted by her dark nipples underneath the gauzy fabric. So, I concentrate on her shoulder, which is just below my eye level. This close, the scent of rosemary oil from her hair mingles with frankincense and cardamom in her perfume.

"The serving girl from the other night has been boasting of your prowess," says Ankhesenamun. "As your wife, it is only right that I experience this for myself."

The shock of her words brings my head up to face her and I see she is also avoiding my eyes. "Is she really saying such a thing?" I ask.

Ankhesenamun nods.

I feel the burn of shame. I am, in part, relieved the girl did not tell the truth, but she has now doubled my dishonor by causing my wife to think me capable of more than I am.

Ankhesenamun moves to the bed platform. She slips first one shoulder, then the next, out of her robe and lets it fall to the floor.

My limbs turn rigid. I feel like I may topple over but somehow manage the few steps to the bed. Ankhesenamun slips a hand behind my belt and under my kilt, and I try not to tremble. She throws aside the belt and unknots my kilt, tossing it to the floor. Her face falls and her body goes limp.

She sits on the bed, looks up at me and bites her lip. "If you don't want to ..."

"I do!"

She takes in a breath and my face burns. I want to tell her I dream about it at night and think about it most of the day. During my lessons, during archery practice, in the audience chamber. Whenever a halfway attractive woman passes, my swollen member follows her like a dowsing rod and I imagine her spread out before me. But when met with reality, my body cooperates about as well as it does with every other thing I try compelling it to do.

I lean my walking stick against the wall and sit beside her. She presses her mouth to mine. It's warm and she tastes faintly of honey and cinnamon. I return the pressure and feel her lips quivering. I touch her breast, but I cannot stop my hand from shaking, so I remove it.

Ankhesenamun grabs me around the waist, leans back on the bed and pulls me on top of her. Her nipples thrust themselves against my chest and her body heat flushes my skin. I should be out of my mind right now, but no matter how my mind wishes to take her, my body refuses to heed my command. For her part, contradicting her decisive action, Ankhesenamun's body remains stiff and unyielding, which does nothing to help my current predicament. She soon notices, shoves me aside and sits up, leaning against the gilded footboard.

"You would rather have the serving girl," she says, her voice full of hurt and contempt.

I sit up and press my back to the wall. "I don't want the serving girl." For a few moments, I say nothing further, and then I take a deep breath. "I was not able to function for her, either."

Ankhesenamun turns to look at me, eyebrows raised.

"I thought I could," I say. "Everything was happening nicely, and then it was done before it even got started." I brush away a tear, hoping she does not notice.

"Oh," says Ankhesenamun, looking vaguely confused.

"I mean it was all over her belly, dripping down onto her thigh." I make a vague hand motion.

"Oh," says Ankhesenamun again as understanding dawns. She presses a hand to her mouth, but not before I see a smirk. Her sides are shaking. I turn away.

"I'm sorry," she says when she is able to speak. "I am not laughing at you."

She is lying. "The girl expressed her discontent and left," I say.

"She was angry with you?"

I turn back to face her. "She did not expressly say so. She wouldn't dare. She simply glared at me, wiped herself on my sheets and stomped out."

"She is common and not worth your anguish." Ankhesenamun touches my knee. "I do not care if you soil the sheets. If you do, I will simply have that girl assigned to washing our linens."

Though it is Ankhesenamun's intent to instill confidence, I find that thought even more humiliating than the original event. I shudder.

Ankhesenamun withdraws her hand. "If you prefer, we can just talk and in the morning, I will yawn and complain how you kept me awake most of the night with your demands and make everyone in the Women's Quarters jealous."

I smile. "That will not be necessary."

Ankhesenamun relaxes. She pulls herself up against the wall next to me.

"I think you are relieved I cannot bed you tonight."

"Not at all," she says, looking at her hands in her lap.

She is lying again. "Are you afraid to bed a man?"

She doesn't look up. "Of course not. Why should I be afraid of such a thing?"

"Because our father forced you to."

Her head snaps up. Her mouth opens and she seems about to protest but stops. She takes a deep breath. "You were so young. I did not realize you even knew." Her voice is a whisper.

"The one advantage to being thought simple is that people talk in front of you, as if you are part of the furniture." For most of my life, I was thought to be simple. Nefertiti was the first, apart from my mother, to treat me as an intelligent person, but until I was crowned King, few people followed her example. "All of the ladies in the Women's Quarters spoke of it, how they must hide your womanhood so Father wouldn't try and make you give him an heir like he did to our older sisters."

Ankhesenamun stares at me.

"The ladies were afraid you would die from it, like Meketaten did."

Tears are now rolling down her cheeks and I wish I didn't mention our sister. "I was still living in the Women's Quarters the night Father staggered in, intoxicated with poppy, insisting on taking you for a wife right then and there."

Ankhesenamun wipes her eyes with her palms, leaving streaks of black and green across her cheeks. She is quiet for so long I start to think she may never speak again. I am unsure of whether I should hold her or tell her she may go back to her quarters. Before I can decide she heaves a sigh.

"He did not force me," she says. She studies my face, possibly deciding if she should continue. "He tried. He pinned me to the bed and pressed himself against me. He thrust a hand between my thighs, trying to prise them apart. He spoke in my ear, sweet promises that turned to threats when I refused to yield. He slurred his words. I struggled, but he was large, and I was so small." She pauses.

"How did you escape?" I ask.

"The poppy finally had its effect," She says. "He slowed down and then went limp. I managed to lift him enough to crawl out from under him. I cowered in a corner, afraid to stay and afraid to leave, until Mother came, found me clean robes and sent me out of harm's way."

We are both silent. He was my father, and he was the King, the representative of his god. A god in his own right. I should not have such thoughts about him, but then he should not have defied Ma'at by harming his children in such a fashion. "I was not sorry when he did not wake up," I say.

Ankhesenamun's response is barely audible. "Neither was I."

Ankhesenamun

The Kushite ambassador walks backward out of the throne room into the audience hall, bent at the waist. I take the opportunity to study the top of his head. The man has adopted the Kemetian style of dress and wears his hair in the current popular style, which is in origin Kushite. Yet it is different on him – the hair hangs in ropes, not plaits and according to my lady Ast, who boasts of having reason to know, it is not a wig. Two ostriches – the ambassador's gift to the King – are led back down the pillared hall, to be sent to the royal menagerie but not before leaving malodorous gifts of their own across the images of bound captives painted on the floor tiles. Servants rush in to clean up.

I am seated on a throne next to Ay hearing the entreaties of our subjects. It is part of my education.

The next petitioner, a messenger of the Naharin, prostrates himself on the floor in front of Ay. This discomforts me – Ay's rank does not merit prostration, yet he offers no correction.

"Great King," says the messenger, rising to his knees.

I raise my eyebrows at this, but the messenger continues and, again, Ay offers no correction.

"I come from Artatama, the new King of the Naharin…"

I hold up a hand, signalling for him to be quiet. I lean close to Ay and speak softly into his ear. "He must be told not the give the obeisance due to the King to another."

Ay's look hardens. He is reminding me that I am supposed to observe, not participate, but I cannot allow such a lapse go unchallenged. I look back at him.

Ay speaks into my ear. "It would not do for the Naharin to think Kemet is governed by a simple boy. Let them fear our strength."

"Naharin is our ally," I say.

"You have much to learn," says Ay, turning back to the messenger and gesturing for him to speak now.

The messenger swallows, evidently unsure of what just passed between us. His long hair and beard are oiled and curled, every ringlet in place. He wears a woolen tunic covered in complex patterns. "I come from the great Artatama, King of Naharin, your loyal vassal," says the messenger. "He beseeches your Highness to send us gold statues, for Kemet is awash in gold."

Ay nods. "You must tell the great Artatama that Kemet values his friendship greatly. We will send a thousand statues.

How can this be? Ay already told the Kushite ambassador he will ease the quota of gold he must send to the King. How will we provide a thousand statues when we will be receiving less gold?

As the messenger takes his leave, I lower my voice. "How are we to fulfil both requests? One to lower tributes of gold, the other to increase gifts of the same?" Before Ay can glare at me once again, I add, "I ask so I may learn."

"It is simple," he says. "Naharin did not ask for solid gold, so we send statues of wood cased in gold. After the second inundation from now, we order Kush to increase gold tribute again and claim our coffers are being emptied by the demands of foreign diplomacy."

I want to ask what happens when Kush and Naharin both realize the deception, but the next petitioner is admitted and approaches us. Parannefer, head priest of Amun at the great temple at Waset enters. He is enrobed in leopard skin over a linen kilt. His papyrus sandals swish on the hard tiles. He bows deeply, a scroll tucked under one arm.

"Rise," says Ay.

"Great Regent," says Parannefer. "Amun is grateful for your patronage."

Ay nods. "As we are grateful for his blessings."

"Amun is the beneficent father of all the gods," says Parannefer. "Sadly, his priests and temples are somewhat lacking. We have still not recovered from the great heresy."

Ay shakes his head. "A devastating blow. How may we help?"

Parannefer unrolls the scroll. "The temple has seen an upsurge in demand surpassing that which was expected. We shall need ten thousand head each of cattle, sheep, goats and geese, and ten thousand beehives. As well, we shall need one hundred thousand setat of land in the delta region and another hundred thousand spread throughout the length of the river for the raising of grain, vegetables, papyrus, flax and for grazing our animals and producing honey."

My eyebrows shoot up and my jaw drops. I try to cover my momentary lack of control with a cough. Ay does not acknowledge my lapse, but he stiffens beside me.

"The King wishes to support the Temple," says Ay, "but you understand the coffers have been strained these last many years." He makes a counter-offer, which is followed by intense haggling, each side feigning generosity. In the end, the grant of livestock is well below the initial ask, but the land grant is a total of three hundred thousand setat in various locations throughout Kemet so that the Temple may use the income from the land to build up its herds.

I do not understand the reason for the bargaining. The word of the King, and by extension Ay as Regent, is law. He simply needed to state what the gift to the Temple was to be and that should have been the end of it. The grant was exorbitant. That much land would provide far more income than is needed to provide for the Temple. A thought strikes me. That much land would put the priesthood in control of so much wealth that they would be able to fund projects for the crown. Was that Ay's reasoning? If so, what should happen when the priesthood decides to withhold support? Are we to beg permission from Parannefer before embarking on military campaigns or trading expeditions? It would have been better to take that land for ourselves. I will ask Ay later, when we are alone.

I am so absorbed in my own thoughts that I do not notice a change in the room until all down the length of the hall right up to the entrance of the throne room, everyone has fallen to the floor, heads touching the tiles, arms stretched out. I turn to my right and see Tutankhamun has entered from the changing room dressed in full regalia, including the double crown of Upper and Lower Kemet and the false beard strapped firmly to his chin. He is so wrapped in jewels I can scarce see what is beneath it all. A fist-sized scarab hanging below a beaded collar, armbands, bracelets, earrings, rings on every finger. I know well the heft of all that gold and whenever I see Tutankhamun thus attired, I wonder if he finds it a hindrance to his mobility or if the added weight stabilizes him.

Horemheb walks behind as Tutankhamun hobbles the few steps to where we are seated. Ay gets up and bows. Tutankhamun takes his place on the King's throne as Ay hands him the royal sceptre.

Tutankhamun motions for everyone to stand. "We are appearing before you today to give thanks to our loyal servant, Ay."

I look to Ay. He does not appear to be shocked, as I am. But before he bows, I see his lowered eyebrows and his downturned mouth as he glances to Horemheb. I share his unease. Tutankhamun has no great love for Ay.

"Ay should be commended for his handling of affairs, for his steadfast support of your King, not only us, but for our predecessors as well. We are truly grateful for his venerable experience." Tutankhamun's voice is steady and, I think, slightly lower than his usual speaking voice. "Thus, it is with great sorrow that we announce his return to his primary post of Vizier, where he is greatly needed. Horemheb, Overseer of the Generals of the Two Lands shall also be known as the Envoy of the King, Mouth who Appeases the Entire Land. From this moment forward, he shall act on our behalf in this very chamber. All appeals must be brought to him."

Ay's face turns a deep crimson and his nostrils flare, but he doesn't dare question the king in the audience chamber.

Horemheb stands behind the King, looking forward. A smile flickers across his face, but is gone so quickly I am left wondering if I imagined it.

Tutankhamun

A breeze lifts the sycamore branches over my head and brushes my scalp. The papyrus stalks surrounding the pond bend to and fro. Mother kneels on the ground before me, my twisted foot in her lap. I wince when she digs her fingers in a little too hard along the arch.

"I am sorry," she says.

"No need," I say. "It will feel better later." My eyes drift shut. I can hear the faint chatter of Ankhesenamun's ladies from across the pond. From the few words I catch, I gather Ast is boasting of her latest conquest and teasing Henutmire, who's newly married and, thus, now forever bound to one man, though I believe Ast used the word "clod." I can't quite make out the words of Tuya, but they carry the tone of chastisement. I fancy she, a matron with grown children, is defending the institution of marriage, though perhaps she is disparaging it. My eyes open when a shadow falls across their lids. Ankhesenamun stands before me. Her eyes drift to my mother's head. I know she'd like for Mother to leave so she may scold me in private, like a recalcitrant child. I suppose I am that, but I'm not her child, and so I will not give in.

Ankhesenamun sits on a chair beside me. "There was no need to remove Ay from his post. He was doing a fine job." Her voice is even, but her jaw clenches ever so slightly.

Mother straightens her back. "May I show you how to massage Tutankhamun's foot?" When Ankhesenamun doesn't respond, she continues. "As his wife, it is your duty."

Ankhesenamun nods and allows Mother to demonstrate.

"Ay is more valuable as Vizier than as Regent," I say. "Horemheb can be spared from other duties."

"Horemheb is a commoner with no experience," says Ankhesenamun.

"Your mother, the great Neferuaten Nefertiti, was a commoner with no experience," I say. "Yet she was the strongest, most capable person in all of Kemet."

Mother gestures to Ankhesenamun that it is her turn. Ankhesenamun looks at her kneeling on the ground, then up at me. She angles her chair toward mine and places my foot in her lap.

"Still, publicly shaming him was not wise," she says. Her hands are tentative on the arch of my foot, but at least they are warm.

"Start here," says Mother. She places her hands under my leg, below the knee and gently pulls downward. Ankhesenamun copies her.

"I publicly thanked Ay," I say.

"You called him old," says Ankhesenamun.

I smile. "My apologies. Is he not aware of his own age?"

"You would do well not to make an enemy of Ay," says Mother. "He is still strong, and he has many supporters." She demonstrates straightening my foot as much as possible, running her thumbs along the instep, fingers applying pressure to the arch beneath.

"He has the second most important post in the kingdom, next to my own," I say. "How should that make him my enemy?"

She and Ankhesenamun exchange a look. I know they think me naïve.

Mother stands. "By your leave, I shall return to my rooms to lie down."

I nod.

Ankhesenamun's hands gain in confidence as she emulates Mother's technique. "Horemheb is too ambitious."

"I would say the same about Ay. For any other man the post of Vizier would be the ultimate achievement, yet it does not satisfy him."

"Ay's ambition is different. He is too old to want power for himself and, as he has no male heirs to leave his titles and lands to, has no reason to reach any higher than he already has. I am the closest he comes to having an heir. Any ambition Ay has is for me and, by extension, you." She touches my knee. "He is not unsatisfied with the post, he is angry with how you announced it," says Ankhesenamun. "You might have spoken to him in private first."

Ay followed Nefertiti from the feast on that night more than a year ago. I don't believe Ankhesenamun saw him go, or if she did, she did not attach any significance to it. But by morning, Nefertiti was dead. I want to voice my suspicion but seeing them both leave a party is no proof, and Ay was Nefertiti's father, so even if they were seen together after, no one would have remarked on it. Ay is also Ankhesenamun's grandfather, and she would not believe it, so I keep silent. But I will not be left alone with Ay so long as I can prevent it.

"Ay is ready to give Kemet away to the priests," I say. Ankhesenamun squirms. I think this has occurred to her as well. "I overheard the entire negotiation between him and Parannefer," I say.

She stops the massage and looks at me, apparently deciding whether or not to speak. Finally, she does. "I have been trying to think of why he should deign to bargain with a servant. If he wanted to enrich the royal coffers, surely it would have been better to take control of those lands ourselves."

"That is not why," I say. "It was a power play. Parannefer needed to demonstrate that the monarchy depends on the priesthood of Amun to stay in power, while Ay needed to demonstrate that he is willing to be generous but will not allow the priesthood to set the terms. In addition, he has now established himself as a friend of the Temple."

Ankhesenamun frowns. I think she is annoyed that I have thought of something she hasn't.

"This is Horemheb's analysis?" she asks.

"It is my own," I try not to smile.

She sighs. "You may be correct. Still, Horemheb is certainly worse. He is a virtual stranger, and you are trusting him with a most important position. If you need an envoy, it should be me. I am a full woman now, ready to fulfill my duties as Great Royal Wife."

"Even your great mother did not step into her role at the age of fifteen inundations. She grew into it gradually, as you must."

"We do not have the luxury of doing anything gradually," says Ankhesenamun, "not surrounded as we are by those who would take advantage of our weakness."

"We do not have the luxury of rushing in before we are ready," I say. "We have only one chance, we must make it a good one."

"Then we must take it now."

"You are not ready. You are not skilled enough in statecraft."

Ankhesenamun shoves my foot off her lap. I wince as it hits the ground. I do not think she intended to hurt me, but she does not apologize.

"You are a child. You are no judge of statecraft," she says.

"I am the King."

"Yes, and that is the problem." Ankhesenamun stands and walks away.

Ankhesenamun

The servant is adjusting the red and white double crown on my head when Ay bursts into the dressing room.

"May I ask what you are doing?" he says.

I straighten in an effort to appear haughty. "I shall be hearing the audiences today, and if all goes well, from now on." I arrange the pleated folds of my dress, so they drape flatteringly about my hips.

"You are not ready for this."

"Nonsense. You have trained me yourself," I say.

Ay huffs. "Do you know how long your mother was Great Royal Wife before she ever appeared in the audience chamber? Twelve years. Even your father was co-Regent for two years before taking over from his father. The training is not done in a season."

The servant bows to leave. I nod.

"I have watched the running of Kemet my whole life. Leadership is as natural to me as breathing. From my mother, I learned what to do. From my father, I learned what not to do."

"I don't doubt the truth of that last statement," says Ay. "But you were still too young when your mother journeyed West to have learned much from her."

"I was nearly a woman."

Ay moves closer to me. My first instinct is to take a step back, but I dare not show weakness.

"Tell me," says Ay, "is your husband, the King, aware of what you plan to do here?"

I lift my chin. "He is a child. I do not need his permission."

Ay moves to block the entrance to the audience chamber. "Who supports your claim to the regency?"

"I do not require support," I say. "I am the Great Royal Wife. I am upholding Ma'at."

"Wrong," says Ay. "No King can rule without the support of the army and the Amun priesthood and until you understand that you are no monarch." He narrows his eyes. "The King," he utters that last word through tight lips, "has already decreed Horemheb should be the one to take audience."

"Decrees may be revoked," I say.

"They may, but this one has not," says Ay. "How is it that Horemheb is not here this morning?"

"He has been detained elsewhere," I say.

Ay throws back his head and laughs. "Perhaps you will make a respectable ruler yet."

"I believe you will find I already am." My words are bold, yet my insides tremble. "You will also find that I have more support than you realize."

"Not yet, but you may, in time." He looks me up and down. "I shall enter the chamber with you."

I hesitate.

"I shall stand at your right hand and stay silent, unless you should ask my advice."

I don't believe he will stay silent but unless he moves, I cannot enter the chamber at all without summoning soldiers to remove him, and that I do not wish to do.

I nod. He moves aside and allows me passage.

Tutankhamun

Sitting at the writing table in my chamber, I mark time by tapping the end of my walking stick on the floor. Horemheb was meant to meet me here an hour before dawn. When he failed to appear, I sent for him, but he was not in his rooms, nor was he in the audience chamber. By this time, the first rays of dawn must be breaking over the land and glinting on the river. The first suppliants will be there, waiting. I consider going myself. It is my right. Even though I'm waiting, the knock on the door startles me.

"Enter," I say.

The guard opens the door and Horemheb himself enters, prostrating himself.

I stand, leaning on my stick for support and move to a spot directly in front of him. "Rise and explain your tardiness."

Horemheb stands, straightening his kilt. "I beg your forgiveness, Highness. I received an urgent summons in the night."

"You have a standing appointment with me every morning. There is nothing more urgent than that," I say. I have to crane my neck to look up at him, which is wrong. The King should be the highest in the room. Perhaps I should have stayed seated and kept him kneeling on the floor.

"The messenger carried the seal, Highness," says Horemheb.

"That is not possible," I say, but I open the rounded lid of the box on my writing table and rifle through it and pull out the seal ring bearing my names. There is only one other. It belongs to Ankhesenamun.

"He told me thieves were raiding the storehouses of Amun on the East Bank and if I were to hurry, I may still catch them," says Horemheb. "I believed the summons to come directly from you, and so I gathered some soldiers and left."

"Let me guess," I say. "When you arrived at the temple, there were no thieves."

"Only some very startled priests who showed me that the storehouses were untouched."

I nod. "We must get to the audience chamber right away."

Horemheb hangs back so I can take the lead. "This is Ay's doing."

"Perhaps," I say. He may have forced Ankhesenamun to give him her seal, or stolen it without her knowledge, but I recall her plea to make her my envoy instead of Horemheb.

Instead of entering the hall like common suppliants, we enter the dressing chamber to view the proceedings. My suspicions are confirmed immediately. Ankhesenamun sits in the throne, with Ay standing to her right. Before her, still in shadow, the long hall is filled with people. The sun has not yet risen far enough for light from the clerestory windows to reach ground level. Supplicants stand in a queue; spectators mill about the red-painted lotus bud columns. Evidently, Horemheb did not previously share my suspicions.

"How is it Ay is pushing the Great Royal Wife into this role?" he asks. "She is too inexperienced."

He moves to enter the hall. I block his way with my walking stick. The movement catches Ankhesenamun's eye. She looks at me with a contemptuous smile on her face which leaves me no further doubt as to who orchestrated this morning's events.

Horemheb must have seen it, too. "You don't suppose it is the Great Royal Wife herself who is behind this?"

Of course I suppose it. Anyone with any sense must suppose it. "Perhaps."

Horemheb shifts his weight but does not dare move my walking stick out of his way. "Regardless of who orchestrated it, we must put a stop to it immediately. They are both violating your direct order."

I do not move my stick. "I wish to hear how my wife handles herself." I emphasize the words "my wife" to remind Horemheb of his place in the hierarchy.

Ahead of the foreign ambassadors, military officials and various ranks of nobility, a priest is complaining that a peasant has breached the fences housing the sacred cows of Amun so he can steal milk. For his part, the peasant insists the cows themselves trampled the fence and have destroyed his barley crop. The priest will have none of it, demanding that the peasant pay for repairs to the fence.

"The temple shall pay to repair its own fence," says Ankhesenamun. "Furthermore, the temple shall pay a measure of barley equal to double that destroyed by the cows." The peasant prostrates himself, uttering blessings to Ankhesenamun. The priests scowl.

Horemheb leans close to my ear. "That was foolish. The Great Royal Wife should have found a compromise. Make the peasant repair the fence and work to pay fifty times the value of the milk he stole."

"How would that be a compromise?"

"The usual punishment for theft of temple property is a hundred times the value."

I nod, but I don't think the judgment was foolish. The accusation of theft was likely a fabrication designed to relieve the temple of fault. The great Temple of Amun, as Ankhesenamun knows well, has recently been granted an enormous gift of lands and wealth. They can well afford the compensation and they must not be given latitude to abuse the people of Kemet.

I recognize the complainant in the next case in front of Ankhesenamun – a minor noble of Waset. He is accusing his wife of adultery with another nobleman, who accuses the first of adultery with his wife. None of the four deny the charges, though the one wife is certain the child she carries is that of her husband. How can she know that? I must ask Ankhesenamun if women have special knowledge in this area.

After listening to both sides, Ankhesenamun decides that the husbands owe each other nothing. Normally, having relations with a married woman requires payment to her husband, but as both husbands are equally guilty, the debt is canceled out. Deprived of satisfaction, the husbands demand their wives be put to death. This shocks me. It is not unheard of for a woman to die for adultery, but it is far from common. The wives beg for mercy.

Ankhesenamun bangs her staff on the floor. The chamber falls silent. "I will not kill women for the crime of fornication," she says. "However, it is within your rights as husbands to put them out and keep their bride prices, should you so desire."

Both husbands state it is their desire, though neither looks pleased.

"I should insist you each marry the woman you have been fornicating with, for you are both as guilty as they." She turns to the wives. "Is it your desire to trade husbands?"

The sharp intake of breath can be heard all around the chamber. This is unprecedented. The two wives seem at a loss for words, but they finally manage to say, no, they do not wish that.

"You prefer to be cast out?" asks Ankhesenamun.

One of the ladies steps forward. "I have an estate in Iunu large enough to support both of us. It was an inheritance, not part of my bride price."

I glance at Horemheb. He frowns. Perhaps he is as surprised as I am at this suggestion.

This time, it is Ankhesenamun who seems at a loss. "Very well. But what of the child?" She looks to the husbands. "Do either of you wish to claim it?"

They do not.

The two wives seem oddly content with the result. They smile to each other as they leave. Their husbands do not smile at anybody, least of all to each other.

Horemheb shakes his head. "That was a travesty."

I don't respond.

"Their husbands have both been cuckolded, and not only by each other."

Horemheb may think me innocent, but I spent years within the walls of the Women's Quarters. I've seen women take more pleasure in each other's embrace than they ever did in that of the husband who seldom visited.

"The Great Royal Wife is too soft," says Horemheb. "But what can one expect from a woman? She should have granted the husbands' request for death."

I am taken aback. "Is that not extreme?"

"Not at all. A woman who defies her husband can never be trusted." He tilts his head toward Ankhesenamun. "You must move against her now and see her properly chastised or she will become ever more unruly."

I shake my head. "I will speak with her in private, first. The people must see us as a unified whole so they may have confidence they are being ruled well."

"Your father and Nefertiti were a unified whole, yet no one had confidence in their rule."

"Not because of their unity, but because of Father's policies." I frown. Horemheb is right in that it is not so simple. But not only is it inadvisable for me to challenge Ankhesenamun publicly, I am not certain I wish to challenge her at all. She, perhaps, is the one person I may trust not to betray my interests, for my interests are her own.

Tutankhamun, Year 4

(ca. 1330 BCE)

Ankhesenamun

I order the boatmen to stop and launch the papyrus skiffs.

"I don't believe this is the best place," says Tutankhamun. "There is a branch a little further to the east, where great flocks have been seen."

"Great flocks have been seen here," I say. "More than enough for what we will catch today."

Tutankhamun grumbles, but he does not object further.

I climb onto our skiff once the oarsman is in place and arrange Tutankhamun's stool. For him, kneeling is clumsy and difficult, so we must allow him use of the stool even though it unsteadies the boat somewhat. Once I'm on board, I help Tutankhamun climb down while Nebetah helps him from above. Nebetah climbs onto the skiff behind us, with my aunt, the Lady Mutnedjmet. Behind them are Horemheb and his wife, Amenia, followed by Ay and Tey. The others of my ladies, with their assorted menfolk and not a few children, board their own skiffs.

It is my favorite time of year for hunting, when the annual flood is much diminished and vegetation is once again visible above the surface, offering concealment for the ducks, yet the waters remain high enough to allow us easy passage. The skiffs fan out, each nosing a place amongst the reeds along the shoreline but allowing us prime position. Servants on land and by boat have already scoured the banks and found the area to be mercifully free of hippopotamuses and crocodiles.

Tutankhamun nocks an arrow on his bow and holds it loosely at his side. He raises his bow, draws the string, and gives me a nod. I signal to the men on shore to release the hunting cat. The animal rushes into the reeds at the edge of the river, sending up a cloud of ducks, flapping and squawking.

Around me, bows are poised, but no one can shoot until the King does. Tutankhamun takes aim and releases the string. He immediately tips backward. The oarsman is obliged to keep him from upending right into the river. I clutch the sides of the skiff and keep my weight low and center.

When we are stable again, Tutankhamun looks to see where the arrow went. The ducks were so thick, perhaps he managed to strike one. Alas, the men onshore detangle an arrow from some marsh plants. It is fletched with distinctive feathers of royal blue.

We move down the shore a little. I stand, with left foot forward, to take my turn. When I shoot, the release of the bowstring whistles in my ear. My duck drops into the marsh. I catch Tutankhamun's eye and he smiles at me. I hand him back the bow.

His next attempt has the same result as the first, as does the next, and the next. After I shoot a second duck, Tutankhamun doesn't smile anymore.

"You do well with targets on land." I intend to be encouraging but evidently, he does not find it so. He glowers at me.

I look to the other skiffs. The others turn their heads. They look to the shore, or each other. None will look at us. On land, there are no sorted piles of ducks, only my two. None but I dare succeed when the King fails. I remember Ay's words that no King can rule without support, and I know that no King can maintain support if he is seen as weak.

I slide backward so I am close to Tutankhamun's feet and lower my voice so none but he may hear me. "Do you need my assistance?"

"Certainly not," he says. "I simply need to adjust to shooting from water instead of land." He hands me the bow.

I refuse it. "You cannot adjust to shooting on the water if you don't continue doing it."

He half tilts his head toward the nearest skiff and offers me the bow again. "I will practice on the pond, when I am alone."

I still do not accept the bow. "You need to try one more time."

"I am already disgraced this day."

"Then once more will make no difference," I say. When he does not move, I continue. "I will shoot no more today unless you do, and no one else will shoot if we do not. We may return to the boat and head back to the palace now, or you may make one last attempt and then spend a pleasant afternoon on the water."

Tutankhamun grips the bow. "If I try once more, do I have your word that you will take the bow and not try to convince me to keep trying here?"

"Of course."

He sits back. "Very well."

I move so close that I am sitting on his good foot.

He tries shaking his foot to dislodge me. I spread my skirts in front of us, hiding the stool while I grasp its legs.

"You are on my foot," says Tutankhamun.

"Give the signal," I say.

He does and raises his bow. This time, when the arrow looses, the skiff rocks slightly, but Tutankhamun remains steady and a duck plummets to the water. He did not kill it, merely crippled its wing, but a quick wring of the neck from a porter will finish the job.

I clap, and then hold out my hand for the bow. Tutankhamun clutches it to his breast.

"You are the one who said I could not adjust to shooting on the water if I do not continue doing it."

"And you are the one who demanded my word that I would not compel you to keep trying it here."

"I am the King. It is my prerogative to change my mind."

I turn to face the front of the skiff and resume my position. Tutankhamun brings down another duck right away, this time a clean kill. By the time the sun begins to dip toward the western horizon, small mounds of duck carcasses dot the shoreline. Tutankhamun has brought down a total of four.

On the way back to the boat, I remain seated at Tutankhamun's feet, one arm twined around his good leg. He looks down at me and smiles, pleased with himself. I am pleased that he is pleased.

I am removing my rings and bracelets, placing them into the ebony and ivory inlaid box, when there is a knock at my chamber door. I utter my assent to enter, and the guard admits Tutankhamun, who asks to speak with me alone. I dismiss Ast and Henutmire. Ast lowers her eyelids as she passes Tutankhamun in a false display of modesty. His head turns to watch her leave. I sit on the bed, remove my sash and slip one shoulder out of my dress.

Tutankhamun puts up a hand and turns his head to the side. "That is not why I'm here."

I pull my dress back up over my shoulder, my first reaction a sigh of relief. Tutankhamun looks up at the sound and I feel ashamed. Then I wonder why he turned away in the first place. Was he gazing at Ast? Would he prefer her?

One of the serving girls? My words fly forth with more venom than I intend. "Well, why are you here?"

He opens his mouth, closes it, and starts again. "I simply wish to thank you for this afternoon."

I nod, feeling shame once again. "That is not necessary."

"Yes, it is. You made it appear I was strong without letting anyone know it was you propping me up."

"I very much doubt anyone out hunting this day was unaware of the reason your shooting improved so dramatically."

His shoulders slump and I regret my truthfulness. I put a hand on his shoulder. "My assistance was minimal. It was you behind the bow."

"Still," he says, "you might have left me to flounder."

"I didn't do it for you," I say. "If the kingship becomes unstable, we will both suffer."

Tutankhamun gives a quick nod. "All the same, thank you." He turns to leave.

"I am sorry," I call as he raises his hand to the door.

He looks back, one brow raised. "For what?" The question has the ring of a challenge, as if he is asking simply to know if I am aware of the offense caused.

I don't know how to answer. For shouting? For not wanting him? For letting him see that I do not want him? Or simply for failing in my duty? "The kingship is not my sole concern." It is not what I intended to say, but I realize it is the truth.

Tutankhamun's grin lights his face and gives him back the air of the childhood he is just now leaving behind. As quickly as it rises, it is gone. "I am gratified to hear it." He bows as he takes his leave.

Tutankhamun

In a war chariot, there is nowhere to lean, and I cannot use my walking stick and still use the bow. Yet, the motion does not allow me to stand without my stick. So, I must grip the sides of the chariot, and this makes it challenging to fire the bow. Even from this distance, I can sense Ay's glare as my shot goes wide yet again.

When Ay motions me back, I tell the driver to take one more lap. I want to try something different. It may work. The driver obeys me, of course. As we approach the target, I pull an arrow from the quiver attached to the side of the chariot. I lean in, gripping with my elbow over the edge, and grit my teeth against the pain in my foot. The sky is cast with angry dark clouds today, eliminating the sun's glare, lending me a measure of confidence. I pull back the bow string, and let it fly at just the right moment.

I hold my breath as the arrow flies true. Its tip points in the direction of the target, but too high. It sails a full arm's length over the target and falls to the desert sand, well behind it. My position when I shot was low and I overcompensated by aiming too high. On the next pass, I will do better.

Ay is approaching the track, waving. I decide to take the chariot in. There will be more training days, many more. For now, my foot is aching with the vibration of the floorboards and with the unspent moisture in the air.

Ay hands me my walking stick as I descend. I grip the curved handle, carved into the likenesses of bound Kushite and Hittite prisoners. Ay waits until the driver is out of earshot. "In the future, we need to conduct your training sessions in private." He tilts a head toward the stables, where grooms and stable hands mill about. "We do not need servants gossiping about your lack of proficiency in the military arts."

"I am improving," I say. "I nearly hit the target today and I will do it next time, I am sure."

"You had one lucky near-hit," says Ay. "This is beyond the mere incompetence of boyhood. Hitting targets does not require exceptional strength, unlike sword fighting. With swords, one only expects a boy to be bested by a man, but to not even be able to stand in a chariot, that is disconcerting."

I do not speak, for fear I'll cry and prove to Ay that I am still a boy. I cannot change how I am, but I can find a different way. And I will.

"To truly be King, you must be able to defend Kemet from its enemies, or" says Ay, "at the very least give the appearance that you can. Otherwise, the people will have no confidence in you."

We step past the stable yard into the training ground. Menna, my teacher, stands waiting, his lean, muscled torso contrasting with the white of his kilt. He hands me the curved khopesh sword. I hand my walking stick to Ay and accept the sword.

I am not the only one training today. Ankhesenamun is there with her teacher. They fill the air with the metallic clank of clashing blades.

Menna and I circle one another. I can only limp, dragging one foot along. When his sword comes down, I raise mine in a successful parry. But it was a ruse. He lunges, hooking my sword in the curve of his own. My sword is torn from my grasp, and I topple over. I am defeated.

Menna reaches a calloused hand down to help me up. "Never leave your side unprotected, Highness."

I accept his help. Next time, I last but a little longer than the first before Menna has me on the ground. I wish I could stop this nonsense. I will never be able to best a man in hand-to-hand combat. Given time and practice, I will master the chariot, but I do not have the needed for the sword. When I rise, I watch the end of Ankhesenamun's practice session. She has backed her teacher to the edge of the spectators. I glance up at the sky. I mutter a quick prayer to any gods listening, asking for the clouds to send forth a deluge, forcing an end to the combat before I must witness her victory. My prayers go unanswered. The clouds whirl, hunted by the wind, and flee to the south and east over the desert. Ankhesenamun disarms him as I watch.

Menna declares we have done all we can do for this day, Ay hands me back my walking stick. Ankhesenamun waits for me and, together, we begin the trek back to the palace. She offers me her arm to lean on, which I refuse. Instead, I grind the tip of my stick into the sand with each step, seeking to take weight off my aching, twisted foot.

We walk past the west villas with date palms and sycamores peering over mud-baked enclosures. The main palace is in sight and still neither of us has broken the silence. I am relieved Ankhesenamun does not attempt to mollify me by lying about my progress. Most others would. When we are too far away to be overheard, I finally speak. "You are to cease your training immediately. You are a woman. You'll never go to war. It's a waste of time for you, and unseemly."

"I train because you need a consort worthy of the title," she says. "My mother trained daily and was powerful. It was for this quality that our father chose her to be Great Royal Wife."

"Our father was a weak fool," I say. She cannot argue with that.

"In all but his choice of Great Royal Wife," she says. I cannot argue with that.

"You are jealous that I am better than you," she says.

I say nothing.

"My teachers let me win," she says.

This surprises me. "Mine do not let me win," I say.

"As you pointed out, I am a woman and will never go to war. I do not need to be able to win."

Still, I cannot erase from my mind the image of her winning while I struggle to my feet. "You will stop," I say.

"If I stop my training, so should you," she says. "It is just as much a waste of time for you as you are not capable of going to war."

I want to hit her. I want to hit her so hard she falls to the ground just as I did. But she's larger than I, and stronger. Perhaps her teacher let her win, and perhaps he did not, but she would need no such mercy from me. "When we return to the palace, you will bathe quickly and then go directly to my bed chamber."

"I beg your pardon?"

"If you will not obey my command to stop training, there is at least one area in which you must do your duty, and you will do it today."

Ankhesenamun glares at me and stomps off alone toward the palace.

Ankhesenamun

I enter the chamber and send the servants away. Tutankhamun is seated on his bed dressed in his finest kilt and jewels; makeup freshly applied. He did this for me, I realize, and suppress a smile. You are here under duress, I remind myself.

I slip off my robe, let it fall to the floor in a shimmer of gauze. Tutankhamun's eyes grow to the size of small moons and his mouth gapes open. A peak forms in the fabric of his kilt. I touch his cheek and allow my hand to wander down, across his chest. He grabs the edge of the bed with both hands, but I still see the involuntary shiver that runs through his entire body. I consider teasing him, allowing his culmination to occur without entering me at all, as happened with the serving girl. He deserves it after his treatment of me. But I cannot. He has endured one humiliation already today. Another would be too cruel.

I withdraw my hand and lie down on the bed, pulling him on top of me. He rearranges his kilt and I guide him. He wriggles his hips furiously and collapses on top of me, breathing heavily.

Is it done so soon? Has it even happened at all? I am unsure what to do. Tutankhamun raises his head to look at me. The silly, lopsided smile on his face and the dreamy look in his eyes tell me we have, in fact, accomplished what we meant to.

I roll him off me and slam him onto the bed between me and the wall. "You do not command me," I say. "Not inside the bed chamber, and not outside of it. I am here because it is my duty to give Kemet an heir, not because you ordered me here."

Tutankhamun nods. His mouth opens and closes. He appears to have some difficulty finding words. "I am sorry I was angry with you."

I am unsure how he managed to work up a sweat in such a short time, but beads of perspiration roll down his face. When he wipes them away with a hand, he leaves streaks of black and green makeup across his cheek. Like this, he looks younger than his twelve inundations. I wipe away the streaks with a thumb and cradle his head to my breast. If he were not King, he would still be in school, not worrying about fighting wars or producing babies. I ache, knowing I have used him as my father used our sisters. It is not the same, I tell myself. Not the same because I have no more choice than he does, and he is not displeased, but the truth of it does not ease my guilt.

"I am also sorry," I say when I can speak again. "I should not have maligned your military prowess."

"You were right," he says. "I can never fight in a war."

"It was cruel of me to say so."

He pushes away and rolls onto his side. "Yes, it was."

I give him a gentle shove. "My assessment was premature. You are still young, with years yet to master the skills." I hope that is true. The Hatti have been encroaching on our allies, and Kemet may soon need to defend its empire. Still, it may be years before war comes to us.

"Years will make no difference to my sword fighting," he says, "but my chariot skills are improving."

I wish he were wrong about the sword fighting. "There is more to kingship than military training. You will spend the majority of your time in council, or in the temple." His hand finds my waist and slides down to my hip. "You've a quick mind and the ability to think several moves ahead. If your mastery of statecraft continues to improve as it has been, you will be ready to take over the administration of Kemet by the time you reach full manhood." His hand glides across my belly, causing my unsated body to tense. "Are you listening to me?"

"Can we do it again?" he asks.

"Hmmm," I respond. "I suppose."

Tutankhamun

"What is the lesson of the Dream Stele of Djehutymose, the fourth of that name?" asks my tutor, Intef.

I recall the story. The young prince, on a hunting trip, fell asleep beneath the beard of the great Khepri in the shadows of the stone mountain tombs of the ancient kings. In those days, only the regal head and the slope of the lion back were visible above the desert sands. Khepri came to Djehutymose in a dream, promising to make him King if only he would free him from the sands covering him. Djehutymose did so and was given the kingship. I know what answer is expected, but I do not believe it to be the correct one.

I am interrupted in my thoughts by a servant approaching our spot under the sycamores, with a message that Ay wishes to see me urgently.

"Tell my vizier that I will see him once I have finished here."

The servant bows and leaves.

I look from Intef to Mother. "About the stele, I believe the answer you are looking for is that the King is subordinate to the gods and must always follow their directives in order to achieve balance, Ma'at."

Intef beams.

Mother frowns. "You said that is the answer we are looking for. What is your answer?"

"Well," I thought for a moment. "If I recall my history lessons correctly, Djehutymose, the fourth of that name, was the second son, and not the appointed heir to the throne. For him to rule instead of his elder brother would, in fact, be an upsetting of Ma'at, not an establishment of it. So, I believe Djehutymose took the throne by force and later wrote the stele to make it appear his rule was divinely inspired."

Now, Mother beams.

"That is the lesson I must derive from it," I say. "For, although I am the legitimate heir, still I must always project the image of infallibility lest I be usurped myself."

Intef huffs. "Djehutymose, the fourth of that name, was a great king. Taking the throne without the direction of the gods would be most unkingly behavior."

"I assure you, I am intimately acquainted with kingly behavior," I say. "I must end the lesson now. My vizier wishes to speak with me." I order a servant to fetch Ay.

Intef leaves and Mother stands behind me as Ay enters. Ay is tense, his jaw clenching. He is not accustomed to being told to wait. He bows. "Highness, I have distressing news."

I nod. "Tell me."

"The Great Royal Wife has ordered a change to the upcoming Opet Festival. The gods will no longer travel from Ipet-Iset to Ipet-Resyt along the Avenue of Sphinxes, but rather by boat on the river. Are you aware of this?"

I am not, but if I admit it, he will think I am easily duped. "Yes."

Ay seems to deflate. "You might have consulted me before agreeing to a change. As Vizier, overseeing festivals fall under my purview."

Ah. So, he is offended at the encroachment on his own authority. "Do you disapprove of the change?" I ask.

"In transporting the gods by boat, they will miss the offerings at the various chapels along the route."

I think the procession would make a grander spectacle on the water. The Avenue of Sphinxes is relatively narrow, providing fewer viewing opportunities. Crowds could throng the river and every person there would thank me for bringing it to them. New chapels could be constructed at the points of embarkation and disembarkation so the gods would receive all due offerings.

"If you have a grievance with the Great Royal Wife, you must go through proper channels," I say. "Horemheb is the King's Envoy."

"Horemheb is not fit," says Ay through clenched teeth.

"Are you questioning the word of the King?" I say. I feel Mother's hand squeezing my shoulder.

"Absolutely not." Ay bows and backs out of the room.

Mother takes a seat beside me. "When you give someone a task, best to let him do it."

I look at her.

"You granted Ay the title of Vizier to placate him after you granted favors to Horemheb. If you wish for Ay to be placated, you and Ankhesenamun both must allow him to perform the duties that go along with the title."

"I was thinking that perhaps Ay would prefer to be Viceroy of Kush."

I intend it as a joke, but Mother does not laugh. "Ay is a very dangerous person to have as an enemy."

She is right, of course, but I think he would be even more dangerous to have as a friend.

Tutankhamun, Year 5

(ca. 1329 BCE)

Ankhesenamun

Tutankhamun is carried in his sedan chair at the head of the parade. No one may accompany him this time, not even me, so I follow behind, rattling a sistrum. The King alone must honor the god Min to bring fertility to the land, to the people and, perhaps most importantly, to himself. When his chair is placed on the ground and he alights, his rocking gait is solemn; his eyes look straight ahead.

Before the King, the stone god stands on a raised platform decorated with lotus and papyrus. Two ostrich feather fans ripple in the faint breeze. Min's head is topped with a plumed crown. One granite hand grips his erect phallus, the other is raised behind his head, holding a flail.

When Tutankhamun reaches a plot of black earth, already ploughed, he accepts a hoe from a priest. He plants his feet wide apart and begins the process of breaking up the soil. His lean back curves as the hoe arcs above him before striking the ground. When this is accomplished – it takes little time, for it has mostly been done for him – he slides along the rows, dropping grains of wheat as he goes.

When the wheat is sowed, Tutankhamun accepts a scythe. He holds it up so the blade glints in the sun before ritually cutting a sheaf of grain, already prepared for the purpose. He offers this to the god. The crowd roars. King and country are fertile. Yes, he is, I think. Tutankhamun glances in my direction and I have to stop myself from touching my belly.

While a servant scrubs me down with natron, my eyes drift to Henutmire. I pull them away at once, but not without a surge of pleasure at the sight of her rounded belly, oiled and gleaming in the lamplight. I clench my teeth to keep from smiling. I must give nothing away, not before Tutankhamun himself knows.

Henutmire must have noticed my attention, however brief. "Do not fret, Highness. The gods shall bless you soon, I am sure of it." She beams and places a hand over her babe. A servant removes the hand so she can better scrub.

Ast tilts her head and closes her eyes as a servant pours water over her to wash away the natron. "Ah, well, better the two of you than me."

Meryetre snorts and a mischievous smile lights up her plain face. "If half your boasts are true, you'll be birthing five babies before her Highness has even one." She looks to me, eyes wide and mouth agape. "My apologies, Highness, I did not mean …"

I allow myself a half-grin. "Not to worry, I know well your barb was not aimed at me."

"Hmmph," says Ast. "I do not take it as an insult. I enjoy men, and why should I not? So long as I always use the linen soaked in honey and acacia, I shall never conceive unless I wish to."

"Indeed," says Tuya, head tilted, and one eyebrow raised. "I used the same faithfully in the early days of my marriage. You have met my son, Pepi?"

Mutnedjmet, relishing her toilette in silence until now, speaks one word. "Sylphium."

We all turn to look at her. The word is familiar to me.

"It is a plant, known to few outside the temple of Sekhmet, mistress of medicine."

My mother had been a priestess of Sekhmet before marrying my father. This must be how Mutnedjmet knows of it.

She continues. "A spoonful in tea every morning will prevent a child from ever starting. But you must not miss it, not even once."

I am struck by a memory. Mutnedjmet bringing tea to Father's beloved second wife and some of his favorites in the Women's Quarters. On Mother's orders? Is that why so few of his other women produced children when Mother birthed so very many? I gasp and stare at Mutnedjmet. When Father claimed my eldest sister, Meritaten, as wife she began to drink tea every morning, but it was Mother who brought it to her, not Mutnedjmet. Meritaten had no child. My second eldest sister, Meketaten was not so fortunate. She died from bearing too young. Yet, when she found herself as one of Father's wives, she stopped

41

speaking to Mother except to boast of her superior status. Is that why Mother did not prevent her death? Was she unable to or did she choose not to?

Mutnedjmet glares at me, warning me to silence with her eyes. I want to draw her aside, into another room, but am interrupted by noises from the outer vestibule. I wrap myself in a towel and go to investigate. Tutankhamun grins at me, his eyes eager. He moves closer and tugs at my towel. I clasp it tighter.

Tutankhamun must lean in and stretch his neck to whisper in my ear. "Come to your bedchamber. There is another field I wish to plough."

I am conscious of my ladies and servants twittering behind me. "We haven't time now. We must get ready for tonight's feast. It is our duty."

"Pleasure is one of our duties," he says. "We must have heirs."

I half-glance back toward the servants, who are visible through the door, puttering with my bathing supplies and pretending they don't hear. My ladies remain out of sight, but I've no doubt their ears are pressed to the wall. "That has already been accomplished." I hear a gasp, followed by several more and some giggling.

Tutankhamun pulls back and stares at me. "Are you certain?"

"Quite," I say. "I have missed my courses three times now and my gowns no longer fit so well."

"I noticed that, but I just thought you were getting fat."

I glare at him, but he doesn't appear to notice. He drops to his knees by placing his hands on the floor first and then bending his legs. He parts the towel that semi-covers me and kisses the bare flesh of my belly. He lays his cheek against me and winds his arms around my hips.

"I do hope it is a boy," he says, "but I shan't be disappointed if our first child is a girl."

"It is a boy."

He looks up into my face. "How can you be sure?"

"Because the wheat sprouted first."

He stands and bites his lip. "But I just planted it today."

For a moment, I don't understand him, but then I remember the ceremony earlier. "Not that wheat," I say. "The wheat I keep in my private chambers."

"Why are you growing wheat in your rooms?"

"I am not," I say. "When a woman wishes to know if she is with child, she waters pots of wheat and barley seeds with her first morning's urine. If the wheat sprouts first, the child is a boy. If the barley sprouts first, it is a girl. If neither sprout, there is no child."

Tutankhamun's eyes grow wide. "Really? I saw babies born while I was living in the Women's Quarters, but I never knew of this."

"Anyone married to the King would need to keep such suspicions private until she was absolutely certain. Especially so for lesser wives whose child may supplant the current heir. They always have much to fear from the greater wives."

Tutankhamun nods. I know he is aware that, due to his twisted body, any healthy, whole boy child at all would have taken his place, no matter how much younger or how thin the royal blood. I am sure he is also aware, as I am, that given advance notice, his mother may have taken steps to prevent her son being ousted from his position.

"You are not one of my lesser wives," he says, "so you did not have any such concerns."

I did not have any reason to fear his lesser wives before I was with child, but once our son is born, I will need to do what is necessary to ensure he remains the heir. "I did not wish to raise your hopes until I knew for certain. As well, I thought Min's Festival was an auspicious time for an official announcement."

Tutankhamun grins. "It is indeed." He turns to go.

"Wait," I say. "I should be with you when you share the news."

He looks me up and down. I still clutch the towel to my breast.

"I will be ready to dress momentarily." I drop the towel and beckon to the servants to continue. One rinses me with a jug of water, while another towels me off and a third soaks up water from the floor.

Tutankhamun rests against the wall until a servant arrives with a chair for him. "A messenger arrived from the Naharin today," he says.

I shiver slightly as my wet skin pimples in gooseflesh. "So I have heard."

"You did more than hear of it," he says. "You met with the man." There is no use denying it. "Yes, but we mustn't speak of it now. There shall be a meeting in the morning, and you shall be there, along with Ay and Horemheb."

Tutankhamun sighs. "If the military is invited, the news must not be good."

"I don't wish to spoil tonight's celebration."

"I am the King. I should not be hearing of important events at the same time as my Vizier and my Envoy."

He is correct, yet the servants are toweling me off and Kemet's affairs must not become the subject of domestic gossip.

"You do not answer, so it must be bad," he says. "Is there …"

I put a hand up to stop him and take the towel from the girl's hands. "You may go now," I say to all of them. "I will dress myself."

Tutankhamun at least has the good grace to look sheepish. I hold up a finger. "All of you, as well."

My ladies emerge from my bath chamber, still wrapped in towels, though Ast's towel seems to be barely hanging on. They bow to Tutankhamun and leave, arm in arm, with the exception of Mutnedjmet. She simply nods her head and sashays from the room as if draped in her finest linen instead of a damp towel.

Once the door closed behind her, I turned back to Tutankhamun. "You once told me adults spoke around you as if you were not there because they took you to be simple. Do not make the same mistake with the household staff or the ladies of the court."

"I'm sorry," he says, "I will be more careful in the future. Is Naharin at war?"

"No," I say. "There is no war as yet, but our former provinces are resisting our entreaties to return to us."

He nods. "I understand. It is not so bad, then."

I go to my trunk with its image of Tutankhamun and I in the garden. Lifting the lid, I find the dress I wish to wear to the feast, a gauzy green linen shift and slip it over my head. The seams strain a little around the middle, but it will last one more night. "If you think the situation is not bad, then you do not understand."

"I did not say it wasn't bad, only not as bad as I thought," he said. "Our former vassals cannot stand independently. The Hatti wish to expand their empire and they are too big and powerful for small city-states to resist. If they are taken by the Hatti, then the Hatti's reach and power grows, and they may soon be in a position to invade Kemet."

I close my mouth, for I find it has fallen open of its own accord. "Precisely."

"Kemet is the only power big enough to resist the Hatti," continues Tutankhamun, "at least for now. Our only hope to stay that way, and the Naharin's only hope of remaining free of the Hatti is for us to rebuild our empire."

I fear I have underestimated my husband.

"Do not look at me like that," he says.

"Like what?"

"Like you have just discovered I am not simple after all," he says with a frown.

"I have always known you are not simple," I say, "but I did not know you had such a firm grasp of politics."

"I grew up with it, as you did."

Yes, I think, he did. We have been married four years now, and I should have been more current with the state of his education. "What do you think we should do about it?"

He snaps his head up to look at me. I realize he is not used to being consulted. "I am not sure yet," he says, "but I'll think on it this night and be ready with suggestions for the morning meeting."

"I believe you will," I say.

Tutankhamun

I am seated at the great writing table, with Ankhesenamun standing to my right as Ay bows himself into my outer chamber. The young man with him prostrates himself on the floor. I bid them both to rise. I recognize the young man – a lesser military official by the name of Nakhtmenu, and Ay's nephew, but I am unsure why he is in council.

"Highness," says Ay, "I humbly ask that General Nakhtmenu be permitted to attend this meeting."

"For what purpose?"

"As part of his training," says Ay. "Nakhtmenu is one of our army's brightest lights and, with proper direction, may prove invaluable to Kemet."

"His excellency flatters me," says Nakhtmenu, "I am but a minor general."

"If it is an exaggeration, it is but a small one," I say. "I have heard of your heroism in the Western Desert. I daresay that if your early promise proves true, you shall not stay minor for long."

Nakhtmenu bows from the waist. "I am honored, Highness." When he rises, his mouth is smiling, but his eyes are hard.

I glance at Ankhesenamun. The lowering of her brow tells me she is as uncomfortable as I with this request. Yet, I cannot find a reason to deny it, and if Ankhesenamun could, she would say it. I nod. "Nakhtmenu may stay."

Just then, the chamber door opens, and the guard announces the arrival of Horemheb. It seems he is also accompanied by a young man with the curious complexion – ivory-pale skin and flaming hair – of some of the Ribu tribesmen. Paramessu. If any soldier outshines the accomplishments of Nakhtmenu, it is he.

After they rise, I nod toward Paramessu. "I presume this is another of our army's brightest lights."

Horemheb harrumphs. "Our army is in need of strong swords, not bright lights, and young Paramessu possesses such. But that is not why I ask that he may attend this meeting."

I search my memory. "Because of his recent experience in Retenu near the Naharin?"

Horemheb nods. "Your Highness is well informed."

I feel a quiver in my belly. It is not uncommon to admit lesser functionaries to important meetings, but for both the Vizier and the King's Envoy to make such a request the same day seems significant, but of what, I cannot tell. I glance to Ankhesenamun. Though she does not meet my eye, I can see she is frowning. My unease is not unwarranted, then. The stated reasons for both requests are not untrue, and the two men may indeed prove valuable. Yet, a resentful glance between Ay and Horemheb hints that the stated reasons are not the true ones. Still, I cannot find a reason to deny this request any more than I could the first.

I nod, trying not to stare at the general's odd colouring. "Paramessu may stay." I indicate Ankhesenamun. "The Great Royal Wife has spoken with the messenger of the Naharin. She will relay the message to us here."

Ankhesenamun takes a breath. "The Naharin have refused our gifts and our demands for tribute. They have no wish to rejoin our empire." Her eyes sweep the room. "In case not everyone here is aware, we have already been refused by the Kharu, the Amurru, the Dahy and the Kananu. Not one of our former provinces wishes to ally with us again."

Horemheb sighs. "Then we have no choice but to send in the army and take by force what they will not give us by choice."

"We will not be sending any army," I say.

There is silence in the room as the others shift their stances and glance to one another.

Ankhesenamun recovers first. "Forgive me, Highness, but last night you expressed how vital it was that we regain our former territory lest the Hatti take it for themselves before invading Kemet itself."

I nod. "It is equally vital we avoid war if at all possible."

Horemheb scowls. "As your father did. If you follow the same path, Kemet will fare even worse."

I pound the writing table with a fist. "I am not my father."

Ankhesenamun pats my shoulder. I shake off her hand. The others stare at me.

Ay clears his throat. "Highness ..."

I raise a hand to stop him and take a deep breath. "We lost the empire because my father chose not to address the situation. I am suggesting we use strategy instead of might. The Hatti are eyeing those provinces just as we are. If we send an army now, it will be all-out war and I am not certain Kemet can win. Are you?"

"Our troops are highly trained and ready to bring glory to Kemet," says Horemheb.

"Those of the Hatti are also highly trained," I say, "and they possess weapons of black metal, whereas we do not."

"Our chariots are lighter, faster and more maneuverable," says Ay. "This gives us the advantage."

I look to Horemheb. "Do you agree?"

"In principle, yes, Highness," says Horemheb. He glances over at Ay. "However, the Hatti chariots are slow and heavy because they are larger and carry a third man, allowing them to shoot more arrows faster than we can. As well, should our charioteers fall and it comes fighting hand-to-hand, their black metal slices through our bronze with ease."

"So, should we meet the Hatti on the field of battle, you cannot guarantee Kemet will be victorious," I say.

"In war, there are never any guarantees," says Ay, "yet I believe Kemet would prevail."

Horemheb nods. "I agree. We have more than just weapons and archers on our side, we have the gods as well."

I roll my eyes. "Gods."

Horemheb opens his mouth to speak, and I flash him a look that dares him to tell me again how I am like my father. "We have gods, the Hatti have gods, the Naharin have gods, everybody has gods. Everybody's gods protect them in battle, but still one side must lose. It seems to me gods are an unreliable source of military strength."

"Our gods are full of gratitude," says Ay. "Your father deposed them, and you restored them. They shall grant us victory, I am sure."

Nefertiti spent her whole life in the service of Sekhmet, goddess of war, in secret when it was forbidden and openly after my father passed to the Blessed West. She was used and manipulated and, in the end, also passed to the West before she could complete her mission. It seems to me that the gods care little for those who serve them. I say none of this aloud. "No doubt the Hatti are equally confident of the favor of their gods." I shake my head. "No, we must not engage in war. It is what they want – to draw us out, have us commit first so they may vanquish us and keep marching through all of Retenu and into Kemet itself. We must offer the provinces greater incentive to ally with us."

"What, precisely?" asks Ankhesenamun. "We have already offered gold and promised to increase the price of silver and to purchase more cedar wood. Further, we have requested a reduced allocation of tribute. We have nothing more to offer."

"What if we were to treat them as provinces of Kemet instead of as conquered nations?" I glance around the room. A collective gasp circles the room. This is not done. Foreigners are not given status equal to that of Kemetians, nor are they given access to the court.

When no one speaks, I continue, "Each new province would appoint its own governor from among its own people and would send officials to the court here at Waset. I would choose a new vizier for the entire area of Retenu."

"In such an arrangement, we would lose tribute," says Ay.

I nod. "Yes. We would have to pay a fair price for goods."

"That gives us little chance to build the royal coffers," says Horemheb.

"We would not be able to build wealth as quickly as we would like, but at least we would be building," I say. "War depletes coffers. Armies need to be fed, armed, and paid. If there is no reasonable expectation of winning, and thereby gaining tribute, it is not a sound investment."

"Why should the Naharin, or any of our other former provinces, wish to accept this offer in any case?" asks Ankhesenamun. "As tributary nations, they maintain their own rulers and their own laws. They simply pay their annual tribute, and in return gain our protection as well as preferred trading terms. If they become a province of Kemet, within a couple of generations they will no longer be Naharin."

"Within a couple of generations, they will no longer be Naharin in any event," I say. "They become Kemetian or they become Hatti, that is the choice they must make."

"It is their King who must choose, and you are asking him not only to abdicate, but to end his royal line forever."

"If he opts for war, he and his entire royal line will die, for the winner cannot afford to let them live. As a Kemetian subject, he will live, so long as he causes no trouble."

Ankhesenamun rests a hand on my shoulder. "Which would you choose – to die as a king or live as a servant?"

I place a hand on the gentle roundness of her belly and look up into her soft brown eyes. Should I ever be handed such a dilemma, I hope to have the courage to live with the shame of failure rather than condemning them to execution through my own glorious death in battle. "My kingdom is Kemet. I shall never have to make such a choice." I believe it is true. I hope it is true. It will be if we can keep the Hatti from our borders, for no other nation could possibly bring Kemet to its knees.

Ay smiles and crosses his arms. "A confident answer and a correct one. There is no need to allow foreigners into the court."

"Your father was Naharin," I say.

Ay's jawline hardens. "And he did not have any influence at court, did he?" The words sound clipped.

I consider pointing out that Ay himself is half-foreign, as was his sister, Great Royal Wife to my grandfather, and they both exercised enormous power. But I refrain because it would be a reminder that every King since my grandfather, myself included, carried foreign blood. Ankhesenamun carries a double dose, as her parents shared the Naharin grandfather. And now we both pass this blood on to our son. A thought occurs. Perhaps that is the trouble – the Naharin are already too close to the Kemetian throne.

"Are the nobles concerned about the ties of the royal family to the Naharin?" I ask.

"None would ever speak ill of the King or his family," says Horemheb.

"How do they speak?" I ask.

Horemheb shifts his weight. "Of your Highness, only in glowing terms. However, it is known that there are family ties to the Naharin, as well as Naharin princesses among your wives."

I start at this. I think so seldom of the wives inherited from my father. Indeed, several are foreign princesses, given as tribute by their fathers, including the King of the Naharin. I give Ankhesenamun a sidelong glance. Soon enough, she will be too big and uncomfortable to wish to visit my chambers at night. Perhaps I should avail myself of the Women's Quarters. I force my mind back to the subject at hand. "And the nobles fear they will be ruled by a Naharin King in the end?"

Ay, Horemheb, Nakhtmenu, and Paramessu all nod at this. Ankhesenamun crosses her arms and leans against the side of the writing table. Now that I understand the fear, I see that it is not an unreasonable one. "Kemet must not be ruled by foreigners ever again," I say. A thought strikes me.

"The army is ready to do your bidding," says Horemheb.

"We could send the army to the Naharin to fight the Hittites," I say. "Or we could send an envoy directly to the Hatti King asking for one of his daughters to be married to the King of Kemet."

Ay and Horemheb both frown, as do Nakhtmenu and Paramessu. Ankhesenamun, however, nods. "It is worth considering," she says. "There would be the addition of one Hatti individual to the court, not a sudden influx of dignitaries and functionaries. Furthermore, the princess would never be Great Royal Wife, so her sons would not succeed to the throne, and there is no worry that Kemet will become Hatti."

"And Kemet would have a source for weapons of black metal," I say. "We could demand some as part of the dowry."

"Why should the Hatti give us that which makes them strong so that we might use it against them?" asks Ay.

"If we receive none as dowry, we still may be able to trade for it," I say. "In any event, there is no harm in asking."

"Even without the black metal, it is still a worthy plan," says Ankhesenamun. "We would save the costs of war and enrich our coffers at once. And if we are not at war, we have less need for new weapons."

"If one is certain of winning, one does not need to bargain," says Horemheb. "It will be seen as weakness."

I ponder this for a moment. "Not if we bargain from a position of strength, set the terms and are prepared to walk away. We decide what must not be compromised and do not waver. Then we make concessions on less important points and allow them to think they have won."

"They will see right through such a ruse," says Horemheb.

"No doubt," I say, "but the Hatti can be no more assured of winning a war than we are and so may be open to pursuing an honorable peace if it is offered."

Ay and Horemheb look to each other.

"Is this your decision?" asks Ay.

"It is."

"Very well," says Horemheb. "We will meet later to draw up the terms of the offer."

I nod. After they have gone, Ankhesenamun sits on the corner of the writing table facing me. She studies me intensely.

"Do you approve?" I ask.

"Your plan has great merit," she says. "Though I do not believe it will succeed."

My heart drops. "No?"

"The Hatti will not accept that which must be non-negotiable for us," she says. "No daughter of Kemet can be given to a foreigner in marriage, so there will be no princess from the Women's Quarters sent in exchange. The Hatti are not a subject nation hoping to win your favor. They are an independent nation intent on conquering us and will not agree to a trade that places them in an inferior position."

I slump in my seat. I had thought my scheme to be perfect.

"Still," says Ankhesenamun, "it will buy time. There will be no war during negotiations. We must prolong them as much as possible. With luck, by the time they break down, we will have won back our former provinces." She places a hand on my shoulder. "It was well done."

I resist the urge to beam at her, though I sit a little straighter.

Ankhesenamun

Sunlight sparkles on golden sand. I feel the heat of it through my sandals as I lead the priestesses, shaking the sistrum to the rhythm of the drum to the rear and the clappers of the dancers alongside. Ahead, the priests carry the stone gods in their golden litters – Amun, his wife, Mut, and their son, Khonsu. My back pains, as it does frequently of late, and I wish I were free to stop and stretch.

The procession turns toward the path down to the valley where the Westerners reside in their tombs. To our left are the temples of my forebears. My grandfather's, surrounded by black statues of Sekhmet, erected in vain hopes of averting plague. Those of the third and fourth Djehutymose and, most beautiful of all, that of Hatshepsut, with its tiers of columns melding seamlessly with the cliff face.

Ahead, the passage rises into the hills and as we top the crest, the view below opens up into a series of folded hills and wadis. I close my eyes briefly. The music pulses through my body and I feel something else, besides. A presence? Mother always told me she could feel the presence of her goddess. I always suspected she more than felt it. In a rare unguarded moment, I caught her tilting her head, as if listening to things unseen and unheard by others, or perhaps only unseen and unheard by me. I scan the sky. The feeling is gone. Apart from white clouds scudding on the horizon and a distant hawk circling, it is empty. I am unsure whether this means this goddess, Mut, and her male counterparts, are not present or if I am simply unable to detect them. I hope it is the latter.

Winding our way along the path, I see the canopies spread out on the valley floor, in the open space in front of Mother's tomb. A sudden gust of wind in the narrow basin billows the brightly colored linens, straining against the poles holding them aloft. Offerings of food, of roasted antelope and ostrich, baked fish, baskets of pomegranates and grapes, wine and bread, honey and sweetmeats, are already piled high. The breeze greets us with tantalizing aromas, causing my mouth to water, my belly to rumble and the child within to squirm as if the scent can penetrate my flesh and stoke his appetite as well as mine.

All of the nearby tombs – those of my great-grandparents and their parents and grandparents – boast similar offerings. My grandparents, Amenhotep and Tiye, lie in the nearby Western Valley and, though I cannot see their tomb from here, I know they are likewise honored this day. My sistrum falters as I pass my father's tomb. Its facade stands empty and alone, as it does every year. The Kemetian people wish to forget him almost as much as I do, and I am relieved not to be duty-bound to feign affection for him. I bring my attention back to the music. The dancers leap and gyrate to the wail of pipes and lute against the relentless rhythm of drums.

The priests gently set the gods down by the entrance to the pavilion. I approach Mother's tomb, laying down my sistrum in front of the food offerings. I take the necklace from around Mut's neck and place it next to the sistrum. I whisper a brief prayer to Mother, hoping she is well in the Field of Reeds. I kneel at Mut's feet, praising her, thanking her for her bounty, and asking her to bless my child and grant me a safe birth.

The ceremony done; we gather beneath the canopies. The gods rest before us, that we may feast in their names. As I take my place at the table, a cramp slices through my belly. I halt for a moment, but the pain is gone as quickly as it came. Tutankhamun, already seated, glances up at me, concern in his eyes.

"Are you unwell?" he asks.

"Simply tired," I say, hoping it is the truth. Menwi, the servant who assists with all the palace births has assured me it is common for a woman with child to ache in the early days, but this was different from the pains of weeks ago. Sharper, more intense.

Nebetah, to Tutankhamun's other side, catches my eye and I look away. She is not so easy to fool as my husband, and her concern worries me. I am glad for the distraction when Ay, Tey and Mutnedjmet arrive and take their places beside mine.

Flagons of wine and plates of food appear before us – roasted gazelle, braised goose, honeyed figs. As we eat, the dancers spin around the gods, leaping into the air. Beside me, Tutankhamun smiles, tapping his good foot with the rhythm of the music.

For the sake of appearances, I eat, but I do not taste. I feel no pain, just a nagging discomfort. I have to resist the urge to shift my weight so that none will notice. Even with the canopy shielding the brilliance of the sun, it grows unbearably hot. The linen of my dress clings to my skin and perspiration beads down my back. Yet the dampness between my legs feels too great to be sweat. I wait for the dance and the music to reach a crescendo, when no one is watching me, and then I look. The white linen is stained bright red.

When the next serving girl approaches, I beckon her near. In a low voice, I instruct her to send my steward with a robe immediately. When he arrives, I instruct him to bring my litter to the edge of the camp. I settle the robe around my shoulders before rising and push my chair under the table.

Tutankhamun lowers his brow. "You do not intend to leave now."

I turn from him and walk toward the spot where servants are approaching with my litter. The breeze stirs behind me and Nebetah grasps my elbow. "I shall accompany you, as shall Mutnedjmet." She turns her head and gestures behind her. My other aunt rises and follows us.

As I pass the goddess, I glance at her granite face and cast one last plea for my child. Mut is the Mother of Kings. Surely, she will help me. She continues staring implacably toward the desert. I feel lost.

On the ride back to the palace, the pains start in earnest. I must lean on Nebetah to make the walk back to my chambers while Mutnedjmet goes to summon Menwi. Nebetah helps me to my bed, fetches towels herself to wad between my thighs, then lies next to me and cradles my head on her shoulder, as my mother used to do.

My other ladies appear. "You should not have left the feast," I say.

Tuya and Meryetre kneel beside me. "Where else would we be, Highness?" says Tuya.

Menwi arrives, carrying about her shoulders a great, bulging satchel that would bend the spine of a lesser woman. I grab her sturdy wrist. "You must stop this."

She lifts the satchel over her head and lowers it to the floor, removes the towels from between my legs and after a brief inspection, shakes her head. "There is nothing anyone can do." From the satchel she removes a small, pink granite statue of Taweret.

I shudder. Menwi would not have brought the goddess of childbirth into my chambers if she believed my pains would stop.

Menwi's sharp eyes follow my gaze. "She is here for you, Highness. To see you through this day."

Nebetah pats my hand. I pull it away from her. "No. The child lives. He was moving less than an hour ago."

Mutnedjmet kneels by the bed. She and Nebetah exchange a glance.

Henutmire, so close to her own birthing time, turns pale.

Menwi eyes Henutmire. "Leave," she says. "This is no place for you right now."

Henutmire glances at me, tears in her kohl-lined eyes, before fleeing the room.

Menwi turns to Ast. "You best go as well, lest you be cursed yourself when you bear children."

My insides twist at this cool acceptance of my loss.

Ast folds her slender arms. "I have no fear of curses."

Menwi shrugs.

"We must go to the birthing pavilion. Do all the chants and prayers," I say.

"They will not help," says Mutnedjmet.

"Get out," I tell her.

"She speaks the truth," says Menwi. "Besides, there is no time. The way is fully open."

Sobs wrack my body. When my midsection squeezes in the attempt to expel its contents, I clamp my hands around whatever is within reach – the bedclothes, Nebetah's hand, someone's hair – and resist. I will not bring forth this child until it is ready.

I hear Menwi's gravelly voice. "Send for some poppy. Now."

I stiffen my body all the more. "I will not take it."

"You will if I have to pour it down your throat," says Nebetah.

"If you do not deliver well, you may sicken and die," says Menwi.

I turn to look at the wall. "I do not care."

Nebetah takes my chin and turns my head to look at her. "I care. So does Tutankhamun. So does all of Kemet. You will do your duty and live."

When the poppy arrives, Ast holds the bowl while I drink deeply, hoping for an oblivion which does not come. Instead, I am forced to endure the process. Within moments, my limbs become too heavy to move and, though there is no longer any pain, I feel my body disgorge the life it held for too short a time. I hear voices echoing, as if issuing from a canyon.

"Take it away." Nebetah's face hovers in and out of view.

"The mothers generally fare better when they see the child, even hold it," says Menwi.

Nebetah moves aside.

"It is a girl, Highness," says Menwi, holding out a linen-wrapped bundle.

I roll half to the side and Menwi places the bundle beside me. A small head is visible. I try to move an arm to lift the sheet off her, but I'm still feeling the effects of the poppy. A hand reaches out and does it for me. The child, curled up, fits neatly into the palm of my hand, yet she is perfectly formed. Her ten fingers are formed into tiny fists. She has been wiped clean, and veins show through translucent skin. Her lashless eyes are closed and on her face is a look of repose. If not for the lack of movement in her chest, she could be sleeping.

"Do not worry, Highness," says Menwi. "The birth went well, and you will recover. There is no reason you should not have many more children."

Tears stream down my face. I try to wipe them away, but my arm falls uselessly at my side.

Nebetah dabs my tears with a cloth, then curls her body around me.

"We shall take her to the embalmers," says Mutnedjmet. "She will live in the Field of Reeds. Our ancestors will care for her until you join them."

I want to join them now.

Tutankhamun

I cross into Ankhesenamun's bed chamber as quietly as possible. The smell of blood hits me, along with something more, something dense and indefinable. I tap my walking stick in front of me and allow it to settle into the floor before taking a step with my lame foot. Then I lean on my stick as I bring my good foot forward. Slowing down the movements makes me unsteady, but as I approach, I see her hair is damp and there are dark circles under her eyes. I don't wish to disturb her. She has endured enough. When I near the bed, I kneel carefully, but at the last moment, the stick falls from my hand, and I stumble to the floor. I am unhurt, but unable to catch the stick before it clatters on the tiles. Ankhesenamun's eyes open.

"I was trying not to wake you."

"I wasn't asleep. I knew you were here."

"Menwi told me she'd given you poppy."

"She did. Before. I would not take it again after." She gestures toward her night table. A full bowl rests there.

I want to reprimand her for not easing her pain, but I know why she won't take it. I, too, am haunted by the specter of our father staggering around the palace and Ankhesenamun has even more reason to hate the poppy than I.

I squeeze her hand. "I am so sorry."

Her eyes widen. "What are you sorry for?"

"I was cross with you for leaving the feast. For ruining the festival," I say. "I didn't know."

She shrugs and shakes her head. "I did not wish for you to know then," she says.

"You didn't wish for anyone to know, but my mother did. I should've seen it as well. Why did she not tell me? Why did you not tell me?" Even to my own ears I sound like a petulant child, and I know it's unfair to be angry with her now.

She strokes my scalp. "We hoped there would be nothing to tell." Her voice catches as a tear escapes and rolls down her face.

I take her hand and hold it between my own. I must be the one offering her comfort, not the other way around. This is where I prove my manhood, not on some distant battlefield.

I climb into bed, and she shifts so I can lie beside her. I put an arm around her shoulders. "You may cry if you wish. I won't tell anyone."

She laughs even as the floodgates burst open. She buries her face in my chest, where tears and snot blend with the vestiges of black and green makeup from earlier in the day. She cries until the tears dry up and still her body heaves. I hold on, whispering into her hair until she is finally exhausted and sleeps. Only then do I allow my own tears to fall.

Tutankhamun, Year 6

(ca. 1328 BCE)

Ankhesenamun

The gilded coffin in the form of the god Wesir rests in a niche in the Temple of Mut, the great mother. As always, I place a hand over its hands and rock it gently back and forth. At first, I came here daily, then every two or three days. Now I make it a weekly habit, after beginning of the week ceremonies at the great Ipet-Iset Temple, I take the avenue south through two sets of pylons, through the gates started in my grandfather's time and only now nearing completion, so I may return to see her. This week, I am doubly thankful to Mut: for caring for this small one, and for granting me another. The barley sprouted just a few days ago. That should mean the child is a girl, though the prediction was wrong with the last one. But boy or girl, there is a child, and for that I am grateful.

I prostrate myself at the feet of the goddess. Mut proved hard and unforgiving when I begged her to save my child's life, but perhaps she acted so in order to keep the child with her. I beg the goddess to protect the babe in the Field of Reeds until I may join her. Midway through uttering my thanks, I am stopped by the sound of the door and familiar stop-drag step. I turn to see Tutankhamun approaching.

"I am sorry to disturb you on this day."

My heart stops. I hope he has not heard me, for I do not wish for my secret to become known for a while, lest Mut prove equally treacherous this time. "There is nothing special about this day."

"It is the day you spend with our daughter, after ceremonies at Ipet-Iset."

I relax. "I was not aware you knew."

"I know," he says. "I also visit here at night sometimes."

I shake my head. I didn't know this.

He continues. "I would not disturb you if it were not important, but a runner has just arrived with a message from Retenu."

From Retenu. Not from the Hatti. Not their response to the latest round of marriage negotiations, then. "I was not expecting news. Were you?"

He frowns. "Not from Retenu."

"What is it?"

"It is not a direct messenger," he says. "It is a runner, the end of a relay, which has been speeding toward Waset with news of an urgent nature."

I let out a breath. "We should meet him in private."

"He waits at the Council Chamber."

I hook my elbow in his and we walk together. Using me to take some of his weight, Tutankhamun can move a little faster. We sway together down the corridors in the manner we have been moving together since he was small. For the first time, I notice his height is now equal to mine.

Outside the council chamber, next to the guards, a dusty individual sits in a chair with a flagon of beer. When he sees us approach, he rises, places his beer on the seat and prostrates himself on the floor.

"Rise and follow," says Tutankhamun as we enter the chamber. He sits on a carved wooden chair behind the writing table, while I stand to his right. The messenger bows deeply.

"I understand you bring news from Retenu," says Tutankhamun.

The messenger rises, but keeps his eyes fixed on the floor. "The Hatti are advancing. Already the Kharu and the Amurru have fallen. When the first runner left, the Dahy were under siege."

The moment I heard of the messenger's arrival, I feared some such news, but it is worse than expected. Now, all that stands between the Hatti and Naharin are the Kinanu, a ragtag mob of nomadic goatherds. All that stands between the Hatti and Kemet are the Naharin.

"Unfortunately," says Tutankhamun, "we did not have advance notice of your arrival, and so have not had the opportunity to prepare a feast in your honor. However, I have already sent word to prepare comfortable quarters for you so that you may rest. You shall dine in the hall tonight." Neither his face nor his voice betray any emotion and I am proud of him.

The messenger bows again and backs out of the room. Once he is gone, I sit on the corner of the writing table.

Tutankhamun places his hands flat on the polished ebony surface in front of him. "I suppose we have the Hatti's response to my latest offer of marriage."

"We did not expect them to accept," I say.

"We did not expect them to violate all the rules of international diplomacy by attacking our allies during negotiations."

"The Kharu, the Amurru and the Dahy are no longer our allies," I say. "Nor are the Kinanu or the Naharin. Father drove them away."

Tutankhamun drums his fingers on the writing table. "We have no choice. We must go to war now." He glances up at me, a question in his eyes, as if hoping I will see what he does not.

I must disappoint him. "War is our only option."

He nods. "I shall meet with Horemheb immediately. He has kept our forces at the ready. We shall leave within the week and arrive about a month later. We may be too late to prevent the Dahy from falling, but with luck we shall help the Kinanu prevail and form a shield in front of the Naharin."

"With luck."

Tutankhamun rises. "I shall also send my steward to prepare my own chariot and weapons for travel."

"You will not go with the army." It is not an order, but nor is it a question.

"I will not sit safe in Kemet while my soldiers die in my stead. Only the poorest King would consider it.

"If you go into battle, you will return as a Wesir-King and Kemet will be left without a ruler."

Tutankhamun glowers at me. "I am as capable as any soldier." He does not believe it any more than I do.

"Given a few more years, perhaps, but you are young and untested, and you would be facing career soldiers." It is a lie. He is near enough to manhood that he would be almost of an age with much of the enemy. I maintain eye contact, tamping down the urge to gawk at the accursed foot.

Tutankhamun clenches his jaw. "I will not need to fight. Merely the sight of the King at the head of his mighty army strike fear into the hearts of the strongest Hatti and they will run."

Still, I must force myself not to break eye contact. True, he has gained considerably in height, yet he is still small and slight. I doubt very much he will cut an intimidating figure on the battlefield even should he manage to hide his crippled foot. It is difficult enough for the two of us to maintain our authority whilst being pulled in opposite directions by Ay and Horemheb. I cannot imagine how I should manage on my own with an infant.

"Your people need you to survive. You have been leading our slow return to Ma'at, but the balance is yet precarious, and without you we should all be plunged back into chaos. Without an heir, I fear I shall be unable to hold Kemet together on my own." I do not bother hiding my tears, in the hopes that they may move him.

Tutankhamun nods and he speaks in a voice so low I must strain to hear him. "Fine. I shall not go."

He gets up and walks out without waiting for me to accompany him. It occurs to me that he may grow to resent me for keeping him from this opportunity for glory, but at least he will live.

Tutankhamun

Hooves clop on the paving stones, chariot wheels whirr, and feet march in time to drumbeats as the parade approaches down the main avenue of Waset before the grand temple. Horses' heads appear first, topped with undulating plumes of red and blue. Sunlight sparkles on their bridles. Whoops erupt from the assembled crowds, and I strain my neck to see the archers drawing their bowstrings and posing. As they draw nearer, I can see the forelegs of the lead horses, lifting in unison, their glossy hides contrasting with the strong muscle rippling beneath.

When the procession reaches our dais, Ankhesenamun and I toss out necklaces and rings to the triumphant soldiers. Horemheb, in the lead chariot catches one and holds it up to the admiring throng. Not to be outshone, Paramessu, following Horemheb reaches behind as a jewel sails over his head and he grasps it.

Snatches of conversation from below our dais reach me. For once, it seems, Ast is the brunt of teasing from the other ladies instead of the perpetrator. Rumor has it that, despite her long condemnation of marriage, she is about to be caught at last, and by her own choosing.

"Kheruef is unique among men," says Ast.

"They are all unique until you marry one," says Tuya. Her tone has the ring of irony, perhaps Ast's own words thrown back at her.

With regret, I return my attention to the spectacle before me. Had I gone with the army, as I should have, I would be riding at the head of the parade right now. A King should never merely watch from the sidelines. Ankhesenamun smiles at me, and I turn away.

"Surely you are not displeased at our victory," she says.

"At the victory, no." I know she understands the true source of my displeasure, but I have managed to avoid the topic for the past few months and have no desire to address it now.

"You made the right decision. Kemet is once again building its empire and still has its King. Ma'at is less precarious than it was before the army marched."

"The people should be cheering for me," I say.

Her eyes widen. "I was not aware you desired such adulation."

"I don't, but if we care to stay on the throne we must be adored by the people, and for that to happen, I must not send others to do my duty for me."

"When I wanted to die, your mother told me it was my duty to live. It is yours as well, like it or no. You cannot rule from the Field of Reeds."

I give her a sideways glance, contemplating if I should broach the subject I have been thinking on for some weeks now. After opening and closing my mouth twice, I decide now is the time and drop my voice lest I be overheard. "At least, should I die now, I would not be leaving Kemet without an heir."

Forgetting all protocol, Ankhesenamun whips her head around to look at me, mouth gaping open. She quickly recovers and resumes her placid, forward-looking gaze. "How did you know? I have told no one. Not even my ladies suspect."

"I wouldn't be so certain of that," I say. "You're getting fat again."

Tutankhamun, Year 7

(ca. 1327 BCE)

Ankhesenamun

I quicken my step so that I may reach Nebetah before she leaves the palace. "I hear you are going to the chariot track," I say as I approach. "Might I accompany you?"

She glances at my expanding girth.

"I have no desire to ride, I would not endanger the King's son," I say. "I merely wish to watch. When I see the horses run and wheels rolling and you holding the reins, I can almost feel that wind in my own face." Nebetah smiles at me. "You are a true daughter of your mother. I shall be glad of the company." She glances at the woman-child trailing me. With each step, the girl's slender legs lift with the all the grace of a gazelle. Her liquid-dark eyes, accentuated with kohl, only enhance the resemblance. "Ast's replacement, I presume?"

"My apologies, Aunt," I say. "May I present the Lady Kawit. She arrived early this morning and I have promised to show her the grounds."

Nebetah eyes her up and down. "You look young. Are you sure you have seen twelve inundations."

Kawit lowers her eyes. "Yes, Lady."

"Hmph," says Nebetah. "We shall see what the next few years bring before we entertain your father's petition."

Kawit's father has been trying for a marriage between Kawit and Tutankhamun for some years now. He thinks to further his cause by placing her in my retinue. Though any of my ladies may become my rival at any time,

I would not usually deliberately invite such a one into my charge. But her father is quite ambitious and, given her youth, I thought it preferable she become my ally before being presented to Tutankhamun as a possible wife.

When we arrive, there is already a horse with chariot galloping around the circuit. Even at a distance, I can see the driver, bow in one hand, leaning to the right. "I was not aware he was out so early." We lean against the circumference rail to watch.

He draws his bow and nocks an arrow, waits for the right moment and releases. The arrow sails true, directly into the heart of the target.

Kawit claps her hands.

"He practices often," says Nebetah, beaming. "He can do what everyone says he cannot, it just requires more work."

"I know it." I say so because I do not wish to quell her mother's pride, yet my own heart constricts. Tutankhamun's chariot skills have indeed improved. I fear these newfound accomplishments will bring overconfidence and recklessness. To cover my own apprehension, I speak of other matters. "He grows as well in mastery of statecraft. The plan to stall the Hatti through marriage negotiations was his own, not Ay's or Horemheb's, and not mine. He has an innate sense of when to apply force and when diplomacy is the better course of action. I believe my mother would proud to see him justify her faith in him."

"I have always been proud of him," says Nebetah. "But now he is a man, it is time you step aside and allow him to run Kemet as he was born to do." She looks to me. "You know this is so. Besides, you shall soon be occupied with motherhood."

"My mother had six children yet still managed to run the country."

"Yes, because your father refused to do so, and the land was in chaos."

"The land was in chaos because my father refused to rule yet would not allow my mother free reign. Had she truly been in power, as she later was, Kemet should have been glorious." I give her a side glance. "Perhaps I should be the one to rule."

Nebetah opens her mouth, aghast. She stutters, as if trying to decide how to respond.

"Do not worry," I say. "I speak in jest. I think my illustrious grandparents left the better example. Tutankhamun is King, and I shall stand behind him, wielding my power in private, as is proper."

The chariot comes to a stop several arm spans in front of us and Tutankhamun descends, holding out a hand. A servant appears with a walking stick. Tutankhamun accepts it, and approaches us, grasping the rail with one arm as he swings himself underneath it.

"Magnificent, darling," says Nebetah, running a hand over his scalp and kissing him on the cheek.

Tutankhamun pushes her hand away. "Enough, Mother." He eyes the guards, who remain passive and the groomsmen, who turn away to hide their smiles.

He places a hand on my belly. "You, surely, are not riding."

"She has come to watch me," says Nebetah.

"Stand with me," I say.

"I wish I could." He kisses me on the cheek while twining an arm around my waist. "But I am due back in the palace." He releases me and takes the path back, turning once to look at me and smile. He nods at Kawit, who smiles openly before remembering to bow her head.

Already the groomsmen are leading fresh horses with a chariot to the track. Nebetah tucks her robes into her sash and ascends. With a word and a flick of the reins, they're off. The wheels blur with motion. Nebetah's hair ruffles in the wind behind her as she makes myriad tiny movements, constantly shifting her weight with the minute changes in terrain.

As the chariot thunders past me, I close my eyes and feel the rumble in the earth. Grains of sand pelt my face and arms, and I picture the palace and the great temple flying past in turn. A flutter inside draws my hand to my belly and I feel selfish for my own yearning. It is not very long, after all – another four months and I shall be riding and training with swords again. In the meantime, I can still shoot a bow. Perhaps when Nebetah is done here, she will do some target practice with me.

I feel a tug on my sleeve. "Shall we retreat to the stables, away from the flying sand?" asks Kawit.

I shake my head. "You may go if you wish. I shall stay as close as I may."

The girl looks longingly at the stable but remains by my side.

When the horses tire, Nebetah brings them in. Two groomsmen stand by in case they should be needed, but Nebetah insists on always caring for the animals herself. As do all of the women in our family. Kawit moves to help, but I motion for her to stay. I untie the horses from the chariot, inhaling their scent from the downy spot behind their ears – sweat mixed with animal musk – while Nebetah removes their bridles. She hands me one lead and takes the other, walking ahead of me. As we near the stable, her horse tries to back away. She coos to calm him. He rears and she releases the lead, lest she be dragged by it. My own horse shies away.

Nebetah sees me and grabs the lead from me. "Go!" she screams.

It happens in slow motion. The lead horse's hind leg rises and kicks out. "Watch out!" I reach for her, but arms are pulling me back. A hoof connects with Nebetah's cheek. She flies up and seems to float to the ground, landing in a crumpled heap on the sand.

The animals bolt, running into the desert. When the arms holding me let go, I rush to Nebetah and kneel beside her. Her left jaw has been crushed. The flesh of her cheek is in ruin. Blood gushes across her mouth and nose, pooling in the sand below her head. My stomach lurches and I turn just in time to avoid retching all over her.

People are running around us, and I stop one, asking him to send for the physician. "It's already been done, Highness," he says.

A man I recognize as a groom brandishes a pitchfork. Serpentine coils are impaled on the tines. "A cobra, Highness. It was hiding in the shadows of the stable wall."

Her eyes are closed, but her chest is rising and falling. She lives. Blood continues to flow. I tear at my skirts, and even though my heart tells me it is futile, I press the wadded up linen strips to her wound to stop her life from seeping out.

I lie down in front of Nebetah, as close as I can get, careful of where I am touching her. I want to cradle her head against my shoulder as she once did for me, but I fear hurting her worse. Even more, I fear that hurting her worse is not possible.

I do not know how long I am there before the physician arrives. His servants move Nebetah onto a rectangle of coarse linen. One at her head, and one at her feet, they lift the corners and carry her. I walk beside her back to her rooms in the palace and sit by her bed while the physician works.

I get up to send a servant to inform the King of what has happened. When I return, Nebetah's eyes are open, and tears are flowing. Her face has been cleaned and there is a gaping hole in one cheek. Where there should be teeth and bone, there is blackness. The physician is using tweezers to pluck out bits of debris. I swallow against the bile rising in my throat. I must not shame myself again.

"Does it pain you very much, Aunt?" As soon as I ask, I know it is a ludicrous question.

She closes her eyes a gives the faintest hint of a nod. I send the nearest servant for poppy.

The physician gives me a hard glare and motions me to the side. "The Queen Mother has lost most of one side of her jaw. She will not be able to drink the poppy."

"She must be able to eat and drink, or else ..." I do not finish the thought, not even silently.

He drops his voice. "It will make no difference."

I resist the urge to shake my head, not wanting Nebetah to know the peril she is in. "You are wrong."

"Head injuries such as she received most often kill within days, if not hours. But even should she survive that, she would almost certainly be facing blood poisoning."

I return to Nebetah. She is fingering the ruin of her face. When she sees me, she grabs my wrist and speaks. The words are garbled. I kneel and lean my head close to hers. She repeats herself and it sounds like, "Take care of my son."

I take her hand and press it to my cheek. "Always. With you to help me for many years to come."

She rasps again and I think she is thanking me for the lie.

The chamber door bursts open, revealing a dark silhouette blocking out the flickering rush lights in the outer chamber. Immediately, I recognize the kilted figure with the twisted foot. I rise to greet him, thinking to talk to him first, spare him some of the shock of seeing his mother in this condition. But when he sees me, his eyes widen, his walking stick falls from his hands, and he must grab the doorway to keep from falling over. I run to support him, and he touches my face. "You are hurt. I was told it was Mother, I did not know it was you, too." He picks at my bloodied clothing.

I take his face in both my hands. "I am fine. It is not my blood."

He wraps me in his arms and rests his head against my cheek. I can feel his body shaking.

I push him away and glance toward Nebetah's bed. "It is very bad." I take a breath. "The physician does not expect her to live."

"He is wrong." Tutankhamun releases me and I retrieve his walking stick for him.

"I hope so," I say, though I do not believe it.

Tutankhamun

Ankhesenamun hands me my walking stick and places a hand on my chest. "The horse kicked her in the face. It is not pretty." Her voice is low, presumably so that Mother does not hear.

I nod and approach the bed. The chamber stretches before me, the images of ducks and papyrus along the walls eerily elongated. I manage the few steps up to the bed platform, gripping my stick until my knuckles turn white so I do not tremble. Before daring to look down, I steel myself and clench my jaw. She must not see any reaction that may cause her fear or worry for me.

It is worse than I feared. Mother's face has caved in. Her left eye droops over the sunken hole of her cheek. Her right eye follows my movement. I want to weep but fight it.

A servant brings me a chair and I sit beside Mother, holding her hand. I am not aware of the passage of time until the chamber is dark and servants start bringing in candles. I look around. Ankhesenamun is gone. When did she leave? Mother's eyes are closed. Fear stabs me in the belly until I hear a rattling breath.

More time passes and a hand lands on my shoulder. I jump.

"I am sorry, I did not mean to startle you," says Ankhesenamun. She has bathed and changed her clothes. "Come to your chambers. Take some rest."

"I cannot leave her. What if she should need me?"

She nods, as if she expected that answer. "Then I shall have a cot brought in here."

"I shall not sleep."

She kneels beside me. "Do you wish me to stay with you?"

I do not, but also do not wish to offend her, so I nod. She rests her hand on mine. After a time, I feel her moving and when I look, catch her wiping at tears. When she sees me looking, she whispers, "I am so sorry. It is my fault." She leans into me and sobs.

I am taken aback. "What do you mean it is your fault? I was told there was a cobra in the stables. Was I told wrong?"

"No." She wipes at her nose. "I was leading one of the horses for her, and when it spooked, Nebetah took it from me instead of moving out of the way of her own horse." Her voice hitches but she recovers. "If I had not been there, she would not have been kicked."

I look from her to Mother, lying on her bed. "If you had not been there, she would have been leading both horses alone. It likely would have happened in any event. It is the will of the gods"

Ankhesenamun glances sidelong at me. "Do you believe in the gods?"

I take a deep breath. It is not a simple question. When we were young, we were taught there was but one god, the Aten. When our father died and I became King, we were told there were many and our father's reign was doomed because he spurned them all. Yet, we have brought them all back and still we are dogged by tragedy. I glance down at Ankhesenamun's belly. There is hope. I shrug. "I believe there are gods. If not, how else would the world exist? Though, I sometimes think the gods are granted both too much credit and too much blame for that which transpires in the lives of men."

Ankhesenamun looks to the figure on the bed.

I nod. "Yes, as I did just now about Mother. It is likely the gods had no part in this."

She takes my hand. "Mother believed in the gods. Truly believed."

"Yes. Her faith was such that it made me believe so long as I was in her presence."

Ankhesenamun sits back and looks about to speak, but then turns away. When she finally does speak, she says, simply, "Is it our doing? Nebetah's injury, the loss of our child, perhaps even Mother's death? If we believed more in the gods, would they be kinder to us?"

I lean forward and place my elbows on my knees. "I don't think the gods care a whiff about belief, only for reverence. We honor them in every way possible. We can do no more." I pat her hand.

She nods.

While I am looking at Ankhesenamun, I feel a hand brush my other arm. Mother is awake, watching me through her one good eye. She inclines her head, a weak attempt at a nod and her mouth moves. I shift from the chair to the side of the bed and lean in to hear what she is trying to say. The faintest brush of air tickles my ear and goes still. Her chest has stopped its movement. I raise my head to look upon her face. Her eye is pointing toward the ceiling, seeing nothing.

I touch her shoulder. When she does not move, I shake it gently.

"She is gone," says Ankhesenamun.

"No," I whisper. "No. She lives." I take Mother's hand and hold it against my cheek the flesh is clammy and limp.

Ankhesenamun seats herself next to me on the bed, saying nothing. In vain, I fight back tears. "How could she leave me?"

Ankhesenamun strokes my back. "She would never have gone by choice."

I turn away from her. I don't want her soothing words. I want to be angry. "Go," I say.

She opens her mouth, as if to protest, then nods and leaves me alone with Mother.

I watch Mother for a while, willing her to resume breathing.

She does not.

"What do I do now, Mother?"

Ankhesenamun

After descending the causeway connecting the palace to the mortuary temple of my grandfather, the great Amenhotep, the third of that name, we pass by the row of black basalt statues of Sekhmet, their lion heads staring in the direction of the palace. Sekhmet guards against the plague. I wish there were a goddess who guards against frightened horses.

As we proceed toward the front of the temple and the assembling funeral procession, the two great statues of Grandfather come into view. So massive are they that, were I to approach closely and on foot, I would find that the mere platforms on which they rest are taller than I. In utter serenity, they gaze upon the river.

Tutankhamun and I dismount and walk directly behind the coffin on its oxen-driven sledge, him leaning on me. Bearers hold a canopy aloft over our heads. It reduces glare but has no effect on the heat. Sweat pools beneath my breasts and belly. I feel the heat acutely of late, and it seems the babe does, too, for he has grown as sluggish as I. A dull ache blossoms across my forehead, exacerbated by the wailing of the mourners, the rattling of sistra and the bellowing of the sacrificial bull. My back spasms.

By the time our column snakes its way past the temples of my ancestors, up the hills and starts down into the hills and wadis where the Westerners rest, I am wishing I requested a litter for the entire way. My feet are heavier with each step, and I struggle to draw enough breath. As we continue our descent, a flash of deep blue appears in the edge of my vision, but when I turn to look, it has gone. Once more, I see it to the other side, this time I catch a glimpse of a woman in white linen, wearing a blue crown and the little breath I possess is drawn away for a moment. I blink my eyes and when I open them again, she has gone, replaced by shimmering heat waves above the sand. It is simply the desert playing tricks.

A breeze passes around us, cooling me as it dries my damp clothing. It whistles past my ears, seeming to utter, "I am with you always."

I turn to Tutankhamun. "Did you say something?"

He appears startled. "No."

I knew he did not, and, more, I knew whose voice I heard. It is not the desert playing tricks, but my own heart. The last funeral I attended was that of my mother. It is no surprise that I should be thinking of her now, at the funeral of my husband's mother. The circumstances are similar, both having died suddenly and unexpectedly. I tell myself this over and over again, for the alternative is too distressing to contemplate. It is not my mother's restless spirit I fear, but the possibility of its existence, which would mean the existence of other spirits I do not wish to encounter. I am thankful we will not be passing near my father's tomb. Another thought occurs which chills me despite the heat. If Mother's spirit yet wanders the desert, did she not vanquish the demons of the Duat and enter the Field of Reeds? Shall she wander, lost, for millions of years?

The entrance to Nebetah's tomb is open to the sun. From the outside, all that is visible is a long corridor, stretching into the cliffside, perhaps all the way down to the Duat, the underworld. We come to a stop, and I sway, swept by a wave of dizziness.

"Are you well?" asks Tutankhamun.

"It is the heat, nothing more."

Now that we are no longer in motion, he takes his arm from mine, wraps it around my waist and pulls me closer. "It is your turn to lean on me."

Nebetah, in her coffin, is lowered from the wagon and propped up in front of her tomb. Priests purify her with clean water and natron, followed by incense. We are near enough that clouds of the smoke waft over us. My head reels and my legs wobble. I clutch at Tutankhamun, but he teeters. Blackness.

A pain in my belly jolts me awake. I'm lying supine, staring at the sky. The surface I'm lying on is swaying. It takes a moment for me to realize I'm being carried in a length of linen. The motion roils my stomach, and I roll to one side barely in time to vomit onto the sand below. When I retreat back and curl around my aching midsection, Mutnedjmet appears beside me.

"You are awake, Highness," she says. "I need not ask how you feel."

"It hurts."

"It shall pass in a moment," she says. "I have already sent ahead for the birthing pavilion to be made ready; in case it is needed today."

I squeeze my eyes shut in a vain attempt to keep the tears inside. "It is too soon."

She pats my hand. "Not very much too soon."

By my reckoning, there is still six weeks remaining. Might a child live at this stage? I prefer not to find out. I relax a little as the pain eases. Perhaps it will not return. "Where is Tutankhamun?"

"He must stay to perform the Opening of the Mouth."

"Of course he must. It is his duty." I say this, yet I selfishly wish he were here with me.

"If it pleases you to know this, he had to be forcefully reminded of exactly where his duty lies," says Mutnedjmet.

I smile. It does please me, and I remain blessedly free of any pain. I stretch out, close my eyes, and breathe deeply, willing my womb to be still. I doze a little, the motion and the heat conspiring to drain my reserves of strength. At the outset, the cramp feels like those that accompany my monthly courses. I tell myself it is no more than that, and certainly nothing to fret over. Yet, instead of abating, it increases. When I can stand it no longer, I cry out.

Mutnedjmet orders my bearers to stop and lower me to the ground. She kneels beside me. "We are almost back at the palace. Can you walk the rest of the way, Highness?"

"I am not sure I should."

"The pains will be easier to endure if you do."

I look up at her. "Are you certain?"

"I spent many hours walking your mother around while she was birthing you and your sisters."

Just then, the pain releases its grip. "It is done. Perhaps there will not be another."

Mutnedjmet arches an eyebrow. "Perhaps, but if there is, it will be difficult for you to rise while it is happening." She holds out a hand.

I stare at the hand for only a brief moment before accepting it and allowing her to help me to my feet. I sway a bit but find my balance and manage to walk unaided through the palace gates. I glance to my right, toward the birthing pavilion set up within the palace grounds, against the outer enclosure wall. "I shall go to my chambers."

"Are you certain, Highness?" asks Mutnedjmet.

Before I can respond, another pain seizes me. All I can do is grit my teeth and nod. Mutnedjmet slips an arm around my waist and, taking much of my weight, walks me toward the pavilion. From a distance, I can see Menwi's robust figure. My ladies – Meryetre, Tuya and Henutmire – also await. When they see me, they run toward us.

I shake my head and clutch at my belly.

Mutnedjmet plants herself, feet apart on the flagstones. She turns me to face her and places each of my hands on one of her shoulders. "Breathe," she says.

I try. Hands massage my back and Menwi's voice instructs me to stop fighting.

"It is too soon." I cry. "I must stop it."

"It will stop, or it will not," says Menwi. "The only choice you have is whether to ease your suffering or make it worse."

When the pain eases, my body is trembling. Tuya and Mutnedjmet walk me to the pavilion and lay me down on the bed. The scents of fresh lotus and convolvulus fill the space, servants having brought vases full of flowers. I examine the canopy above in detail while Menwi's fingers probe. The coarse linen wafts in the breeze, the corners held aloft by papyrus stalk columns twined with ivy. When Menwi removes her hand and sits back, I scoot back, sit up and close my eyes, fearful of what she is about to say.

"The way is only partially open," says Menwi.

I open my eyes. "Is that good?"

Menwi tilts her head. "It is uncertain. Most likely, the pains will continue until the babe is born, but there is a chance they will stop and not start again for many days, or even weeks."

My whole body sags in relief. "I pray to Mut it is so."

"So do I," says Mutnedjmet.

"But if it is not, will the baby live, born so soon?" I ask, eyeing the statues of Taweret and Bes in the corners, here to protect mothers and babies during childbirth

"Also uncertain," says Menwi. "There is a chance he may."

There is a chance. There is a chance. Regardless of what happens in the next few hours, there is a chance my baby will live. "What do I do now?"

"Everything I tell you," says Menwi. "For now, rest. When the pains come, walk." She intones: "I am Heru who conjures so that she who is giving birth becomes better than she was, as if she was already delivered. Look, Het-Heru will lay her hand on her with an amulet of health. I am Heru, who saves her." She repeats this three more times and then retrieves from the satchel by the bed a clay amulet of Bes and binds it to my forehead.

For her to recite the traditional prayer, she must believe I will deliver this day. Indeed, the pains do not stop. I alternately rest and walk with Mutnedjmet or one my ladies.

I have just completed a circuit of the courtyard with Henutmire when she whispers in my ear. "The King approaches."

I turn to see Tutankhamun. "I shall take over now," he says to Henutmire and allows me to lean on him instead. I lead him toward a column so I may have something solid to lean on when I need it.

"You should not be here," I say.

"I am the King. I may be wherever I want to be."

If that were true, and Mutnedjmet did not deceive me, he would have been here from the beginning. "How went the ceremony?"

"Perfectly. Mother is well equipped to navigate ..." He stops when I clutch at the column, moaning and he calls for help.

"What is the trouble?" shouts Menwi. "Why is there a man here?"

"You speak to your King, madam."

"If you were Amun himself, I'd say the same thing. No men near the birthing pavilion."

"The Great Royal Wife is in great pain. She needs help." "The Great Royal Wife is soon to give birth," says Menwi. "In this, she is no different than any other woman."

By this time, I am returning to myself enough to open my eyes. Tutankhamun's eyes are wide and his voice low as he gestures to me. "It is always like this?"

"Yes," chorus Henutmire, Tuya and Meryetre, even Mutnedjmet, for though she has never borne a child herself, she has seen the truth of it many times.

Menwi softens. "As soon as there is news to tell, you will be informed."

Tutankhamun pats me on the shoulder. "I shall pray fervently to Het-Heru and Mut. To Amun and Khnum, even Bes and Tawaret and every other god who may help."

I watch him leave, wishing he could stay, yet knowing he would be of no use if he did.

Some hours later, Menwi orders me back for another examination.

"There is no progress, Highness," she says. "All is exactly as it was before."

I smile. "Then it will stop."

"Unlikely," says Menwi. "Your pains are mere minutes apart and strong." She hesitates.

"What is it you are not telling me?"

She swallows. "When I examined you the first time, I thought the babe moved a little. This time he did not, even with my prodding."

"He has been quite calm lately."

"When was the last time you felt him move?"

"Yesterday. Or perhaps the day before."

Menwi looks at the floor.

"It is the heat," I say. "It makes us all tired and lazy."

Mutnedjmet and Menwi exchange a look. "Perhaps," says Menwi.

"What is wrong?" I ask, though I fear I already know.

"Lie back, Highness. I must check again," says Menwi.

This time, as she removes her hand an ache builds, starting at the base of my spine and radiating around my whole body. Menwi and Mutnedjmet help me to sit.

"What have you done?"

"You must birth this child sooner rather than later," Menwi slides me to the edge of the bed. "You need to squat on the floor now."

"It is not time. You said the way is not open yet."

"This is how we open it."

Menwi instructs me to walk and then squat and repeat. Only when my legs can no longer hold me does she allow me to lie down.

"I need to use the chamber pot," I say.

Menwi sits next to me and rolls me onto my back. "Step onto the bricks." She arranges two bricks, each decorated with images of a mother just having given birth under the watchful eye of Het-Heru, by the side of the bed.

"Not now," I say. "I need the chamber pot." But she does not relent, and I clench my buttocks so as not to disgrace myself as I place a foot on each brick.

At a word and a gesture, Mutnedjmet and another lady take a place on either side of me, helping me to squat.

"Support her back." Menwi turns to me. "It is not the chamber pot you need. When the next pain comes, you must push."

The babe is small. Only two pushes are required. After I've lain back down on the bed and Menwi places the linen-wrapped bundle in my arms, I lift the wrapping to inspect. A girl. More than double the size of my first child, yet almost small enough to fit into my two hands. She does not respond to my caress.

"I am so sorry, Highness," says Menwi.

"No!" She is so perfect. Surely, she is merely sleeping. I fold the wrapping over her tiny body, leaving her face free, and sob into the soft linen.

I am disturbed by someone shaking my shoulder and realize Menwi has been speaking.

"Allow Mutnedjmet to take the babe to the embalmers."

I clutch my child closer and shake my head.

"We are not finished, Highness," says Menwi. "The afterbirth still needs to be delivered." She sends one of the ladies for poppy.

"Must it be done now?"

"Your pains have stopped already. The longer we wait, the more difficult it will be."

I turn my head away. I do not care.

"If you do not deliver it, you will bleed and it will not stop," says Menwi.

I look at her. I want Nebetah to tell me I must do my duty, as she did last time, but she is not here.

Mutnedjmet touches my head. "I will take her to the embalmers, and, after, she will go to the Chapel of Mut with her sister so you may visit them both. When you are ready to go West yourself, you will bring your two oldest children with you to the Field of Reeds." She holds my hand, gently moving it so she may take the babe. I allow her to.

Someone offers me a bowl of poppy, which I drink.

Menwi tugs lightly on the remnant of cord still protruding from me. She probes inside with her fingers. "The way is closing. We do not have time to wait for the poppy to take effect." She produces a scoop-like instrument with a long handle.

I struggle to scoot backward.

Menwi glances to the side. "Hold her down."

All of the ladies in attendance appear, each one holding down my limbs, pressing me to the bed.

Menwi hands me a rag and orders me to bite down on it. "It must be done." She advances with the scoop. "Best if you do not move, Highness."

A searing pain tears me from the inside. My body convulses or would if it could move under this weight. When my vision falters and I feel my consciousness ebbing, I welcome it.

I'm woken by a light so dazzling I must shield my eyes. When I become accustomed to it, I see it is the sun setting across the desert. Silhouetted in black is a single oarsmen atop a barge moored in a canal. Standing in the bow, a lone figure looks at me. I cannot make out the features, yet I am drawn to this solitary being.

It seems as drawn to me as I am to it. It steps from the barge, balancing with one arm out, as if carrying something in the other.

Just as I realize who this personage is and open my arms to run to her, the scene fades, becomes superimposed over the inside of my bedchamber. I can hear voices, echoing as if from the distant cliffs:

"Make her comfortable ... nothing more can be done ... the priest ..."

When Mother reaches me, the desert becomes real again. She puts an arm around my shoulder. Her hair smells of her favorite perfume – lotus and myrrh. I close my eyes and breathe her in. She nudges me and holds up the squirming bundle in her arms. It is a wee babe with dark curls and soft, brown eyes.

I hold out my hand to touch her but stop short. "Is this?"

Mother nods. "Your daughter."

I am confused. "She lives?"

"No, she does not."

I raise my head and, with my eyes, follow the dark slash of the canal. It descends underground.

Mother follows my gaze. "The entrance to the Duat."

"Then I have also passed to the West?"

"You have not yet decided. You may stay and enter the Duat, or you may return to your life."

Tears choke me until I can barely speak. I take the child from her – my child. I rock her in my arms and kiss her head. "I wish to go with you."

"Would you leave behind the husband who needs you?" asks Mother.

"He is a man now. He no longer needs me."

"You are wrong. Without you, he will stand alone against all the forces that would see him ousted from the throne."

"I do not believe I am very much protection in that regard."

"It is your duty to make the attempt."

I look at her. "You told me it was my decision to stay or to go."

"It is. I am here to see you make the correct one."

"You sound like Nebetah, I was just now wishing she would tell me some such thing." It occurs to me that, perhaps, this is a dream borne of my wishing. Earlier, I imagined I saw Mother, and now I am dreaming her. Then I see Mother's face. Tears stream down her cheeks as they never did in life and the look of anguish in her eyes makes me instantly regret my words.

"The last time Nebetah did tell me to do my duty, I wished it were you." Tears now stream down both our faces.

Mother takes my face in her hands and her voice breaks as she speaks. "I am glad Nebetah could be with you when I could not." She takes the child from me. "We will both be here when you are truly ready for the Field of Reeds."

I watch them walk back to the barge. Just before stepping aboard, Mother turns to me. "Never turn your back on Ay."

Before I can ask her meaning, the desert is replaced by my bedchamber. I take a breath. A face appears beside me. A young lady-in-waiting kneels by the bed. Kawit. "Send for the King," I say.

Tutankhamun

When I enter her chamber, Ankhesenamun is sitting up, leaning back against a pillow squashed between end of the bed and the wall. There are dark smudges beneath her eyes and bones jut through her sallow skin, but she is alive, and when I kiss her forehead, her flesh is blessedly cool.

She looks me up and down. "You are wearing your robes of office."

I accept the chair offered by a servant and sit. "I was in the audience chamber."

She lowers her eyebrows and looks to the window, flooding with morning sun. "You need not have listened to audience alone. Surely, we could have canceled for one day and gone together tomorrow.

I pat her hand. "Beloved, you have been ill for weeks."

She starts to talk but stops with her mouth half-open and cocks her head, as if listening to something. She frowns. "That is not possible. It was but a few hours that I slept."

"You bled." I take a breath. "I saw the sheets. I know not how you still lived. And then, just as you seemed about to recover, you burned with fever and clutched at your belly." I close my eyes to stifle tears. "You did not know me, you kept calling for your mother."

She starts at this.

"I thought surely …" I cannot continue.

She touches my arm. "I am here now."

I hold her and kiss the top of her head. She mumbles something I can't quite hear.

She repeats herself. "I want to see our daughter."

"There will be time for that. Right now, you must rest."

She pushes away from me and swings her legs over the side of the bed. "Is she in the Chapel of Mut already?"

I move to her side. "Still in the embalmers' tent, but you are not strong enough yet."

She glares at me and stands. The moment she does, her knees buckle, and she falls. I help her to her feet and sit her back on the bed. "You are not strong enough."

"I rose too quickly, that's all."

She looks me in the eye, and I know she means to go regardless of my opinion on the matter. I send a servant to arrange a litter for her and then send another servant to arrange a litter for me. Perhaps Ankhesenamun will mind being carried less if I am not hobbling beside her.

The porters lower the litters to the ground outside the Temple of Ipet-Iset. From there, I allow her the illusion that I am leaning on her as usual. The embalmers' tent is in the outer courtyard. We stop outside the open door-flap. I tap the flagstones with my walking stick and ask that we be given some privacy. The workers prostrate themselves before leaving.

Our daughter is dwarfed by the table on which she lies. The linen wrappings give her puny limbs substance, and I am glad her mother shall see her with at least the semblance of plumpness.

Ankhesenamun strokes the tiny head. "I am so sorry," she whispers. I think she is talking to the child until she faces me. "If only I had taken a litter instead of walking in the procession, perhaps our child would live."

That is not what Menwi told me. She believed the babe had died a day or two before the birth. I wonder if Ankhesenamun knows this.

"Next time, I will do better. I shall take no risks, and our son shall be perfect. I swear it to you."

With a shock I realize she does not know the rest. She cannot know, for she has been largely senseless since the birth. I glance from side to side, hoping someone will appear to relieve me of the responsibility of being the one to exterminate her hope. Yet, whatever shows in my face must alarm her.

"You do not believe me," she says, "and I do not blame you."

"I never doubt you," I say. "You are the most capable person I know." I look to the entrance flap, but as no help appears imminent, I continue. "Menwi says you will not conceive again."

Ankhesenamun's mouth moves, but no words form. She shakes her head. "She is wrong. She must be wrong."

"It was a difficult birth, followed by a difficult illness. Many times, I thought you would join our daughters in the West." I do not add that I am relieved she can no longer bear children, for if that were possible, I would never lie with her again for fear the next would be the end of her.

Her body begins to shake. I try to put an arm around her, but she shakes it off.

"Ankhesenamun." She's silent, so I repeat her name. "Ankhesenamun."

She ignores me still or, perhaps, she does not hear me. Her gaze has become fixed on a table full of embalming tools and jars of natron and of unguents. She steps away from me, moves around our daughter, and approaches the table. She runs her fingers over the tools – hooks and knives, tweezers and awls – until they hover over the bronze handle of an obsidian blade. I realize what she is about to do. I scramble to her side and grab the hand holding the knife before she can plunge it into her other wrist. I squeeze the wrist and force the blade from her hand, slicing my own palm in the process. Red droplets fall to the flagstones as the black stone shatters there. I stamp on the pieces, further pulverizing them.

Ankhesenamun pounds my chest. I grab her wrists and hold them still.

"Let me go!" She pulls her arms, attempting to free herself. She eyes the scalpels on the table.

"I won't."

She pulls a hand free and punches me square on the jaw. Leaning against the table for support, I spin her around and grab her around the waist, pinning her arms to her sides. I lean my head against hers and hold her, willing her rage to soften into tears.

Still, she struggles. "I don't want to be here."

I don't ask what she means because I am afraid I know. "It is …"

"Do not tell me it is my duty to live."

That is not what I was about to say. I meant to tell her it will be better with time. Perhaps that is the wrong thing to say, but I am unsure if there is a right thing. "I am still here," I say.

She attempts to pull away again. "You are no help. You never feel anything. Our children are both dead and you do not even grieve."

I release my hold and spin her around to face me. "How dare you tell me I don't grieve for my children. Their loss wounds me more than I have words to say it, but I thank Amun that I have not lost you, too. For the past many weeks, every moment I was not at my duties, I spent standing vigil over you. I had every priest of every god in all of Kemet saying prayers for you, sacrificing bulls and sheep ..." my eyes burn and my throat closes, stifling my words.

Ankhesenamun drops to the floor, hugging her knees. Her ribs are heaving. Dark lines of red blot her clothing and her skin wherever I touched her. She mumbles something incoherent. I lower myself to the floor next to her and caress her cheek with my uninjured hand.

"You must put me aside," she says.

"Never."

She wipes at her eyes. "You must. I cannot give you the heirs you need."

I inspect my wound. Blood no longer flows, but I make a fist anyway to prevent the cut from reopening. "The Women's Quarters are full of women capable of producing children, but not one of them is capable of ruling by my side as Great Royal Wife."

She looks at me. "I do not want your pity. I want you to do what is best for Kemet and replace me."

"You are what is best for Kemet." I falter. "You are what is best for me." I cannot keep the catch out of my voice. "My mother and my children are all in the West. You are all I have. You are the only one I may trust." I am now sobbing like the child she thinks I still am, and she must hate my weakness as I do, yet I am powerless to stop. "Please don't leave me." I wait for her to turn away in disgust, to tell me I am not worthy of kingship. That I am not worthy of her.

Instead, she cradles my head against her shoulder. "I will stay for you."

We hold each other.

Tutankhamun, Year 8

(ca. 1326 BCE)

Ankhesenamun

It is my first trip outside the palace grounds since the day everything changed. Where once Tutankhamun depended on my support to make the trek, I shall be depending on him for a time. He is now both taller and heavier than I, and though I have recovered well from my illness, still I tire easily.

After descending the causeway, instead of proceeding east along the line of Grandfather's temple, we turn to the south, where a new temple is rising. Stone pillars grow out of the golden sand, along with two colossal statues flanking either side of what, once completed, will be the entrance pylon.

I hear a sharp intake of breath behind me and am thankful for it. Perhaps the others are so struck they have not noticed my own awe. The statues are idealized likenesses of Tutankhamun, standing with hands at his sides and one foot forward. The white of the kilts is so bright it almost hurts the eyes, and it contrasts handsomely with the red-brown of torsos and legs. The lips are fuller than in life, but the remainder of the faces are truly his, the sculptor having captured the youthful glow and the intelligence in his eyes. Tutankhamun leaves me to stand between his effigies and turns to face the assemblage. He assumes the same pose, with left foot forward. We all dutifully applaud, feigning no notice of how one flesh foot curls under, while both stone feet are straight, nor of the walking stick now tucked under one flesh arm.

Tutankhamun raises his arms and gazes forward without smiling. In the moment just past the peak of the applause, he holds up a hand for silence. "You see before you the colossi that will mark my House of Millions of Years once I have passed to the West. Come and see the beginnings of the House itself.

Before following him, I glance behind me. The entire court has gathered to celebrate the inauguration of the House and its sentries. Almost as one, they fall in line behind us to view the foundations, the half-risen pylons and the rows of columns. Tutankhamun indicates where the walls will be. "Here, will be the story of my own divine birth, in which Amun took my father's form and visited my mother."

It is his way of distancing himself from the crimes of our father, while simultaneously aligning himself with the traditional gods of Kemet. It is a move not without precedent, for Hatshepsut made the same claim in her own House of Millions of Years. More than a century later, there is none left alive to say her claim was untrue. It shall be the same for Tutankhamun and those years of chaos shall be forever erased from history.

When Tutankhamun turns to continue the procession, Ay moves to his side. "It is quite modest. A King must proclaim his greatness for all to see." His eyes glance to Grandfather's temple, making a clear comparison and finding Tutankhamun lacking.

Tutankhamun responds as if he did not notice the snub, and instead addresses himself to the court. "This is but the beginning. Year by year, I shall add new rooms and colonnaded halls and gateways. By the time I am ready for the Field of Reeds, it will be a marvel to behold." He now glances to the nearby temple himself. "And shall dwarf all others."

The crowd listens with rapt attention. He leads the way slowly, but with a strength I have not seen in him before. During my illness, he has become steady, independent, and not only in body. His voice brims with confidence. With a pang, I realize it is because of my illness. Because I was not there, he discovered he no longer needed me. I'm caught between pride at his transformation, and regret that I had no part in it. Fear, as well, seeds itself in my belly. I cannot give him heirs and he doesn't need me to rule. He keeps me only because I am his last tie to childhood and when he no longer needs that....

I am relieved when the presentation is done, and we emerge back into the sands. Servants have erected canopies and spread blankets near the edge of the now-flooded fields that separate the royal temples from the river so that we might dine before returning to the palace. I resolve to not think on the uncertainty of my position and enjoy the meal. Ay, with his wife, Tey, sits beside Tutankhamun before Horemheb may usurp that spot. Horemheb and his wife, Amenia, sit with Ay and Tey.

Before I can take my place, Mutnedjmet waves to catch my eye and I tilt my head to invite her over as my Meryetre, Henutmire and Tuya take their places near Tutankhamun, leaving space for me. I search for Kawit and spy her lingering by the temple door. I beckon to her. As Mutnedjmet makes her way to me, Nakhtmenu places a hand on her waist and whispers something in her ear. She responds with a scowl and removes the offending hand.

"Shall I send Nakhtmenu to his bedchambers without any supper?" I ask as she approaches me.

"Please no, I fear that is what he wants," she says. "Though he would like for me to be there as well."

"You do not find him appealing?"

"He is a clod." She reaches for a fig and pops it into her mouth.

"I did not realize you were so choosy."

She raises her eyebrows. "You make me sound wanton."

I rather think it is her behavior that makes her appear so, not my words, but I choose not to say it.

She tilts her head in the general direction of those seated to Tutankhamun's right. "I do have standards." She deliberately keeps her gaze pointed at me, but there is no mistaking whose chiseled thigh she is indicating.

Horemheb is resting with deliberate casualness, not looking at us. Just as it occurs to me that their ignoring of each other is no accident, Mutnedjmet continues, her voice lowered.

"Besides, why should I lower myself to Nakhtmenu when that will be waiting for me later?"

"He already has a wife," I say.

"All the better," says Mutnedjmet. "He shall never expect me to fill that position."

I open my mouth to warn her of the dangers awaiting, should she be caught, but realize there is no need. Mutnedjmet is unmarried and, thus, unlikely to face any punishment at all. At worst, Amenia may be granted a divorce. I wonder if Horemheb would mind.

My attention is caught by Kawit and a young nobleman wearing an elaborate, curled wig and fine linen robes. He touches her hair and her cheek. Kawit blushes, but at the same time, shrinks from his touch.

"I see you thinking," says Mutnedjmet. "You are envious of me, perhaps."

"I am the Great Royal Wife. Why should I envy you?" It sounds haughtier than I intend.

I order a passing servant to tell Kawit she is needed here.

Mutnedjmet laughs. "Every moment of your life is planned. You must be here, or there, you must do this. You must marry the boy your mother chooses for you."

I avoid looking at Tutankhamun. "She did not make such a poor choice."

"Perhaps not, as husbands go." She leans in closer. "I cannot imagine he has much fire in the bedchamber."

Kawit approaches me in time to hear this. She keeps her eyes down.

My cheeks burn. "Bedding is for the begetting of children. He has proven himself adequate for the task."

"Adequate." Mutnedjmet rolls the word around on her tongue. "Adequate. Precisely what one seeks in a lover." She fights not to laugh as she turns her back to the royal party. Mutnedjmet points out a particular well-built guardsman and raises one eyebrow.

I cannot believe she is suggesting I betray Tutankhamun, and Kemet, in such a manner. "He is a servant."

Mutnedjmet whispers in my ear. "Then order him to serve you." I no longer fear bedding, as I did in the early years of my marriage, but neither do I desire it. Most certainly, I have no wish to seek it out from other men. Mutnedjmet leans toward Kawit. "Perhaps you would care to try him out?"

"Lady?" says Kawit.

Mutnedjmet tilts her head. "The guardsman. He is a considerable improvement over that fop you were speaking with just now."

"It was talk, nothing more," says Kawit.

"Come now," says Mutnedjmet. "I know all about the shenanigans of the ladies-in-waiting. I used to be one myself."

"I am sure I don't know—," starts Kawit.

"Ah," says Mutnedjmet, nodding. "You have your sights set higher than a mere guardsman. You are hoping to land yourself in the King's bed."

Kawit's head snaps around to look at me. "Highness, I—." "Leave the girl be, Mutnedjmet," I say. Kawit's shock is so clear I think she must believe I resent her because her father wishes Tutankhamun would take her as a wife. I am amused she should think I would feel threatened by her.

Mutnedjmet pulls me back to her.

"Sooner or later, the King will turn away from you."

Before I can stop myself, I flinch.

"Ah," says Mutnedjmet. "He has already."

"I have been unwell; he has not wished to impose."

"Impose? You are his wife. Men do not 'impose' on their wives. They simply take what they want."

The protest dies on my lips. I know this to be true for most men. Besides, "impose" was my word, not Tutankhamun's. When I begged him to take me so I could prove my ability to conceive again, he vowed he would not until I accepted there would be no more children. He said he did not wish to give me false hope and see those hopes dashed again. My attempt to end my own life lay unspoken between us. I believed he was afraid I would succeed next time, but perhaps it was a pretext to distance himself from me. After witnessing my weakness in the embalmers' tent, he must know I am not the rock of stability he has relied on. The one he no longer needs.

"Do not fret. You are truly fortunate," says Mutnedjmet.

I look at her. "Fortunate?"

She drops her voice to a whisper. "Now that you can no longer bear children, you may do what you please, so long as you are discreet. You need never worry about needing to seduce your husband so he might think your child his."

The background murmuring of voices is blocked out by the sound of my own heartbeat. Until this moment, I was not aware the defect in my womb was public knowledge. Lights flash around the edge of my vision and my heartbeat quickens. I feel lightheaded. I sway a little.

Mutnedjmet places a hand on my shoulder. "Are you unwell?" She no longer speaks softly.

Tutankhamun's head swings around. "Beloved?"

I nod. "I am tired. Nothing more."

"You always tell me you are simply tired immediately before you collapse."

I take a deep breath and smile. He is quite correct. "This time it is the truth. I am not about to collapse." I'm not certain when I say it, but it does turn out to be true. The light-headedness passes.

"Do you wish to return to the palace?"

I shake my head. "I wish to remain and celebrate the building of your House of Millions of Years." I sit beside him.

He squeezes my hand.

Tutankhamun

As I prepare for bed, there is a knock on my chamber door and the guard informs me Ankhesenamun requests permission to enter. I nod.

She stands in front of the door. "I was not certain you would be here. I thought perhaps you were visiting one of your other wives."

"Not tonight." She gives me a look as pained as if I struck her. Surely, she knows I visit the Women's Quarters. "You know I must."

She nods. "It is your duty."

I motion for her to enter. She sits beside me on the bed. "I'm sorry," she says.

"Please, stop apologizing. Our loss is no failure of yours."

"I mean for how I behaved last time I entered your chamber." She pushes a lock of hair behind her ear. "It was unbecoming."

"It was grief."

She heaves a sigh that seems to emanate from the soles of her feet. "I don't wish to be alone now."

I pull her close to me. "You will never be alone, so long as I am alive." Her heart thumps against my chest and her breath is warm on my neck.

She shudders and I think she is crying, but she pulls back, and her eyes are dry. She traces my mouth with her finger and kisses me. "Do not send me away again," she whispers.

"Never," I say.

The boat rocks, but Ankhesenamun shifts her weight in a dozen places at once, rolling with the waves as if she were born on the water. Her body tenses and she plunges her spear into the water. An instant later, she withdraws it. The fish is pierced through the dorsal fin and it wriggles off the point, plopping back into the water.

Ankhesenamun's body sags, but she throws me a smile. She's not discouraged, for it was a fine throw. She nods to acknowledge applause from Horemheb, Ay and the Viceroy of Kush, Huy, accompanying us in a second skiff. Huy is the reason for this outing – he has lately arrived in Waset with news of our distant province.

My turn, and I must brace myself to avoid tipping the papyrus skiff and rolling myself, Ankhesenamun and our oarsman off into the river. I grit my teeth against the pain in my foot, resentful of Ankhesenamun's easy grace. It is unfair that the gods afflicted me instead of her. The moment I see a flash of silver, I plunge the spear into the water and pull it back up with a fish wriggling on the end. Ankhesenamun, kneeling in the center back, applauds loudest and I feel a flush of shame for my momentary bitterness.

Huy steps into position, crouching his squat body to one side, one powerful arm raised, and bests all of us. He brandishes his spear with two large perch cleanly impaled through the center.

Ay claps him on the shoulder. "It stands to reason the Kushite is the better fisherman. Living in such a backwater province, there is little else to fill one's days."

Huy knocks the fish from his spear into a basket. "If only that were true." He wipes his brow with the back of his hand and withdraws to the back of the skiff, allowing Horemheb to assume throwing stance in the front.

"Trouble in Kush?" I have heard rumblings, but nothing truly alarming.

"It is why I have come so hastily to Kemet. There has been an uprising of the people."

"Then you must put it down," says Horemheb, scowling.

I can guess at what he is thinking. We need our resources in the north, to keep the Hatti at bay. Diverting our armies to Kush would present the perfect opportunity for an invasion of the Naharin.

"It has been crushed, but I cannot say it will not happen again," says Huy. "The people are dissatisfied. They wonder why we must send our gold and ivory to Kemet, why we must spend our time hunting for skins and feathers and slaves to be shipped north. Why should we not keep our bounty for ourselves?"

I wonder if this is truly the Kushite people talking, or Huy himself. "And what do you answer when the people speak treason?" I ask.

"Rest assured, Highness, I do not countenance such talk."

"I do hope 'not countenance' means you relieve the offenders of their heads," says Ay.

"Or drown them," says Horemheb.

"Or both," says Ay. "Cut off their heads and throw the corpses into the river in a large public ceremony so the people will see that those who speak against the King lose both this life and the next."

My belly churns and I swallow the bile that rises. For his part, Huy pales, or at least turns a few shades paler than his usual night-darkness. I glance to Ankhesenamun. She listens intently, with no appearance of being disturbed by the revelations. Of late, she has mastered the art of appearing inscrutable.

"I have tried," says Huy. "Seeing their fellows executed only feeds their anger. Every such death causes another riot. Another work stoppage. I haven't enough soldiers to enforce the peace." He looks at me. "I need you to send me more."

I take a stab at inscrutability and hope I come close. "I must discuss this with my advisors."

"What is there to discuss?" asks Huy. "If you do not send the army, you will lose Kush."

Ankhesenamun

Ay pounds a fist on Tutankhamun's writing table. "The nerve of Kush. They think Kemet is weak. They know of the trouble with the Hatti and think to take advantage while we are distracted."

Tutankhamun sways back and forth, leaning on his walking stick. "And should we engage with the Kushites, the Hatti will think the same and quite possibly choose that moment to attack Naharin."

"Yet we cannot afford to lose Kush," I say.

"We must send the army, of course," says Horemheb. "I do not see that we have any choice."

Tutankhamun shakes his head. "Nor do I. But perhaps we need not send the entire army. Kush is small and the land enclosed by the river and by desert, as is Kemet. It could be held by a smaller force. The rest may march to Retenu in case of attack by the Hatti."

"We cannot send enough men and arms to hold off the Hatti," says Horemheb, "but, perhaps, the Hatti will not know this."

Ay straightens. "This time, the King must ride with his army. The Kushites have no respect for a leader who does not fight with his men."

"No," I say.

At the same moment, Tutankhamun says, "I will go."

"It is too risky for you to fight," I say. "Kemet cannot lose you."

"I do not plan to fight," says Tutankhamun. He raises his chin and widens his eyes. "My mere presence will inspire the troops and give them the strength to keep fighting."

"Not if those troops witness you tumbling from your chariot and getting trampled by your own horses."

Tutankhamun faces me, nostrils flaring, his empty hand clenching into a fist. He wants to strike me. I stare back at him and do not flinch.

"Leave," he says.

I blink. "I beg your pardon."

"I said leave. If you cannot think rationally on this matter, you are no help to me."

"The King is quite correct," says Horemheb. I glare at him, and he waves a hand. "About traveling with the army. It is his duty, as it has been the duty of all Kings before him." He turns to me. "The army will protect him and deliver him safely back to your arms."

Tutankhamun turns several shades of red.

Horemheb tilts his head. "You have a wife who treasures your company. That is a rare gift."

My own face burns. To my shame, I was thinking not of the loss of Tutankhamun, but the loss of my own position should he not return.

Ay places his hands on my shoulders and looks into my eyes. I want to turn away but know he will see it as weakness.

"Granddaughter," he says. "The King is right. He must lead the army; it is his duty. It is how he will restore Ma'at to Kemet."

I note he refers only to Tutankhamun restoring Ma'at, not to me. I fear that once Tutankhamun is away from Waset, away from me, Horemheb may convince him to grant power he should not. With a shiver, I consider the possibility that Horemheb, and perhaps Ay as well, wish Tutankhamun dead. Should he die without issue, either of them might make a play for the crown. I study Ay's face – the web of creases, the saggy jowls, the rheumy eyes. Surely, he has no designs on kingship at his venerable age. But Horemheb is in a position to make a valiant attempt, should he so desire, and the army would likely support him if he did.

Yet, I cannot prevent the inevitable. Tutankhamun must lead our army. But while he is gone, I shall rule Kemet and Ay may not find me as pliable as once he did.

Tutankhamun

The projectile sails over the crenellated battlements, bounces across the courtyard and comes to a rolling stop before the inner fortifications of the military settlement. A soldier runs to retrieve it and I watch as he grasps it by dark, spiralled hair. As he nears, I recognize the blank, staring eyes of Huy, Viceroy of Kush.

I put a fist to my mouth to stop the rising bile and swallow hard. If I pause and look thoughtful, perhaps the battle-hardened soldiers surrounding me will think I am merely contemplating my response.

"Are you quite well, Highness?" asks Horemheb.

"Fine," I say, "but the Kushites are clearly done with negotiations. It is time to act."

"With respect, Highness, the time to act was upon our arrival weeks ago," says Horemheb.

I flash him a look. "It would have been remiss of us not to try. War is expensive."

"Yes, Highness."

"Prepare to attack." I turn to walk back to my barracks.

Horemheb sidles up alongside me. "May I speak, Highness?"

I nod.

"I understand you are to lead the initial charge."

"Yes." My belly roils and I fear it may attempt to purge itself again.

"With your permission, you shall be flanked by Paramessu and myself." At a sharp glance from me, he continues. "You ride through the center of our troops, Paramessu and I shall approach from the left wing. We shall time it so that you are out in front for all our forces to see you leading them to victory."

I nod and swallow.

"Once you reach the enemy lines, veer to the right on my signal and not before. At that point, Paramessu shall fall in to your right and slightly ahead, while I follow directly behind you. After the initial pass, I shall escort you to the rear with the officers while the remainder of the chariot corps takes its run."

"No, I must remain on the field of battle as a rallying point for my soldiers."

"You shall be on the field."

"Far to the back, out of the fighting," I say. "That is the coward's way."

"The Great Royal Wife was right about one thing," says Horemheb. "Nothing will destroy morale faster than you being impaled on an enemy sword in full view of the men."

"You do not think I can fight." I instantly regret saying it. He and I both know I cannot, and it was unwise of me to risk a truthful answer to such a question.

Horemheb makes a noise in his throat. "Men need a leader and that is you." He claps me on the shoulder. "When Kings do fight, they are always surrounded by the best fighters who must fend off both his attackers and their own. Frankly, you contribute more to our effort by staying clear of it."

I understand his response for the face-saver that it is. Nonetheless, I appreciate it. "In that case, I will stay out from underfoot."

"I am grateful, Highness."

I return to my rooms and prepare. A servant winds the formal linen kilt around my waist and fastens the leather belt. The bronze scales jingle as my armor is lowered over my head and I slip my arms into the sleeves. After the blue war crown in placed on my head, a servant applies kohl to my eyes so that I may look more impressive to the enemy and to protect against the glare of the sun.

When I step into the chariot and loop the reins around my waist, the troops are already assembled in columns of four, with the battalions of chariots positioned on the wings. The aisles are each wide enough for a chariot to pass. I steer to the center. Through the gap I can see a broad expanse of field ending at a solid wall of round shields. Though I cannot see them yet, I know the Kushite archers stand ready on the flanks and in the rear. My stomach quails at the thought of those fabled warriors standing against us instead of with us. I pull back on the reins. I consider staying where I am, in the rear. It is where I will spend the majority of the battle at any rate. Small loss if I never leave it.

The horses paw at the ground. They are anxious to be running, even if I am not. I look from side to side. Our troops stand with swords and spears ready, waiting only for me. I signal the horses. The chariot lurches.

Soon, I am thundering along too fast to concern myself with anything other than my purpose. A cheer erupts from the infantry as I pass, rising in volume with each turn of the wheels. I raise my bow and ready my arrows. The moment I am just shy of firing range, I let loose. In my peripheral vision, I see a chariot approaching on either side, arrows flying.

Enemy soldiers raise their spears and drop into fighting stance. With leopard skins draping their taut muscles, they appear truly fierce, and I must remind myself that my generals will not allow me to come to harm or I would turn tail and disgrace myself in front of my entire army. I am nearly within striking distance and ready myself for the turn. But Horemheb's signal does not come. A quick glance to my left tells me he is still advancing. A spear is raised in my direction. I watch the soldier aim, but still Horemheb does not signal. As the soldier moves his arm back to fire, he is struck in the throat by an arrow flying in from my right. Paramessu. The soldier roars in defeat, yet as he dies the roaring gets louder instead of fainter. I wonder how this can be and realize it is Horemheb, who is nearly upon me now. I must have missed the signal.

I pull to the right with such force the chariot tilts onto one wheel and I have to grip the sides and throw my weight against the turn to prevent capsizing. Once righted, I find myself between Horemheb and Paramessu, as planned. We circle back behind the troops, keeping close in to stay clear of the light chariots racing toward the enemy line, bombarding them with arrows.

Behind the lines, I watch as the infantry moves in, under cover of the archers. Without chariots of their own, the Kushites begin to fold. It is over by midday.

After a light meal, I take the throne inside the walls of the garrison. Soldiers line up to deposit severed hands at my feet. Always the sword hand, never the other one, so we may know how many of the enemy were killed. Soldiers are given a piece of gold for each hand. Gold mined in Kush, the same gold for which the dead rebelled. It seems fitting. By the time the line is halfway done, the pile of severed hands begins to putrefy in the blazing Kushite sun. My stomach roils and my earlier meal threatens to expel itself. I cover my face with a fold of my linen robe and motion for my fan bearers to waft the breeze away from my face. The situation improves only slightly.

At day's end, a feast is arranged for the officers. The scent of spit-roasted beef spills out of the dining hall and drives the odor of decaying flesh out of my nostrils. Upon my entry, after all have risen from their bows, they applaud and cheer. I cheer along with them, thinking it is in honor of our victory today.

Paramessu raises a cup. "In honor of our King, Son of Amun, who outshone all of us today with his show of courage."

The cheer dies on my lips, and I look around. This is for me? "But I have done nothing extraordinary today, unless you count managing to not fall out of a chariot."

"His Highness is modest as well." I recognize the voice as that of Nakhtmenu.

Paramessu turns to address the room. "His Highness's words are unassuming, but I witnessed him stare down the Kushite forces, daring them to attack."

As I recall, they were more than willing to accept that dare.

Paramessu continues. "And then veering off in a turn that is the envy of every recruit to the chariot corps. Impressive, Highness."

Not knowing how else to respond, I nod and accept the praise as my due.

Horemheb approaches and whispers low in my ear. "Next time, ignore the enemy and watch for my signal. Should you be speared or have your head crushed in tumbling from your chariot, I'd be the one left to face the wrath of your wife." His eyes glint with amusement.

I speak equally low. "Noted."

Ankhesenamun

"Highness."

The sound pulls me from sleep. I open my eyes to see Kawit's face mere handspans from my own. She carries a rushlight to keep the darkness at bay. The flame flickers, casting shadows on her face, making her dark eyes seem even larger than usual.

I sit straight up. "What is it?" I feel a lump in my throat, as I have not since hearing of our army's victory. "Is it the King?"

"Yes, Highness."

My hands start to shake.

Kawit continues. "The army has arrived two days earlier than expected. They are camped outside the city."

Why should they have arrived early? Did they have cause to hurry? "The King is healthy and whole?" I ask.

Kawit hesitates. "I suppose I would have heard if he were not."

I let out my breath. They are simply ahead of schedule, perhaps eager to return to families. "Yes, I suppose you would." I swing my legs over the side of the bed to the floor and rise to my feet. "Come, there isn't a moment to waste," I say as I head for my bath. "We must stage our celebrations two days earlier than planned."

My ladies are grouped below me, but I sit alone on the dais, fighting the urge to race up the road. I sit as straight as it is possible to sit, stretching my spine as far as I might so I may catch a glimpse of him sooner. At first, the procession is a smudge at the gates of the city, wavering in the heat haze. As it approaches, it resolves into horses and chariots and men. I can distinguish Tutankhamun's lopsided stance from a distance, but while I expected him to ride alone at the head of the parade, another rides beside him. It is Horemheb. Though I take care not to show any reaction on my face, it concerns me that Tutankhamun should show him such obvious favor.

Tutankhamun allows the horses to run. He nears me, grinning like fool. His joy is so infectious I cannot keep from smiling in return. His attention wavers for but a moment when he nods at one of the ladies. From my vantage, I cannot tell which, but my belly quivers when Kawit returns the nod, blushing gracefully.

Tutankhamun waves to the chest of jewelry beside me. I pick out a necklace and hand it to him. He fires it behind him into the line of soldiers and waves for more. Soon, I am scooping out great handfuls of gold and jewels and waving for the procession to continue so that they might all have a chance at catching the bounty sailing around their heads.

I do not remember when I last laughed so heartily.

At the feast, the mood is high all around. The air is permeated with the sounds of talk and laughter, the heady scents of frankincense and rose blending with roast fowl and fish.

After the final course has been served and the guests are drowsy with too much wine, Tutankhamun raises his cup and asks for silence. All turn to watch him, expectantly, as the background noise reduces to a dull murmur. He calls forth Horemheb and shakes his hand.

"In recognition of your years of outstanding service to the Crown, I hereby grant you a place among the nobility." He hands Horemheb a gold pectoral brooch inlaid with lapis, carnelian, and glass. It depicts the Heh, the god of millions of years, flanked by twin Heru falcons, the whole topped by Tutankhamun's name. "You are no longer a commoner."

A profound silence has fallen on the dining hall. I can almost hear the thoughts as everyone attempts to understand the true meaning of this announcement. I glance at Ay, down the dais from me. He shows no emotion on his face, but the muscles of his jaw are working.

Once Tutankhamun and Horemheb return to their places, Ay shoots me a look and leaves. I have no wish to confer with Ay at this moment, but I have lost all appetite for food, drink, and merriment. Tutankhamun is so engrossed in conversation with Horemheb and Amenia, who by extension has now been elevated to the nobility herself, I doubt he will notice my absence. And so, I leave without a word.

I decide against stopping to see Ay. I need time to ponder this latest development without his voice nattering in my ear. But when I arrive at my chambers the guard informs me Ay is waiting inside.

I find him in my sitting room, standing with his hands behind his back. "I did not summon you," I say.

"We are family. I do not need to wait for a summons."

"I am tired," I say. "Whatever brings you here can wait until morning."

"We need to discuss the King's latest move and what it means for the future of our family."

"There is nothing to discuss. The King has made his decision."

Ay paces. "It was beyond rash to confer such favor on a commoner. One might think he meant to name Horemheb his heir."

"I am certain the King has thought through all of the ramifications." Truly, I hope he has not. For if he has, it bodes ill for me. "However, if you have concerns, you must bring them directly to his Highness. Only he can explain his rationale."

Ay does not respond. There is no need. He and I both know Tutankhamun has no need to justify his choices to anyone and, if he does have a grander plan in mind, he is hardly likely to reveal it to Ay.

"I should think you would have concerns yourself," says Ay. "He insinuates that you are not capable of bearing children."

I freeze. He does not know. It is not the subject of gossip, then. "The succession does not depend on my ability to bear children. The King has many wives and concubines capable of producing children. There is no need to name an outsider as heir."

"Unless it is the King who is at fault," says Ay. "No woman has yet borne him a child, save you, and those two are dead."

I do not give him the reaction he seeks, but I ache at the words.

"Perhaps it is the King who is unable to sire children."

"He has sired two."

Ay raises an eyebrow. "Has he?"

I cannot hide my shock. "How dare you imply I would betray my husband and my King."

"Hmmph," says Ay. "You would hardly be the first woman in your untenable position to take such steps."

I hear myself give a quick intake of breath before I can compose myself. I wonder if he is speaking hypothetically, or from knowledge, but dare not follow through on the thought. The only two other women in my position he has known well were my mother and my grandmother. Either one committing such an act may undermine not only my position, but Tutankhamun's as well. "We do not know the King's intentions in this matter," I say. "Perhaps he has no intention of making Horemheb his heir. If he does have that thought, he is only being prudent. I remain confident there will be an heir, but if it never happens, it is wise to lay the groundwork in order to avoid civil war after the King passes to the West." I surprise myself by defending that which so pains me, but I realize I am correct. Tutankhamun must act to maintain Ma'at, no matter the personal cost to me.

"Should that become necessary, the King must keep it within the family," says Ay, "and not pollute the royal blood with that of a commoner."

I raise an eyebrow and glare at him. He is a commoner, and well he knows it. Well, he also knows that his common daughter is my mother, and his common sister grandmother to both me and Tutankhamun. "It is far too late to worry about polluting the royal blood with that of commoners." I watch him grind his teeth. Now I know the reason for his outrage is not concern for me or for Kemet. He seethes because Horemheb has been granted the honor he himself has been denied.

"My family has become royal through three generations of marriage. Horemheb cannot say the same."

"Nor could your family, three generations ago," I say. "Nor does it matter. You cannot be the heir. You are far to advanced in age to take the throne now. You would not live long enough to lead Kemet. You also have no male heirs to inherit, nor are you likely to produce any."

Ay's face turns red. "I am the one who put your mother on the throne of Kemet, and I am the one keeping you there now. I can remove you at a whim."

I will myself not to tremble. I am not so foolish as to think him weak, but he does not have the hold on either the military or the priesthood he once did. "I am the Great Royal Wife, and you are an advisor, nothing more. You will carry out my will and that of the King, or I shall be the one removing you."

Ay advances on me, one hand raised. I remain still and stare into his eyes. "Go ahead. You know the punishment for striking the Great Royal Wife."

Ay's hand shakes, but he drops it and walks away. I let out a breath. I give it enough time to be sure he has gone and tell my guard that no one save the King himself is to be admitted into my rooms without prior permission.

Tutankhamun

I draw my bow and sight down the length of the arrow. Four targets are set up along the track. I notch the first arrow and let it fly. It splits the target. I pull out the next arrow and fire it almost immediately. It misses, but the next two hit, not as well as the first, but hit, nevertheless. Rounding the bend in the track, I see a small white smudge against the railing. I guide the horses in and jump out of the chariot, handing the reins to a groom.

Ankhesenamun smiles. "You are very much improved. Your time spent with the army has done you good."

I nod. I do not tell her how, for me to ride and shoot well, I must balance on the side of my foot, and that it pains far more than usual for days afterwards. "I had little opportunity for practice while on the march."

"That is not how I hear it," she says. "Everyone speaks of how you charged the Kushite army and pulled away, pulling away only barely in time to avoid being impaled on their spears."

I open my mouth to tell her the truth but decide against it. If she knew I froze on the battlefield within reach of enemy spears, she would raise Sekhmet, goddess of war herself, to prevent me ever going on campaign again. "That didn't require any particular skill," I say.

She slips her arm around mine and I lean on her, grateful to be able to take some of the weight off my foot.

Ankhesenamun starts on the path back to the palace, glancing around to ensure we cannot be overheard by the guards. "I wish to speak with you about Kawit."

Ah, so that is the reason for her visit to the chariot track. I hoped she merely wanted my company. "What of her?"

"Is it your intention to take her as a wife, as her father wishes?"

I take a deep breath. "She is yet a year, perhaps two, away from marriage."

"Still," says Ankhesenamun, "she is losing her youthful scrawniness." She glances at me. "Do not tell me you have not noticed."

I clear my throat and do not look at her. "I would not be a man if I failed to notice such a comely young woman."

She falls silent as we pass by the West Villas, and I gaze at the foliage draping over garden walls.

I am the one who speaks first. "She is your lady. It would be best if she remain so."

"You need sons and Kawit appears to be capable. More, she is willing."

Ankhesenamun looks to me with apparent calm, but I see the muscles of her jaw working and know it pains her to speak of this. I would not add to her pain by telling her the truth, that some nights I dream of Kawit and wake with an urgent need. That if Kawit were a baseborn woman, she'd have been warming my bed for some months already. That I might have used my position as King to take the girl as I wished, in spite of her noble birth, save for Ankhesenamun herself. Should I give in to my lust, she would forever see Kawit as a rival, though that she could never be. And should Kawit bear me a son … I have lived too long in the royal court not to know how lesser wives and concubines become haughty when they start to think themselves above their station. Never could I place such a viper amongst Ankhesenamun's ladies.

"I have wives and concubines enough already. I have no need of more."

She nods. "We must also speak of your promotion of Horemheb."

"What do you wish to know?"

She stops and looks at me. "Is it your intention to name him heir, should your many wives and concubines fail to provide you with a son?"

I resume walking. "That shall not be necessary. I shall have many fine sons." I do not meet her eyes. It has occurred to me, as I am sure it has to her and to most everyone else, that if I could father children I would have done so by this time. "However, it is only wise to have a contingency plan, should I be taken suddenly to the West."

She nods. "I thought as much, and I said so to Ay."

"He questioned you on the matter?"

She shifts her weight and looks to the ground. This causes me to wonder how often she and Ay discuss policies in private.

"He thinks that any contingency plan should remain within the family, as is tradition."

"Does he have an idea how to accomplish this? You and I are the only direct line heirs left."

"Though he did not say so, I believe he means himself."

I let out a breath. "He is as much a commoner as Horemheb."

Ankhesenamun sighs.

"Beloved?"

"He threatened me."

I stop and turn her around to look at me. "Did he hurt you?"

She shakes her head. "No. He wanted to, but that was not his threat. He said he is the one keeping me on the throne, and he can remove me at his leisure."

I shiver and I am not sure if it is with rage at Ay or fear for Ankhesenamun.

"I dreamed of my mother when I was ill. She told me never to turn my back on Ay."

The hair on the back of my neck rises.

"It was a trick of my own mind, nothing more," she says. "I missed her desperately at that time."

I chew my lip. "Or perhaps she felt your need and traveled from the Field of Reeds to deliver the message."

"What do you suppose she meant?"

I am not sure she wants to hear my thoughts on this matter. Ay is, after all, her grandfather, and I have no proof, only a feeling. On the other hand, she must know of Ay's potential for violence if she is to stay safe. "Do you remember the night of the feast, when your mother announced she would raise Ptah to supreme god?"

She nods.

I lick my lips. "When your mother left the banquet hall, Ay followed her."

"That is hardly unusual. She was his daughter, and he a trusted advisor."

"Who found your mother's body the next morning? Who brought you the news?"

Her eyes widen. "You do not think ... that is not possible."

"I do not know if it is true, but it is most certainly possible. It is rather convenient for your mother's death to occur at the exact moment she thwarted Ay's plans to consolidate his power by raising up the priesthood of Amun."

She clutches at the necklace around her throat. "Ay would never have killed Mother. She was his conduit to power."

"And now you are."

She places a hand over her mouth.

"Ay is constantly grasping ever closer to the throne. I elevated Horemheb in an effort to check Ay's power. Ay is smart enough to see it and is not happy about it."

"What are we to do?"

"Ay has powerful supporters," I say, "for now. They can be removed, but it will take time, for it must be done with discretion."

Tutankhamun, Year 9

(ca. 1325 BCE)

Ankhesenamun

Ay gestures to the conical mud structure and bows his head to Tutankhamun. "Time to inspect the grain, Highness."

Tutankhamun eyes the spindly ladder leading up to the hole at the apex of the granary. At the beginning of each year, he climbs rung by agonizing rung, with me stabilizing the bottom of the ladder and all the officials pretending there is nothing amiss. This year, Tutankhamun merely nods toward me and says, "Henceforth, the Great Royal Wife shall perform this duty."

Ay's head snaps around to me and I keep my face passive. Tutankhamun and I discussed this previously. Taking over small duties of the King will demonstrate an elevation in my status to second in command yet will not raise fears that he is becoming his father as raising me to co-Regent would.

I tuck the hem of my skirts into my sash and clamber up the ladder. At the opening, I reach in and pull out a handful of golden barley. I hold my hand out, open it, and turn it over, allowing the grains to fall. They dance in the wind, catching sunlight as they spin in eddies to the ground.

I speak from deep within my chest so all may hear me. "The grain is clean and good and ready to prepare into bread and beer for the Beautiful Feast of the Opet."

As I descend, I glance down the row of granaries. Dozens of them, all full to bursting. We have enough stores to bake the twelve thousand loaves, and brew the four hundred jars of beer, to be given away at the festival, and still have plenty to last until next harvest. The flood waters lie sparkling on the fields, visible from the granaries. The river has risen high this year, but not so high that the fields will drown. The past year was bountiful, and this one promises to be even more so.

Tutankhamun takes my hand when I step down off the ladder.

Ay addresses Tutankhamun. "I have taken the liberty to arrange a litter for you at the head of the procession."

"It will not be necessary."

"Highness," says Ay, "I beg you to reconsider. Crowds throng the Avenue of the Sphinxes during the Feast. Were you to be carried above their heads, many more would be able to view the glory of their King."

It is a transparent fib. He means that the multitudes would not see Tutankhamun leaning on me. The common people seldom see the King, so do not know of his twisted foot. They would have little confidence in a King unable to walk unaided, so in public Tutankhamun wears long robes to hide his foot and leans on me to hide his need for a walking stick. Instead of a crippled King, they see a husband and wife devoted to one another. They love us for it, but perhaps it does not suit Ay's plans. If Tutankhamun does not walk, there is no need for me to be by his side. It is not normally the duty of the Great Royal Wife to precede Amun to his temporary home at Ipet-Resyt. Remove me from public sight often enough, and the people shall forget me. Once the people forget me, it becomes easier for officials to ignore me.

Tutankhamun starts on his way out of the granaries. I follow, along with Ay. "It is not necessary because the procession will take the river route both outward and inward," says Tutankhamun. "I shall ride in a barge at the very front."

I attempt to hide my surprise, yet I must acknowledge the cleverness of the plan. Being carried overland implies weakness, but on a boat Tutankhamun may be seated and he will simply appear to be mirroring the image of Amun following behind him.

Ay shakes his head. "The river route would be depriving the priests of the honor of carrying the god, his consort and son."

I expected Ay to praise this innovation of Tutankhamun's as it removes me from the picture as effectively as his own plan, but of course he is concerned with maintaining the privilege of the priesthood. Perhaps he fears being blamed for the loss of it, which would erode their support of him. Perhaps I could plant the idea that Ay orchestrated the move to the river, but decide against it. It may reduce his support among the priesthood and reduce his power, but Ay may respond by attempting to seize more power elsewhere.

"The god and his family must still be carried from Ipet-Iset Temple to the water steps. This will require priests," says Tutankhamun. "More priests must accompany the gods on their journey over the waters, and again more to carry them from the landing into the Ipet-Resyt Temple. If we assign more priests than strictly necessary at each leg of the journey, there will be as many as needed on the seven legs of the overland trek. All shall be able to participate, as usual."

Ay nods. I am unsure of whether he truly approves or is simply allowing the King to think so, though I cannot think of why he might object.

"An excellent plan, Highness. The Great Royal Wife shall be waiting at the water steps to accompany you to Ipet-Resyt Temple." He glances to me, the hint of a smirk on his lips.

Tutankhamun shakes his head. "Oh, no. The Great Royal Wife shall accompany me from the beginning."

The rest of the way back to the palace, I do not look at Ay.

Tutankhamun

Despite my statement to Ay that Ankhesenamun should accompany me the entire procession, there is one small part in which she may not participate. Only the King, and the priests, may enter the deep recesses of the Temple to meet Himself.

In the Festival Hall, behind the sanctuary of Amun, resides the Barque of the Divine Living King. Within is my own ka-statue. The doors to the shrine are open and I shiver as I behold my own likeness, for this is unlike any ordinary statue. It is the place where my life-force shall reside after I have passed to the West. It is where I shall return, time and again, for millions of years. The priests dress the statue, pour libations over its head, and burn incense. When the shrine doors are closed, four priests lift the miniature barque, and we proceed westward to Amun's sanctuary.

I stare into the eyes of the god's ka-statue. My father taught me all idols are false idols. The gods are not real, save one. Since my father's death, my advisors and teachers have taught me that all the gods live, and it was their disfavor that brought down my father and his empire and has come close to destroying all of Kemet.

"Highness?"

A priest, bowing, hands me the implements I am to use in the ceremony. The purification of the god with natron and incense is now complete and all are waiting for the Opening of the Mouth. I accept the adze and touch it to the god's mouth, so he may speak and eat, and to his eyes, so he may see. The granite eyes do not look vengeful. They do not look approving. They are entirely void of emotion. It is the same each year. I do not know if it is because Amun does not exist, or simply that he is not in residence in his statue at this particular moment. Perhaps he only enters his statue when no one is looking so that he may observe without being observed. Perhaps he seldom visits his statute because it is kept hidden, and he would be staring into the dark alone. I decide that when I become a god after passing to the West, I shall not visit any ka-statues buried in my tomb or hidden in temples. I shall visit the grand statues at my mortuary temple so that I may see the desert and the river, the people and the animals, and feel once more I am among them.

We travel, with the Barque of Amun, to a smaller temple outside the greater one. It is here I perform the Opening of the Mouth for Khonsu, the son of Amun. That accomplished, we proceed, followed by an ever-growing number of priests now carrying three small barques and proceed along the avenue to the Temple of Mut, wife of Amun, mother to Khonsu. On both sides of the avenue, ram-headed sphinxes watch as we pass. Once Mut's eyes and mouth have been opened, we leave her temple, now accompanied by four barques, and turn toward the river. Halfway there, we halt at the sanctuary of Kamutef, an aspect of Amun, the "bull of his mother," who created himself. I leave offerings of incense and flowers at the feet of the god. Here, we switch priests to carry the barques, lest these ones tire and drop one of the gods.

A number of boats are queued at the water steps, now flooded almost to the very top. Ankhesenamun waits by the head barge. Upriver, the elite of the military stand ready to advance along the banks. Kemet's finest are in war kilts topped with leather bands, riding chariots, astride horses or on foot. Horemheb is at the head of the column in his chariot, the horses topped with feathers of blue and red. Paramessu is in the chariot beside him.

Leaning on Ankhesenamun, I cross the plank to board the first boat and we take our seats on the waiting thrones. A hush falls on the throng as word travels up the riverbank of the gods' arrival. The delay seems interminable as each barque is loaded on its own boat, but at last the lines are undone and workmen tow us downriver. The military keeps pace with us on the bank, Horemheb's horses pressing the crowd away from the shore. Cheers and ululating cries ring in counter point to drums and flutes and cymbals. I raise a hand and turn toward the throng so that they might look upon their King and receive his blessings. Beside me, Ankhesenamun is silent, hands folded in her lap.

At the Ipet-Resyt landing, we are greeted by Ay with Tey, holding bouquets of lotus and lilies, cornflowers, and roses. Nakhtmenu and Mutnedjmet are leading cows adorned with bells and feathers. The workmen tie up the boat and we wait until the barques of the gods have been unloaded and taken up by fresh priests, and then allow them to go on ahead before debarking ourselves.

Ankhesenamun and I fall in directly behind the shrines and their bearers, followed by Ay and Tey and Nakhtmenu and Mutnedjmet with their fattened beasts. We stop and assemble inside the courtyard of the temple while the priests lay down their burdens and float the ships in the sacred lake where they will remain for the days of the festival.

Nakthmin and Mutnedjmet relinquish the cows to priests, who walk them to the lake under the eyes of the gods. The priests scratch the cows behind their ears with one hand while holding an obsidian blade in the other. One stroke and the animals fall, bright red pooling in the dirt, a flood mirroring that of the river, nourishing our Black Lands, readying them for planting, renewing gods and King and people.

I accept the crook and flail from my bearer and step forward, balancing awkwardly on my walking stick. Standing between the two sacrifices, I turn to face the assemblage. To a man, they feign not to notice my shuffling gait, although by now they are so accustomed to it perhaps they no longer pay it any attention. Ankhesenamun breaks her air of studied indifference to throw me a smile. I hold out a hand and motion for her to come join me. She arches her eyebrows but does as requested.

When she stands beside me, lotus flower in one hand, I begin my practiced speech. "This year, the Ninth year of the reign of Nebkheperure Tutankhamun, has been blessed with an auspicious beginning. The river flood is neither so low as to threaten famine nor so high as to molder the crops in the fields. Our armies have subdued the rebellion in Kush and our empire is at peace. May we all rejoice this year and for many more to come. With the blood of sacrifice, the land is revived, the gods are reborn, and your King and Great Royal Wife are renewed in strength."

Ankhesenamun stiffens at my side, but otherwise shows no sign of surprise. Her inclusion in the ceremony is an unexpected honor, but a necessary one. None must be allowed to forget who rules Kemet.

In the front row of the gathering, Ay glares at Ankhesenamun with narrowed eyes.

Ankhesenamun

For the duration of the festival, the temple is open to the ordinary folk of Waset. Indeed, all of Kemet, for many have traveled from as far away as the Delta to the north or the First Cataract to the south. Some farther, perhaps.

Tutankhamun is occupied distributing loaves of bread to the people streaming through the gate and winding around the temple itself to where I am rooted in a pavilion by the lake with my ladies. We oversee the pilgrims, accepting their gifts in exchange for the chance to pray to the gods and seek an oracle of one of the deities.

Supplicants present a fatted duck, neck recently wrung or a bundle of vegetables or a delicate bottle of perfume, according to their means. I nod and wave them on. Servants collect the tokens. The food is sent to the kitchens, where it will become part of the Beautiful Feast; material goods are distributed amongst the priesthood.

The wind carries the questions asked of the gods to my ears, most similar. Will my fields produce this year? Will my daughters marry well? Will my son succeed in his exams? All ordinary questions asked by ordinary people. Following the question comes a cheer or a sigh of relief if the boat carrying the god tips forward, or a more disappointed sigh if the boat tips backward. I must force myself not to glance at the small temple to the Aten, erected by my father, with its columns in the forms of both Mother and Father, though the difference between the two is so subtle, it is difficult to distinguish between them. Father has been given Mother's rounded hips, while she has been given his excessively elongated face. Even here, in the sanctum of Amun, the Aten has infiltrated. Yet, he does not interfere with the homage paid to his rival. Amun, for his part, seems unruffled by the interloper. Perhaps they have declared a truce. Perhaps the war between the two was nothing more than the fancy of men. Or, perhaps, both are powerless and any stories to the contrary simply false comfort.

Mutnedjmet fans herself and eyes the sun, only an hour past midday. "Still many hours before we may stop listening to this senseless babble."

"You do not envy them?" I ask.

"Certainly not," says Mutnedjmet.

Tuya makes a show of looking away, but her eyes keep drifting back toward us. Meryetre stifles a yawn. Henutmire is absent, having lately borne a child.

Kawit shivers. "No, Highness. What is there to envy? Once the Festival is done, they will return to drudgery in the fields."

It will be another month yet before the waters have receded enough for planting to begin, but I do not correct her. Instead, I think three months without work year after year sounds blissful. I think enjoying a festival, instead of presiding over it sounds blissful. Most of all, I think having no greater concern for the future than marriage prospects or the next crop yield would be the greatest gift the gods could give. Tutankhamun and I might have been prosperous farmers, or perhaps with his intelligence he might have been a scribe, and I might have had the running of a small household. A peasant woman holds out a handful of moldering vegetables. I nod my acceptance, for it is not my place to refuse, no matter how poor the offering. The vegetables will at least feed the livestock.

It occurs to me that, had I been born a commoner, I would have been able to choose my own husband, and that most certainly would not have been my young brother. I wonder who I might have chosen, had I been free to do so. A merchant perhaps, or an army officer. Yes, a man who is away on campaign for months or years at a time, giving me much time to myself.

I cannot expect Kawit to understand, though Mutnedjmet has an inkling. They enjoy a freedom I have never known, yet they envy me because all they see is power, not the fears or the constant vigilance that are the bedfellows of power.

A woman's voice reaches my ears from across the water. She wants to know if her son, currently burning with fever, will live. This is quickly followed by a choked sob. I stretch my neck to see if it is the peasant with the moldy vegetables who asks, but her face is obscured. I ache at this connection between the woman and myself and am reminded that no life is without sorrow. Perhaps I am guilty of the same skewed perception as my ladies. Perhaps I envy because I do not understand.

After waving on the next pilgrim, Mutnedjmet speaks to Kawit. "I did not expect to see you here. Aren't you usually holed up in the Delta at this time of year?"

"During the season of harvest, Lady," says Kawit. "Though, I am thinking of remaining in Waset this year."

This surprises me, for she has not mentioned it before. "Your family shall be greatly disappointed if you do not join them."

"I am a grown woman now and cannot be expected to abandon my post simply because my parents wish to travel," says Kawit.

"I have other ladies," I say. "I can manage without you for a couple of months."

Kawit opens her mouth, then closes it.

I am sorry I spoke so quickly and put a hand on her arm. "I shall miss you greatly, but I would not dream of ordering you to miss your family retreat. You must treasure those times, for they are not given to everyone."

Kawit frowns and turns to speak to Mutnedjmet. "You have been spending much time with Nakhtmenu during the Festival."

Mutnedjmet stops fanning. "I am not spending time with Nakhtmenu, we are simply performing ceremonial roles together."

Kawit nods. "Call it what you like, but it is no secret how Nakhtmenu feels about you."

Mutnedjmet reaches behind me to swat Kawit with her fan. "You, young lady, would do well to stop spreading gossip."

Kawit is undeterred. "You do not find him handsome?"

"Not nearly so handsome as he finds himself."

Kawit laughs, evidently thinking the remark a joke. "You should be flattered. A woman of your years being pursued by one of Kemet's most desired men."

Mutnedjmet turns, her eyes bulging and a tiny vein in her neck throbbing so I think it must soon burst.

Kawit blanches. "Forgive my forthrightness, Lady, but you are past the first blush of youth."

I choke back laughter, but not before Mutnedjmet turns her glare on me. I shrug. She has spent a lifetime denying the creep of time, but she is my mother's sister and I know her true age. Most women of her years are dandling grandchildren on their knees.

"Tell me, Lady Kawit," says Mutnedjmet, "how go your plans to marry the King?"

Kawit opens her mouth, then closes it and turns away. Tutankhamun has finally, and definitively, refused the petition of Kawit's father and Mutnedjmet well knows it. I feel some measure of guilt, for Tutankhamun made the decision to spare me trouble, but I cannot deny I fell some relief as well.

The pile in front of me has been growing, so I gesture for a servant to come and clear it before speaking. "It is not only during the Festival. I have also noticed you spending time with Nakhtmenu. Is it possible you have changed your mind about him since last we broached the subject?"

She shakes her head. "Not at all. It is my father who is spending time with Nakhtmenu. Tey grows older and is not as able to play the gracious hostess, and so Father begs me to do it."

Something about this disturbs me. Ay never makes a move without a plan and Mutnedjmet never submits to another's will unless there is a benefit to her. Yet, I cannot think what the arrangement here may be.

"Does this mean you have abandoned your other pursuits?" I dare not utter Horemheb's name in front of Kawit or it will be all around the Ladies' Quarters by nightfall.

Mutnedjmet moans low in her throat. "Absolutely not."

They have been discreet; I'll grant her that. In the months that I have known of the dalliance, not a whisper has reached my ears save from Mutnedjmet herself. Horemheb has titles and power and so I do not wonder at the attraction there, but I cannot understand why she might entertain the idea of Nakhtmenu, for he has neither. He is a promising officer in the army, though from what I have seen, his reach exceeds his grasp. Tutankhamun has shown no inclination to grant titles to Nakhtmenu, but Ay favors him greatly. The question is what does Ay intend to do with him?

Tutankhamun

The crowds on the banks of the river bow down as we, their King and their gods, return triumphant after renewing the lands. The flood waters are beginning to recede, having fallen several arm lengths since the start of the Festival a week ago, leaving in their wake the black earth that is Kemet.

We follow the route we took traveling to Ipet-Resyt, but in reverse. Now the gods must be returned to their sanctuaries, refreshed and ready to face the year ahead. My own ka-statue is returned last. I am meant to watch as it is returned to the inner sanctum, but instead I fix my eyes over the top of its shrine and attempt not to dwell on its purpose.

Exiting the temple precinct, I encounter Kawit, who requests to speak with me alone. I instruct the guards to stand outside of earshot.

Kawit stands, eyes down.

I wait for several moments, but when she says nothing, I grow impatient. "You wished to speak with me. Speak. Or am I to guess at what it is you wish to say?"

When she looks up at me, a single tear is tracing its way through her eye makeup and down her cheek, leaving a black trail. "You have turned down my father's request for marriage without explanation. May I ask why? Have I displeased you in some way?"

I am taken aback. I thought the push for marriage was entirely her father's pursuit, not her own. "My reasons are my own and none of your concern."

When I turn aside to take my leave, she calls out. Looking back, I see the first tear has been followed by several more. "Please," she says. "I will do better."

I push aside my feelings of compassion. She does not want me, but only the prestige and the chance at power I can give her. "My decision is final."

I rejoin Ankhesenamun so that we may retire to our chambers to prepare for the night's feast.

"Do you suppose anyone would notice if we did not attend this night?" she asks.

I sigh. "I should think so."

"Pity."

"Why? Did you have other recreation in mind?" I hope the answer to that question is no, for I do not have the stamina.

"Yes," she says. "Sleep. I do not believe I have had more than three hours this entire festival."

I laugh. "Nor I, but it is one more night and then we are done. We may sleep tomorrow."

"When?" she says. "After audience chamber or perhaps between answering correspondence and military drills?"

I let out a breath. My entire body feels bogged down as sodden linen, heavy and sluggish. "I shall cancel everything for tomorrow."

"No, you shan't."

I nod in agreement. "No, I shan't, but I should very much like to. And I will, soon."

She turns her face up to mine.

"In a few months time, when the flood waters have receded and the young plants are sprouting, we shall turn everyone away and retreat to the Shedet for a time. We shall be able to sleep all day if we wish."

A faraway look comes across her face and her mouth smiles, but her eyes do not. She longs for such a reprieve, but she does not believe it will happen. I will make it happen for her. "We will. I promise you."

Her face darkens. "Best not make promises you cannot keep."

"I will keep this promise."

"I do not doubt your intent. What I doubt is that our duties will slacken enough for us leave Waset."

"Highness." The voice startles me as we approach the turn to my quarters. A guard has come searching for us. "A runner waits in your chambers," he says.

"Send him to the kitchens. We conclude the Beautiful Feast of the Opet tonight. I shall see him tomorrow prior to giving audience."

The guard bows. "He has been waiting all day, Highness. He says it is urgent and will not take much time."

I attempt not to sag visibly. "Very well. We shall see him now."

The runner prostrates himself when I enter the chamber. I bid him rise. He is a lanky fellow in a crumpled kilt, still with the dust of the road on his sandals. It must truly be urgent.

"You may speak," I say.

He bows his head. "It is bad news, Highness. Qatna and Ugarit have fallen to the Hatti."

I thank him and bid him visit the kitchen for food and wine.

When he leaves, Ankhesenamun looks to me. "The Hatti already pressure Naharin from the north. Now they box them in from the south."

I nod. "And soon they will squeeze. It is a common enough tactic, but in this case

an entire nation stands in place of a battlefield."

"Soon or late, war will come to the Naharin," says Ankhesenamun. "It is inevitable. We will have no choice but to join."

She is correct. And she was also correct about making promises I cannot keep, for it will be long before we may leave Waset.

Ankhesenamun

Tutankhamun sits at his writing table, tablets arrayed before him. He looks up at me as I enter. His expression is neutral, giving me no insight as to why he has summoned me.

"Is the news good or bad?" I ask.

He smiles. "It is not bad." He motions me to his side and spreads the tablets out before me in chronological order.

My eyes widen as I read the cuneiform markings on the clay. They are from King Tushratta of the Naharin. He wishes to form an alliance with Kemet to drive out the Hatti for good. I return his smile. "The Naharin finally wish to resume our alliance."

"With no concessions," says Tutankhamun. "Though we cannot be sure they will wish to continue said alliance once the Hatti have been defeated."

"We shall worry about that once the Hatti have been defeated," I say. "I presume you intend to accept the offer."

"Naturally. It does mean we must send our army to Naharin."

"Naturally."

His smile widens. "I shall return triumphant once again, as I did from Kush."

I feel a quaver in my belly. Even as a figurehead, he is vulnerable, and I fear he will find the armies of the Hatti to be far more formidable than the rebels of Kush. "I am certain your presence will inspire the troops, just as it did as Kush."

There is a look in his eyes that unsettles me. "This time shall be different. I shall do more than simply ride out ahead. I have been training hard for this contingency and will take part in the battle, as a King should.

I feel as if the air has been sucked out of the room. I cannot breathe. "You must not."

"I must. It is my duty."

"No," I say. "It is not. Kings must be protected in battle."

"I shall be. Horemheb and Paramessu will fight by my side, protecting my flanks and my back."

"That is not enough. You must stay to the back, well behind the fighting."

"The Hatti are more disciplined, more well trained, and more seasoned than the rebels in Kush," he says.

I am relieved he knows this. "All the more reason for you to stay out of battle."

He shakes his head. "All the more reason why I must not take the coward's way. My men must stay strong and keep fighting. The future of Kemet depends upon it."

"The future of Kemet depends upon your survival." I do not know what else to say. We have discussed his physical vulnerability. He is surely aware of it, yet he now stubbornly insists it is not so, that he has finally surmounted the insurmountable.

Tutankhamun stands, leaning on the writing table. "I grow tired of your lack of faith in me."

"I have the utmost faith in you," I say. "You are shrewd and just and possess a strength of will that few can overcome, but you—."

"—Cannot fight. I cannot do that which Kemet demands of me now." He glares at me. "That is what you were about to say."

I do not bother with a denial, for he would not believe it. "You are a man, and all men have both strengths and weaknesses. Do not confuse the two."

"I am not a man. I am the King and that makes me a god. A god does not have weaknesses."

He is correct. In the eyes of the people, he is a living god. I do not often think on the strain it must cause him to always have to project the image of perfection he cannot attain in life, but it must be oppressive at times. As now. I place a hand on his shoulder.

He shrugs off my hand. "You are a mere woman. You cannot understand."

"Perhaps there are things I do not understand, but others I understand very well."

He turns to me. "You still would prevent me from fighting if you could."

A sudden chill possesses me at those words, "if you could." I do not answer. For the first time and likely not the last, my opinion will not weigh in his decision.

He must read my answer in my face, for he responds despite my silence. "I was not asking your advice, simply telling you what will happen."

I turn on my heels and leave, throwing the heavy door closed behind me. He may refuse to listen to words, but he cannot ignore deeds.

I hurry out, through the mostly deserted banquet hall, the slap of my sandals on the tiles echoing around the palm-leaf columns. Once out of the hall, I turn left toward the armory. The startled attendant scurries backward to fill my request for two khopesh swords. Weapons in hand, I head back toward Tutankhamun's chambers. The few servants working in the banquet hall, preparing for the evening meal, eye the swords and step out of my way. None speak a word to me, perhaps daunted by the grim set of my jaw.

When I arrive back at Tutankhamun's chambers, he is sitting at his writing table. A Naharin scribe sits cross-legged on the floor with a fresh clay tablet on his knees. The reed stylus in his hand moves with the rhythm of Tutankhamun's spoken Akkadian, recording every word.

Tutankhamun looks up as I enter, his brow furrowed.

I point to the scribe and then the door. "Leave," I tell him. He places his reed in the pouch at his waist and moves to stand.

Tutankhamun shoots him a glance. "Stay." He takes the reed back out and settles back into position.

"Leave," I say again. The poor man looks from one of us to the other, eyes wide as serving plates. "I have urgent business with the King."

Tutankhamun looks as if he is about to protest, but in the end dismisses the scribe, who hastens out before the King changes his mind again.

I dismiss the guards as well. They eye the swords and wait for Tutankhamun's approval.

"You may leave," says Tutankhamun. "My wife does not intend to assassinate me." He gives me a sidelong glance as if not at all certain that is the case.

"Certainly not," I say.

The guards nod and leave the room, closing the door behind them.

I drop the swords onto the writing table, inches from Tutankhamun's hands. "Choose your weapon."

"Do you challenge me to a duel?"

"More of a demonstration. No harm done, but no leniency given. Choose your weapon."

"This is nonsense," he says.

"Why?"

"Why?" He looks at me as if he thinks me dense. "You are a woman. It is not a fair fight."

"A woman who has had considerable training. I am not the one at a disadvantage here."

A cloud darkens his face. He knows now, if he did not already guess, what my mission is.

"If you think me wrong, prove it," I say. "Show me how much you have improved of late."

"There is no purpose in it," he says. "The outcome will not influence my decision."

We shall see. He will go to war no matter what – he must – but perhaps being bested by a woman will teach him caution and keep him behind the lines. Instead of openly stating this, though, I take a tack far more likely to make him want to meet my challenge. "It will ease my fears."

He looks up at me and takes a deep breath. I have his attention now. "Show me you are capable of fighting, and I shall not spend the months you are away in fear you will never return to me." I do not have to feign the catch in my voice, nor the tear that rolls down my cheek.

Tutankhamun stands and hefts both swords, one at a time. Though they are near identical, one is slightly heavier. He meets my eye as he chooses this one. In a real battle, it would be the proper choice, the additional heft adding strength to his blows. In this charade, however, where there will be no attempt at wounding, the weight will slow him down. Not enough for me to win without superior skill, but perhaps enough to even up the difference in strength between us. He knows this as well as I. Seeing him once more placing me on an equal footing, even when I am out to prove myself above him, makes me want to leave my sword on the writing table and embrace him. Yet if I do not fight him now, he may not return from Naharin, and all would be lost without him.

I tuck my skirts into my sash, pick up my sword and drop into a stance opposite Tutankhamun. We circle, each assessing the weaknesses of the other. His is obvious. His left foot pains him so he cannot put his full weight upon it. He sways a little as he moves. His equilibrium is precarious. I strike to take advantage of it, swinging my sword high so he will be forced to unbalance himself in order to block my swing.

He swings high and bronze meets bronze in a ringing crash. My arm is met with a solidity I did not expect.

He smiles and shrugs. "I do know how to use my weaknesses." His lack of balance was a pretense.

We circle again. This time Tutankhamun is steady, without a hint of a sway. Without taking my eyes from his face, I attempt to keep his feet in my peripheral vision. I can see their general position, but I cannot study them without dropping my attention from the rest of his body. I must remember to ask him to show me later.

Tutankhamun lunges first, but it is another feint, and I recognize it in time to meet his sword. Our swords clash repeatedly, the noise ringing in my ears.

He forces me backward. I struggle to maintain my own footing while, inexplicably, he advances relentlessly.

With my posterior pressing against the writing table, I let out a roar. I move as if to strike high, but swing low at the last moment, aiming directly for his weak leg. Tutankhamun parries but is driven backward. I press my advantage, winning back several foot-lengths.

When Tutankhamun prematurely commits to a high strike, I allow him to swing through while I strike at his forward leg with the flat side of my sword. He raises the leg and strikes at my arm. My teeth rattle with the impact. But instead of toppling, as I expect, he brings his leg back down and scuffles backward.

Sweat beads his forehead and his chest rises and falls at a rate much greater than my own. In a half-moment of eye contact I understand two things. The first is how he compensates for his weakness: by allowing the strong leg to take his weight. The weak one is merely a stabilizer. It is the strong one I must attack. The second thing I understand is that he is working much harder than I. Perhaps because of his ceaseless attack, perhaps because his foot pains him more than he acknowledges. In any event, all I need do is conserve my own energy while he tires.

Instead of parrying the next few thrusts, I keep my sword tight against my body and dodge. Tutankhamun stops and looks at me, eyebrows lowered. The next thrust, I block, but twist to the side so he must turn to face me. His breathing is yet more rapid.

When he attacks, he gives me no opportunity to dodge. I must meet each blow. I aim consistently for his strong leg, but it is the same side of his body as his sword-arm, and he protects it well. The sword feels heavy and my arm trembles. I grab the hilt with both hands, but Tutankhamun smiles. He sees my weakness.

Tutankhamun resumes his attack. He brings his sword around from the side, making it impossible for me to maintain my two-handed grip. When I let go with one hand, the flat side of his sword smashes against my wrist. I am spun around and lose my footing. My sword sails through the air and clangs against the wall.

Before Tutankhamun can point his sword in symbolic victory, I spin around and get my feet under me, hands still on the floor. Instead of rising, I swing one leg around, hook my foot around his strong leg and pull him down. I grab his sword as it slides across the floor and jump to my feet.

One foot planted on his chest, I point his own sword at his throat.

He hisses through his teeth. "You were lucky."

I do not move the sword. "I am shorter, lighter and weaker than any man you will face on the battlefield. I have less training than a soldier and no battle experience. The Hatti will not need luck."

I remove my foot from his chest and offer him a hand up. He stares at my hand for so long I expect him to refuse it, but at last he takes it and eases himself up. I offer him his sword, hilt first. He accepts it, retrieves my sword, and places both of them on his writing table.

I resist the urge to rub at my wrist. It will be bruised and swollen by morning.

"Go," he says.

I reach out a hand to touch his shoulder and he shies away. "Go."

"I only hope to keep you alive," I say.

He sits down at the writing table and stares at me. "I know," he says, "yet I cannot look on your face for now. Please go."

I want to beg him one more time not to fight, but I know all he can hear at this moment is his own humiliation. I nod and leave, hoping my actions have not had the opposite of their desired effect and made him more determined than ever to prove himself.

Tutankhamun

"The army will be ready to march within a month, just after the start of the new year," says Horemheb as he and Amenia disembark at the water steps of Ay's estate moments after we do.

"Excellent," I say. Ankhesenamun stiffens beside me. It is her wrist that is wrapped in a bandage, but she is not the only one still smarting from that encounter.

The outside walls of the estate are lined with white limestone, now sparkling in the evening sun, and shaded by sycamores and fig trees. The gatekeeper, noting the arrival of the royal boat, simply bows his head and steps aside to let us pass.

Horemheb falls in step with me, while Ankhesenamun lags behind to walk with Amenia. Horemheb is stiff, even more so than is his habit, each foot hitting the ground with a dull flap, one after the other. He looks straight ahead, not speaking. Taciturn being his usual demeanor, one might not see anything amiss but for the clenching of his jaw, the grim set of his lips.

"These events are frightfully dull," I say, knowing that is not his true reason for concern, nor mine, but discretion being required in the moment.

Horemheb glances at me, eyebrows raised. "For most wedding feasts, I would agree, but this one promises to be anything but dull, if not in its performance at least in its aftermath."

"True enough." The marriage between Nakhtmenu and Mutnedjmet promises to make life at court interesting indeed. Ay has always had an eye for the throne in the event of my demise or continued childlessness, but with no male heirs has had no real hope of staking a claim until now. This marriage of his daughter gives him a male heir. While Mutnedjmet is advanced in years, she may yet be capable of bearing children, but even if she is not, should Ay succeed in taking the throne, Nakhtmenu would succeed him and, as King, could take other wives. In the event I should not sire an heir, I must consider formally adopting Horemheb. Perhaps, in time, a coregency to solidify his claim. Yet, acting too swiftly would not be prudent. Should I produce a prince of royal blood late in life, would a Horemheb already established on the throne, or even formally designated as heir, be willing to relinquish his power in favor of my son?

Ay's banquet hall is in the center of his home, so that it may retain heat as the day cools into night. There, Ankhesenamun must part from Amenia and join me on the dais with Ay, Tey and the newly joined couple. Unsurprisingly, Horemheb has been relegated to a corner of the room that is clearly visible from our tables, yet far enough away to reinforce his inferior status at this event.

When servants appear with the first courses of cucumbers, dates and stewed figs, and the aroma of roasted gazelle wafts over us, I observe the newly joined couple. Nakhtmenu raises his cup frequently, shouting and calling to the dancers. Mutnedjmet smiles over her cup when she spies me watching, but otherwise eats and drinks sparingly, only occasionally leaning over to speak to Ankhesenamun.

"Nakhtmenu is joyous this night," I say to Ankhesenamun in a low voice, "as he is right to be. He has scored a great victory in marrying so close to the royal family. One would think that Mutnedjmet would be equally joyous, having not only secured a husband at long last, but one who could potentially enable her to sit on your throne."

"One might think so," says Ankhesenamun, "if one did not understand women."

Thinking silence may be in my best interest at the moment, I choose not to respond.

Ankhesenamun continues. "Mutnedjmet is accustomed to living life as she chooses, taking lovers as she chooses. She may find the thought of power intoxicating, but this night she begins to understand the cost."

Yes, the cost. I cannot decide if her words are meant to express regret or resolve. "Will it dissuade her, do you think?"

Ankhesenamun shakes her head so slightly as to be nearly imperceptible. "I do not."

It occurs to me that she has lost a trusted ally. As her aunt, Mutnedjmet has been a friend and confidante her entire life. This night they become rivals. Ankhesenamun must be feeling the loss. Before the sword fight, I would have slipped an arm around her waist, low enough that it would not be observed by those below us, simply to let her know I understand. But my resentment burns, and my eyes fall to the bandage around her wrist and think, perhaps, she would not welcome my touch in any case.

Kawit sits to one side of the room with Ankhesenamun's other ladies. She watches me over the rim of her wine cup. Her eyes, ringed with kohl and dusted with malachite and gold powder, linger on mine a fraction longer than is seemly.

The music changes from flutes to lively drums, jolting me from my thoughts. Mutnedjmet's pet dwarves have taken the floor, rolling and leaping. Their acrobatics are poor, yet the laughter from the audience is deafening. Perhaps that is the point of their performance. Across the floor, one man remains unmoved. Horemheb crosses his arms and looks to the door, giving every appearance of one gauging precisely how long he must stay. I attempt to catch his attention without being obvious, for he and I need to meet again before long to discuss deployment of the troops. And, of course, the ramifications of this marriage. He looks everywhere but in my direction. I wonder if it is the dwarves or me he wishes to avoid seeing.

Ankhesenamun leans over. "Settle down. With you jerking your head back and forth, you resemble one of those Naharin fighting birds."

"Horemheb is deliberately ignoring me."

Ankhesenamun puts a finger to her lips and tilts her head to indicate Mutnedjmet to her other side. Mutnedjmet watches the dwarves as they roll to one side of the room, but her eyes do not follow them as they move out of her field of vision. Instead, she looks down at her table, or off to her husband's table. Everywhere but in the direction of Horemheb. It takes me some thought before I understand the meaning.

"How long has this been going on?" I keep my voice low.

"I have known of it nearly two years."

My mouth drops open. "Two years? Does Ay know?"

"I should think if Ay knew, he would have killed Horemheb by his own hand."

I think for a moment. "Or eliminate the problem by marrying her to Horemheb's chief rival."

Ankhesenamun looks at me. "Possibly. Still, I think it unlikely that Ay knows. It is not talked about in the Women's Quarters. I have heard nothing about it, save what Mutnedjmet herself has told me."

"Should I die without issue, Mutnedjmet shall be well placed to become Queen no matter which contender wins the throne," I say.

Ankhesenamun shoves away her plate, rejecting a significant portion of lentils and onions. She drains her wine. A serving girl appears to remove the plate, another one to offer more. Ankhesenamun waves her away. I do not blame her. I, too, find myself with a sudden loss of appetite. More so, perhaps, because I know I shall soon be leaving her alone at court.

"You must watch Ay closely while Horemheb and I are away on campaign," I say. "Ay's ambitions will know no bounds now."

Ankhesenamun shoots me a hard glance. "There is no need to remind me of Ay's ambitions, nor of the steps he may take to see those ambitions fulfilled."

"Tomorrow we must meet in private to discuss strategies for dealing with Ay while I am gone."

Ankhesenamun sighs. "I was doing this job while you were snivelling at your mother's knee."

"I am no longer a boy," I say, "and you no longer need to do the job alone."

She turns to me. "Yet, I will be alone. You shall be away for months, at least." She squeezes her eyes shut, but not before a tear trickles down the corner of her face. "If you do not return, I shall be forever alone, caught between Ay and Horemheb."

"I shall return."

"Do not overreach your abilities." She waves her injured wrist in front of her face. My cheeks burn at the reminder. "Kemet needs you to live and so do I." Her voice chokes and she coughs to cover it, lest someone else hear her sorrow. She leans closer and drops her voice to a whisper. "I cannot do this without you."

"You are more than capable of it, but there will be no need," I say.

"You cannot know that. We must add that to our agenda for discussion." I glance up and find that Horemheb and Amenia have left. "If I do not return, marry Horemheb."

Her eyes widen momentarily. She arranges her features into a more passive expression before speaking. "I do not believe I heard you correctly." "He would be your best choice."

"Best of a poor lot, perhaps."

I put an arm around her waist. "Do not fret. The Hatti shall be defeated, I shall return to you whole, and we shall have our time away in Shedet."

She looks up at me.

"I have not forgotten my promise. By the time the army returns, the fields may be grown tall, but still, we can take a little time."

She looks away. She knows as well as I that, if the campaign is prolonged, the harvest may be in, the fields flooded again, and new crops sown before I return.

She does not believe it will happen, so I must show her. I will start the arrangements now so that we may go as soon as possible after I return, however long that may be.

After the feast, when we have returned to the palace and I to my chambers alone, I hear a disturbance in the corridor. When the guard opens the door, I stand up, hoping Ankhesenamun has come and am disappointed when the guard tells me the Lady Kawit is requesting permission to see me. I instruct him to allow her into my sitting room and I take my place behind my writing table.

The scent of cardamom and cinnamon precedes her into the room. She has changed since the feast. Her robes are of translucent linen, showing off her henna-darkened nipples and the dark triangle below her belly. I am thankful the writing table hides my involuntary reaction. "I am told ..." my voice cracks and I cough to cover it up. "I am told you need to see me."

Kawit sits on the corner of the writing table and runs a finger down my chest, raising a ripple of gooseflesh. "I saw you watching me at the feast. I thought, perhaps, you wanted to see me."

I move to stand up, then think better of it. "If I wanted you, I would have sent for you."

She glances down to my lap and smiles. She reaches as if to untie my sash, but I grab her wrist. She stares at me, wide-eyed.

"You would turn me away, despite your desire?"

"I don't desire you," I say.

She flicks her eyes downwards. "Part of you does."

I wonder how old she is. Surely, at least fifteen inundations by now. A woman, to be sure, but a young one. I almost laugh aloud when I remember I am but little older than she. "No matter the demands of my body, I do not roll the daughters of noblemen around on the furniture. It is unseemly." I gesture at her attire. "Now, go, and in the future, do not appear before me in something that is unfit to wear for any but a husband."

She juts her chin forward. "You could be my husband."

"You already know my decision on that matter."

Her face falls. "Yes, but you have never explained why. Am I so displeasing?"

"You are not," I say, "but you are the Great Royal Wife's lady and I do not think she would approve."

"The Great Royal Wife does not have a say in the matter."

This time I do not even try to stifle my laughter. "The Great Royal Wife has a say in a great many matters, including everything that happens in the royal household, and well you know it." I do not add that, right now, Ankhesenamun has more need of allies than I do of another wife.

"Concubine, then?" Her voice is low and her lip trembles. Is she truly so besotted?

"Concubine is below your station," I say. "Not worthy of a woman of your birth."

She pretends to scratch an itch, but instead wipes away a tear. "Concubine to the King is preferable to ..." her voice trails off.

"Your father would be insulted by such an arrangement," I say. I rise and place a hand on her shoulder. "You are young and beautiful. I am sure there are many noble men who would treasure you as a wife. I will speak to your father ..."

Her chest heaves and her sobs fill the air. "My father will disown me when he discovers what I have done."

My initial reaction is that she feigns emotion in an attempt to manipulate me. Tears lead rivulets of black kohl down her cheeks and her nose reddens from her wiping at it. When a lady pretends despair, she does so delicately, so as not to mar her appearance. I sit beside her on the writing table and place a hand over hers. "Tell me what has happened."

Tutankhamun, Year 10

(ca. 1324 BCE)

Ankhesenamun

It is still dark, and stars twinkle outside the window when Tutankhamun nuzzles my neck. "Did I wake you?"

"Yes, but it does not matter," I say. "I would rather spend these last hours with you than waste them on sleep."

As Tutankhamun's hands caress my breasts and slide down my body, as he removes the alabaster headrest from under my neck and places it on the floor I pray to Aset and Het-Heru and Mut and Bes and Taweret and any other gods who care to listen, even the Aten of whom I am forbidden to speak, as I already have three times this night, "please, please let a child start now." I don't speak it aloud, for I do not wish for Tutankhamun to hear my desperation, yet I have been giving sacrifices for the healing of my womb since the sentence of barrenness was passed on me, and so I silently repeat the words until he collapses, panting, on top of me.

I kiss his cheek, pull him closer, cradle his head against my shoulder and change the words of my prayer: If he is taken from me, please do not leave me childless.

I intend to stay awake the rest of the night, breathing in the manly, musky smell of his sweat and his seed, but I must have fallen asleep, for the next I am aware, the bedchamber is full of pre-dawn light, tinting everything in shades of purple. I am turned on one side, my headrest still on the floor. My shoulder and neck ache from the unnatural position. The bed sways and I turn over.

Tutankhamun is sitting up, slipping on his sandals. He bends down to kiss my forehead.

I sit up. "You were going to leave without saying good-bye?"

"We shall see each other again before I leave."

"In the temple, along with the entire court and the army officers."

He shifts to one side, brushes the hair from my eyes and touches my cheek. "Do not be angry. I wished to carry with me the perfect image of you sleeping."

This unexpected response brings a lump to my throat, and I cannot think of a response.

"You looked very like a goddess in repose," says Tutankhamun. "Het-Heru, with your long eyelashes brushing your cheek and a string of drool hanging from your lips."

I brush the back of a hand against my mouth. Tutankhamun laughs. I punch him in the shoulder, and he pretends it hurts.

"There is one thing I must discuss with you before I go."

"And yet, you were trying to leave while I slept."

He looks at the floor. "Perhaps it would be easier to discuss in the temple."

In the temple. Surrounded by people, where I must control my reactions. Icy cold grips my heart. "What is so difficult to say that you cannot say it when we are alone?"

He takes a deep breath. "I have taken your lady, Kawit, as a concubine."

Kawit. It is his right to take concubines, even wives, as he desires. Still, Kawit. The lady closest to me. "When did this start."

He clears his throat. "On her return from the Delta."

Two months. I nod. "I am glad you told me yourself, though there was no need. It is your ..."

"She is with child."

I feel as if the air has been sucked from the room. Surely, the gods could not be so cruel. They would not deny me a child while giving one to Kawit. "She is certain?"

"Quite," says Tutankhamun "I need you to watch out for them both while I am gone. I have left documents in the archive acknowledging her child as my own and also instructions to hold a wedding feast immediately upon my return. I have given a copy to Horemheb and must leave another copy with you."

I press my lips together and close my eyes. I open them when I feel a hand on my shoulder.

"I know this must pain you," says Tutankhamun. "Please know that I would rather throw myself on my sword than cause you a moment's grief, but I must take any chance given to provide Kemet with an heir. By the grace of the gods, an heir will soon be born, and he must be protected at all costs, no matter who his mother is."

I close my eyes just long enough to stop the tears threatening to spill. He is correct. "While you are gone, I shall ensure that Kawit's child is acknowledged as your heir."

"Thank you," he says as he rises to leave. At the doorway he stops and turns. "I shall return to you."

I say nothing. At the moment, I am not certain I want him to return.

Tutankhamun's dark figure, silhouetted against the mid-morning sun, turns to face me. His head, topped with the blue war crown, is held high. The kohl surrounding his eyes is black as night, and sharply defined, giving him an air of maturity he has not quite earned, but is growing into. He stands straight, and with his twisted foot hidden under his long kilt, the walking stick planted on the floor beside him speaks of authority instead of weakness.

He holds out a hand and I join him in the temple courtyard. The army is assembling, preparing for their procession out of Waset and on to Kadesh to meet the Hatti.

When Tutankhamun takes my hand and presses it to his lips, I wonder if he shall ever do so again.

There is but one throne on the dais this day. As I take my place, Mutnedjmet takes a lower seat to my side, and Ay and Tey takes seats to my other side. The army forms ranks; Tutankhamun in front in his chariot.

Kawit appears carrying wreaths of flowers. She passes some to me first. I cannot meet her eyes. She hands some to Ay and Tey and as she leans over to deliver wreaths to Mutnedjmet, my eyes are unwillingly drawn to her belly, where there is a small, yet distinct, swelling. Oh, my husband the idiot. She is at least three months gone, which means the child was conceived while she was away in the Delta. It is not the King's child and well she knows it. I think back. Never has she mentioned to me a lover in the Delta, nor did she behave as if there were one. On the contrary, she did not wish to leave on holiday this year and she was greatly relieved to return to Waset. Yet, clearly, she has a man. Or did, about three months ago. I vow to find him and expose the pair of them before someone else discovers the lie.

The procession nears and stops in front of us. Tutankhamun winks at me and bows his head, and I hurl a wreath of flowers at him. It hits him in the face, but he catches it as it falls and tosses it back into the air laughing. My heart aches at the thought that this might be my last sight of him, and I know, no matter what he has done, I want him to return to me. I want him, not only for

Kemet, but for me. While he is away, I shall deal with Kawit and when he does return, he will find a peaceful household, and a devoted wife, waiting for him.

He turns and leads the procession through the main gate and down the road toward the distant border and the even more distant Kadesh. As the back of his helmet fades to a blur and then disappears, a thought occurs to me. Should the gods deny my pleas, and fail to give me the son we need, we must take the one that is available. I glance at Kawit. She is waving to the retreating army, tears in her eyes. Some of the soldiers were lately stationed in the Delta. I wonder if one of them is the true father. I must find out who it is and be rid of him permanently. Perhaps a generous payment of land near the first cataract. Perhaps a distant posting where an accident might befall him. Who else would know? Too many to bribe? If I have no inkling of the truth, perhaps there are very few, perhaps none.

I devise a plan. I shall give the gods one last chance. If I am not now carrying the son Kemet needs, Kawit's child will be born as the Horus prince and will rule Kemet and no one but me will be any the wiser.

Tutankhamun

Facing the mighty Hatti is an altogether different prospect than facing Kushite rebels. For one thing, Hatti have chariots, as we do. True, their chariots are heavy and difficult to maneuver, but they can carry two archers and a driver, whereas ours have room for only one archer. Where they depend on strength, we must depend on speed and stealth. Thus, instead of charging enemy lines alone, I employ a driver so that I may fire my arrows while he drives us away from opposing fire. At least, that is how Horemheb presented his suggestion to me, and I accepted in the same spirit. I am grateful he did not mention the presence of a driver would ensure I do not drive straight into a spear as I nearly did last time.

For another thing, when the driver turns the horses down the aisle between our assembled soldiers, both Kemetian and Naharin, instead of a solid wall of shields facing me across the battlefield, I see an aisle identical to our own, with a Hatti chariot charging in my direction. Their king in the position of main archer, resplendent in bronze scales and gleaming helmet.

As my chariot breaks free of our troops, I see the Hatti arranged in columns, as we are. The main body of the troops, with swords and shields, take the center ground. To each side, ranks of chariots, horses pawing the ground and drivers holding them back, wait their turn to run.

I reach into one of the many quivers lashed to the sides for an arrow and as I do, I check the tension of the belt binding me to the chariot. I raise my bow, nock the arrow and stare down the Hatti king, who is aiming his bow at me. The floor rattles under my feet and I clench my teeth against the pain, willing my body to stand straight.

I pull back the bowstring, but do not release it even when I am in range. Instead, I watch the Hatti king, waiting for the slight shift in his stance, the upward tick of his bow. When I see it, I shout, "now!" The driver veers into a turn so sharp the chariot teeters. I lean with the motion, grasping the chariot frame between my elbow and chest and let my arrow fly. The opposing chariot swerves out of the arrow's path. Shouts go up around both sides of the field and the ground thunders with the feet of men and horses.

Before my own chariot can retreat, I am surrounded by my own men screaming with battle frenzy. My driver takes me to high ground so I can watch the battle with some of the reserve officers. I descend and enter the pavilion, out of the sun, while my horses are unhitched and led away. A servant is waiting to hand me my walking stick. The plain stretches out beneath me. On the far side another hill rises, where the Hatti have staked their high ground.

Our archers wreak havoc amongst the slower moving Hatti. Even with reduced firepower, we can strike quickly and decisively and retreat before they can find us. Our foot soldiers fare considerably less well. The Hatti black swords cut through our own, and those of the Naharin, as if they were reeds. I look for Horemheb's chariot and find it, and him, mustering more archers to cover our soldiers, but he cannot spare many, for still he needs to keep the Hatti archers at bay.

The Hatti king does not retreat. I can see his gilded chariot and plumed horses in the midst of the fray, surrounded by a phalanx of guards. I seethe at being left on the sidelines. I am King. I have no business allowing my men to fight and die for me. I should be leading them.

I turn to my driver. "Come," I tell him.

He gives me a bemused look but follows me nonetheless to the grooms. I order them to ready the chariot again. They get up to obey.

"Highness?" says the driver.

"We are going back to the battle. It is our duty."

The driver looks to the field and hesitates a moment. I know Horemheb has ordered him to mind me and keep me away from the fighting. Yet, I also know the injury this causes his soldier's pride. Besides, I outrank Horemheb. He nods and smiles. "Yes, Highness."

"What is your name, soldier?" I ask.

"Ahmose, Highness."

I nod. "It is an honor to serve with you, Ahmose."

He nods. "The honor is mine, Highness."

When the grooms bring the chariot around, Ahmose takes his place as driver. I ascend and consider not using the belt. More freedom of movement would aid me. Too much movement, though, may unseat me altogether. In the end, I fasten the belt and give Ahmose the signal to move.

Orderly ranks have collapsed into a maelstrom. The two forces are so thoroughly comingled it is difficult to identify to which army individual fighters belong. Most of the Hatti archers have abandoned their chariots in favor of hand-to-hand combat, where they have the advantage. Our own chariots circle, occasionally picking off a lone Hatti archer, but seldom daring to fire into the mass of footed soldiers, for fear of striking one of our own.

The Hatti king remains in his chariot, still surrounded by his guards. He circles the battle, lobbing arrows into the melee, apparently not caring if he hits one of ours or one of his own.

I turn to Ahmose. "To their king."

His eyebrows shoot up. "Are you certain, Highness?"

"If the king falls, the battle is over," I say.

Ahmose glances up at me from under a furrowed brow. I can all but hear him thinking that is precisely his fear. "The Hatti king is well guarded, Highness. Your own guards do not even know you are here."

"Then you must keep me away from enemy fire."

He clenches his jaw, but nods. I do not blame him for his reluctance. It is a perilous mission, and if I should fall, Ahmose would be punished. Even so, he signals the horses to run. My battle cry joins the chorus of pounding hoofbeats, metal on metal and the cries of the victorious as well as the defeated.

We circle around to surprise the king from behind, where he is least protected. As the chariot picks up speed, the motion pains my foot. But this is no longer the first charge. I do not need to cut an impressive figure. I need only to kill. I lean into the side, grasping with my elbow to steady myself while I aim. My first arrow hits a Hatti archer in the neck. As he falls, his partner sets loose an arrow.

Ahmose steers me out of harm's way. The chariot lurches as we fly between enemy chariots and pass a few of our own. My good foot slips and I slide down inside the chariot, hanging by the belt. In desperation, I cling to the sides, unable to regain my footing. "Retreat!" I shout.

When we are clear of the battle, I readjust the belt and stand. The pavilion sits atop a hill. As it nears, I squeeze my eyes shut. I have no children. I have no empire. I cannot even fight. Worse yet, my army has just witnessed my cowardice. I wish I thought to use a rough chariot and remove the plumed headdresses from my horses. At least then, my ignominious retreat might have gone unnoticed. The clamor of battle has dulled to a nondescript roar, yet it is enough to remind me that the last sight some of my men will ever see is that of their king abandoning them.

"Return," I say.

For a moment, Ahmose looks as if he did not hear me, but then he turns the chariot once again.

I loosen my belt a little. More slack will allow me to rise, should I fall again. "Stay on the periphery, so I may shoot more freely."

"Do you still wish to target their king, Highness?"

I nod.

Ahmose circles around and we approach the field from behind. I fire several arrows, some finding their mark. The king is in sight. He is surrounded by four chariots, each with two archers and a driver. Even should I manage to kill all of those guards, they would be promptly replaced by others. My one chance is to shoot through a hole in the line of defence.

I ready my bow and nock an arrow, but as we approach the gap between chariots, they pull together to close the gap. We drop behind to approach the other side with the same result.

"Highness," shouts Ahmose, cocking his head to the side.

Several chariots have broken ranks and are heading straight for us. I nod. We have no choice but to engage. I ready several arrows and shift into my usual position, leaning to the side. Firing in rapid succession, I take out both of the archers in the lead chariot. Two other chariots overtake the first, arrows flying. Ahmose assumes a zigzag path to evade fire.

From my left, two more chariots race toward me. On instinct, I take aim before recognizing them as our own. The standard flying above the horses of the first are Horemheb's. Close behind him is Paramessu. I turn back to the enemy. Two of them charge directly at me, side by side. Their arrows sail to the side, engaging only Horemheb and Paramessu. I have little time to wonder why all four archers would ignore me when the two separate and from between them races a third chariot – the former lead, now without any archers.

Ahmose turns in time to avoid a full ramming, but not in time to avoid a sideswipe. I fall against the side. My bow clatters to the ground and is well behind me before I can think of retrieving it. The looser belt allows me to fall further, tangling myself with Ahmose's legs and threatening to drag him down as well. I pull myself up to my knees and untie the cursed belt. Horemheb and Paramessu are busy with their own fight and unable to get to me.

As Ahmose turns, the other charioteer is already racing toward us again, secure in the knowledge that I cannot fire on him. "Go! Go!" I grunt, but it is not necessary. Ahmose is already driving us away. Other enemy chariots are coming at us from another direction. My fingers cramp as I try to knot the belt.

When the crash comes, I am vaulted over the side. I twist to avoid landing on my head, so instead hit the ground hard on my contorted leg. Something snaps and the pain is like a bright light inside my skull.

Agony jolts me awake. Agony unlike any I've ever known, beginning in my leg, and radiating throughout my body. I'm staring at the oiled linen peak of a tent. Someone is screaming. I believe it is me.

The face of the army physician hovers over my own. "Apologies, Highness. We had hoped you would not wake until after the bone was set."

I look down. My thigh is uncovered and there is an angry wound, swollen and red and oozing blood. I turn my head and vomit onto the dirt floor. A pair of sandaled feet walk into my field of vision. I look up to find the feet are attached to Horemheb.

"It is not so bad as that, Highness," he says. "It is a clean break and required but little shifting to move the two ends back in place."

My stomach roils and, though I attempt to swallow back, still I vomit once more. The physician approaches, clearly intending more poking and prodding. I shift the leg away from him and cry out as the pain hits.

"Now, Highness," says the physician, "this is but a small discomfort compared to what you have already endured."

He is correct in that this should be a minor discomfort, but every touch is magnified as he probes with his fingers to check the setting of the bone. I clench my jaw to keep from screaming, but I make no attempt to stop the tears rolling down my face.

To distract myself, I look at Horemheb. "How went the rest of the battle?"

He cocks his head to one side. "Well, we did not win, but neither did we lose definitively. It is not over yet. The Naharin are sending reinforcements and we still have three more units in transit."

The physician completes his task and turns away momentarily, returning with a pot of honey and a stick. He drips honey liberally over the wound.

"A messenger waits to run back to the palace at Waset," says Horemheb. "I wanted first to see your condition so that I may give the Great Royal Wife good news."

I nod.

"We are preparing special transport for you to return as soon as possible."

"No. I must stay," I said. "My men need me to be here."

Horemheb huffs.

"Do not tell me my men need me to stay alive. I am alive and they need me here."

"Do you wish me to speak frankly, Highness?" asks Horemheb.

I nod.

"As you are, you are a burden. We must care for you and defend you constantly. With you safely recuperating back in Waset, we will be free to win this war for you."

I remember the sight of the Hatti king in his chariot. I must stay, yet I cannot deny the truth of Horemheb's words.

"His Highness is correct," says the physician.

We both look at him.

"Oh, perhaps not about the men needing him to be here, that is for more intelligent minds than mine to decide," says the physician. "But he is correct that he must not leave. The trip home would be unbearably painful and may cause the wound to worsen. The longer his Highness can heal before bearing the return voyage, the better."

I nod. "It is decided, then. I shall stay with the army."

Ankhesenamun

I drop the scroll on my writing table. After a few moments, I pick it up and reread to be sure my eyes do not deceive me. I skim past, "For you only, my beloved Ankhesenamun ..." and "... please destroy this letter ..." and land on, "You may suspect that Kawit's gravidity is further advanced than it should be, given her recent return from the Delta. I beg you to conceal this fact and also beg you to forgive the deception. The palace walls have ears, and I thought it safest to confide in you by sealed scroll written in my own hand. The gods have denied us children of our own, yet I have found a way to give Kemet the heir it needs. I beg your cooperation, for I must have your help in order for the ruse to succeed." He signed it, "Your devoted husband."

I laugh. Tutankhamun knows, has known from the beginning, that Kawit's child is not his. Fortunately, I already decided on the same deception he did, else I might have exposed her before ever reading the letter.

After the army departed, I set aside the sealed box Tutankhamun left me, opting not to open it until after I knew if I carried an heir. The first time my courses arrived, still I hoped, for some women are known to bleed with child. Neither the wheat nor the barley sprouted, but that has also been known to be wrong at times. Not until my courses arrived for the second time, did I admit the truth. I carried the box to my writing table, broke the clay seal stamped with Tutankhamun's names, and was surprised to find not one, but two, scrolls inside. The first was the one I knew to expect, the copy of the document acknowledging Kawit as Tutankhamun's concubine and her child as his own.

After reading it, I resealed it and hid it in a cavity concealed by a loose floor tile and covered by the leg of my bed.

The second is the one I now read. It gives no details as to who fathered the child or what steps, if any, Tutankhamun has taken to ensure this man causes no trouble. Using a rushlight, I ignite the papyrus and watch it burn to ashes. This accomplished, I gather the ashes into a small pot and pour them down the toilet, into the pot of sand beneath, whence they will be dumped into the palace sewer pits. Then I leave my chambers, my guard trailing behind me, and send a servant to command Kawit to meet me in the courtyard. The palace walls do indeed have ears.

I sit on a seat under the sycamores by the pond and wait. When Kawit arrives, her head is lowered, and she does not meet my eyes. Since the announcement of her new status of concubine and mother to the heir to the throne, a distance has grown between us, largely of my own making. Believing this arrangement to be a betrayal by both my husband and my lady, I called on Kawit infrequently. Kawit, likely knowing of my antipathy toward her, has not sought me out. More, she has kept her head down in the Women's Quarters and has not given into the airs common amongst women about to birth the next King, though that may be more due to fear of being discovered in her lie than in any regret over losing my favor.

I have not seen Kawit in some weeks. Her belly is now gently rounded. There is no more hiding her condition, even should she want to. Instead of the wrenching of the guts I am used to feeling at the sight of her, I now feel hope. She is saving us. Instead of asking her to sit, I rise and, smiling broadly, invite her to walk with me.

Her eyes widen and she glances back at the guard under the lotus bud columns on the portico. She seems unsure of herself but nods her consent.

As we skirt the pond, I clasp my hands behind my back and assume a deliberately casual air. "It is not the King's child you carry."

Her eyes are round and her mouth gapes open. For a moment, she seems incapable of speech, and then she stutters. "I – I assure you, H-H-Highness ..."

"The King himself has told me." I spread my hands in front of me. "Do not fret. I do not intend to expose you. On the contrary, I wish to continue with the King's plan."

Kawit takes a deep breath. "Why should you wish to do that?"

I decide forthrightness would be best. "Because it is in my best interest to do so. Kemet is in desperate need of an heir."

She nods. "Even so, you cannot be pleased that I carry the child you do not. How does it benefit you to put my bastard on the throne of Kemet?"

I continue walking, savoring the shade of pomegranate and fig trees. "I do not say I am pleased with the situation, but at the moment options are limited." I turn my head to face her. "I am going to be candid. Though no one speaks of it, at least not in my presence, it must surely have occurred to everyone at court that I am unlikely to ever bear a child."

"You are still young, surely you will in time," she says.

"I thank you for the gentle lie, but it is not necessary. The sons of the Great Royal Wife supersede those of all other wives and concubines." I glance at her belly. "Your child is no threat to a son of mine, should I bear one." I stop walking. "Do you know what should happen if the King dies without an heir?"

She shakes her head.

"A fight for the crown, possibly civil war. I shall become a prize for whoever seeks the Kingship and Kemet will be plunged into chaos."

Kawit blanches.

"With a legitimate, acknowledged heir, the succession is assured, Ma'at reigns. If the heir is still a child when the King passes to the West, I become Regent and rule in his stead until he comes of age."

Kawit nods with the dawn of understanding.

"Providing the heir makes you the savior of all of Kemet."

Kawit draws herself up straight and smiles.

"However, should the child's true father start telling tales, the deception will be for nothing."

A cloud darkens Kawit's face. "He shall not cause trouble."

"How can you be certain? Has the King already taken care of him?" Kawit's voice is small. "I do not know."

I sigh. "Then you must tell me who he is so I may look into the matter."

Kawit shakes her head. "No. He will never acknowledge this child as his. Never."

"He may, if he believes he can leverage payment from the crown."

Kawit's eyes widen and she chews her lip. "The King knows. If he has not ensured silence already, he may do so on his return."

"That will not be for many months, perhaps not until after the child is born. If the father does not know he left you with child, he may start counting backward when he hears of the child's birth and realize the truth." I grasp her hand. "We must act now." I hope I do not have to raise with her the possibility that the King may not return at all.

Kawit trembles and a tear snakes a path down her cheek, followed by several more.

I lead her back to the chairs, sit down beside her and stroke her hair. "You need not be afraid to tell me," I say. "No one else shall ever know." I wonder if she does not believe me. Perhaps she thinks this has all been a ruse to get her to confide a truth I had really only guessed at.

She takes a shuddering breath. "It is Wajmose."

I am struck dumb for several moments. "Wajmose, your uncle? The royal perfumer?"

She nods and wipes her nose with the back of her hand.

This complicates things. He is too well connected for a simple banishment. People would note his disappearance and wonder. A bribe, perhaps, and the promise of eternal royal gratitude. Perhaps a promotion, but not one so grand it would elicit curiosity. What if the price of his silence is more than we can pay? What if the price escalates year by year? No, a permanent elimination is needed. One that gives the appearance of an accident.

Kawit leans against me, her chest heaving in great sobs. I put an arm around her, feel a pang of shame for having forgotten about her, and realize she is mumbling something. "I'm sorry, what did you say?"

She sniffs and starts partway through her ramble. "Every year, when we travel to the Delta, Wajmose gives me my own room and he visits at night."

Every year? She is so young now. "How long has this been going on?"

"Since I reached ten inundations. He told my parents I was near womanhood and needed privacy and so he kept me away from the other children."

"Did you never tell your parents?"

Kawit nods. "I told my mother after we returned home that first emergence after it happened. He visited me nearly every night that season."

Liasons of that type between close relations belonged to the gods alone and, by extension, the royal family who is from the gods, but not for other men. I sigh. The punishment for debauching children is castration, followed by death. Unfortunately, a public pronouncement and execution would reveal her child's true paternity. "Yet, your mother still allowed the visits to continue?"

"She said I must have done something to encourage him. That I should dress more modestly, be less wanton and he would not desire me."

"It was not your doing. You were a child." I see again my mother, staggering into my bedchamber in the throes of her own illness to keep my father from me. She sent me away and by morning, he was dead. This girl's mother allowed it to continue. Kawit looks at me. "I tried. I truly did. I wore longer dresses, no jewels, no makeup. He ordered me new clothes and had his own stylists work on me. He'd have me wait for him in my private room at night. This past season, he no longer waited for night to fall. He'd find reasons to be alone with me or simply order me to his office." She sobs. "My mother told me I disgusted her and to keep it quiet because my father would send me away if he found out. That he'd sell me to a sheepherder in the desert."

By the end of this speech, I am trembling as much as Kawit. Partly in remembrance of the fear I felt myself as a child, but mostly in rage. I hope this Wajmose lives so I may throttle him myself. "I wish you had told me this sooner. I wouldn't have permitted you to accompany your family to the Delta last season. Or ever again."

"You would have done this for me?" A new barrage of tears starts.

Of course, she would not have believed I would protect her when her own mother would not. "Does the King know all of this?"

Kawit nods and I understand. Even without the need for an heir, Tutankhamun would have acted the same. Not for Kawit, but for me. And for our sisters. For the ones he couldn't protect because he was too young and too weak. A thought occurs to me.

"You have younger sisters, have you not?"

"Yes, two," says Kawit.

"Has Wajmose been bothering them as well?"

Kawit sucks in a breath. "I do not know. I do not think so. They did not have private rooms in the villa, and I did not notice him ordering either of them to his office or …" She puts her hands to her face. "If I stop going, will he go after them, do you think?"

I think that if his taste is for young girls, it matters not whether Kawit joins her family in the Delta next season of emergence. He will surely choose one of them over the mature woman and mother Kawit will be by that time. More than any other consideration, this makes my decision for me. Wajmose must die and I promise myself it shall be painful.

"Wajmose will not hurt your sisters or anyone else, ever again."

Kawit gazes at me in silence.

"Furthermore, your child shall be treasured by all of Kemet as the King's child. If it is a boy, he shall ascend the throne, in time."

Kawit lowers herself to the ground.

"What are you doing?"

She grasps my hand and kisses it.

I glance at the nearest guard and a couple of ladies on the other side of the pond, out for a stroll. "Get back on your chair right now," I say through clenched teeth.

She does as ordered, her hands folded in her lap. "I only wish to express my gratitude. You and the King have saved me."

No, I think. It is you who have saved us, but I allow her gratitude, for we will need it. Tutankhamun has never sired a living child on any woman, and not for lack of trying. Yet, Kawit is fertile and if we succeed in one deception, we may succeed in two. Or three, or more, if necessary. If Kawit is grateful enough, she will consent to taking lovers I choose to keep birthing children until there are at least two boys. I must keep a lookout for men who will be gentle with her, not overly demanding of me, yet are entirely expendable. If I encourage Tutankhamun to frequent her bed, perhaps not even he need not know her subsequent children are not his. Perhaps, gods willing, they will be.

A servant approaches and bows deeply. "Highness, a messenger has arrived from Retenu. He waits in your outer chamber."

My heartbeat skips a little and I feel as if there is a serpent twisting in my bowels. I stand. "Please see the Lady Kawit back to her quarters." I leave, trusting my order will be carried out while I return to the palace. On my way through the corridors, my legs feel as if they've turned to quicksand, and I cannot decide whether I want them to move faster or slow down. When I reach my quarters, I stop at the door. My head feels shaky, but it nods anyway. The guards open the door and move aside.

In my chamber, a messenger sits on a chair. Seeing me, he jumps to his feet and bows. I move past him and gesture for him to follow me into my office. I dump myself into the chair behind my writing table, hoping the movement was more graceful than it felt. I grip the edge of the table to keep my fingers from shaking. "You have news from Kadesh?"

"Yes, Highness," says the messenger. "Our glorious army fights for Kemet and has every hope of prevailing."

I want to believe this is the full message, but no one would bother sending a messenger to tell me the army hopes to prevail. The army always hopes to prevail until the outcome is decided. My mouth is dry and my tongue sticks to my teeth, making it difficult to form the words. "And what of the King?"

"He has suffered an injury."

"But he lives?"

The messenger nods. "Yes, Highness."

He lives. I listen to the tale of how Tutankhamun broke his leg while valiantly fighting the Hatti king and I care not how much of the story is exaggeration. He lives. The quicksand that started in my legs now travels up my entire body and threatens to dissolve into an amorphous glob.

I stand and incline my head to the messenger. "We thank you for your service this day. Please, go to the kitchens and ask for food and beer. Or wine if you prefer. I believe there is some lovely roast goose left from last night's meal. Service such as yours deserves the very best."

The messenger looks at me, brows drawn, before bowing himself out. No doubt, he wonders why I should be so pleased at news that the King is injured, yet this is almost the best news I could have received. One cannot drive a chariot with a broken leg. One cannot charge enemy lines with a broken leg. One cannot stand on the field of battle with a broken leg. Tutankhamun shall now be well out of the fighting, kept safe by his men.

He lives and he shall return to Waset and to me. Together, we shall rule long and have an heir, two if we are most blessed by the gods. When Tutankhamun is finally ready to travel to the West, he shall be succeeded by a Crown Prince nobody questions. Fleetingly, I wonder if placing on the throne a man without royal blood of any kind would please the gods or anger them. I stifle the thought lest it dampen my mood.

Tutankhamun

"Another blanket." My body is shivering, yet drenched in sweat, and so the blanket covering me is damp. It is that which makes me feel cold. Pain lances through my leg, reaching up to my hips and down to my toes. "And more poppy."

The sound of shuffling feet and the physician appears before me. "I did not realize ..." he stops when he sees my face, swallows, and starts again. "I did not realize you were awake, Highness." He orders an assistant to fetch a blanket. When it arrives, he rolls down the damp one, replacing it with the new one as he does so. As the blanket is rolled down below the wound, the physician leaves the new blanket in a mound by my hip, blocking my view.

"How does it look?" I ask.

"There is much swelling."

"Surely, that is to be expected."

His brow creases. "Of course, but there is more swelling than anticipated. The bandages cut into the flesh." He asks for a blade and the assistant hands one to him.

I rest my head back. "Ah. That is why the leg pains so." Obsidian tears through linen, which pulls at my flesh. I wince.

When it is over, I turn my head toward the physician again. His face is ashen. "What is it?" I ask, though I fear I know. I reach a hand toward the blanket which blocks my view and pull it aside. The flesh surrounding the wound is grey and bubbled in places. Vivid red streaks line my thigh up to my hip. Now my trembling is not only because of the cold. "What can be done?

The physician holds up his blade. "Lancing the blisters may drain the poison."

I nod. The sour smell of decay is released. My stomach revolts so quickly I have no time to lean over the side of the bed. Vomit drips down my face and pools under my cheek. The physician does not call his assistant but cleans me himself with a towel.

The odor of putrefaction is unmistakable, the very same I encountered in Kush, from the severed hands piled at my feet. No matter how I may wish otherwise, I cannot deny the truth. "I am dying, am I not?"

His face contorts.

"The truth," I say.

He nods. "Yes, Highness."

"Will it be long?"

"No, Highness. Two, maybe three days at most."

"Will it be painful?"

He clenches his jaw. "Yes, Highness. The poppy will help very little."

I close my eyes so that he may not see his King cry. "Send for papyrus, ink and writing reeds. I must write a letter to the Great Royal Wife."

"You needn't do so yourself, Highness. I shall send for a scribe."

"No scribe," I say. "This must be written in my own hand."

He looks about to object but notes the look on my face. "As you wish, Highness." He sends his assistant.

When my writing materials arrive, I attempt to push myself up with one hand, but fall back down, clenching my teeth against screaming with the pain.

The physician stands by the bed on my good side and offers a hand. I grasp it with my own and, with a groan and much support, I raise myself to sitting. He sits slightly behind me, supporting my back and, at a gesture from him, his assistant does the same on my other side. The two men spread the sheet of papyrus across my lap so I may write.

I chew the end of the reed, separating the fibers into a brush, then dip it in the ink. My hand shakes as it nears the papyrus, and I am unsure whether I can complete the task or if I should need to call a scribe after all, if I am unable to even manage such a simple thing as writing a letter. I touch my hand to the papyrus, and it makes a squiggle of black, so I remove it, squeezing my eyes shut lest I disgrace myself by crying in front of my subjects.

I feel a touch and open my eyes. The physician has steadied my hand with his own. When I attempt again to write, the words are shaky, yet legible and recognizably mine. I smile at the man beside me and am overwhelmed with gratitude. Though tears fall, I no longer feel it a disgrace.

Ankhesenamun

"Do you wish me to repeat the message, Highness?"

My hands grip the writing table until my knuckles turn white. I shake my head. I have no wish to hear the message a second time. Nor do I wish to open the papyrus, sealed by Tutankhamun himself, now lying before me. "You lie. You have been sent by the Hatti to undermine our confidence." Even as I say it, I know it is not true. Should the Hatti wish to destroy our morale, they would do so with the army, not with me.

The messenger's face blanches. "I assure you, Highness, I have been sent by general Horemheb and no other."

"It is simply not possible." I raise my eyes to look at him. "Mere days ago, I received a message telling me the King was injured, but lives. That he would heal and return home."

"It was the hope …"

"Hope? You dare speak to me of hope?" I take a few deep breaths. It is dangerous to speak so. Should rumor spread that my wits are addled, it could be used as an excuse to wrest the throne from me. I gesture for him to leave. He does.

I crack open the clay seal on the papyrus. The hand, though occasionally unsteady, is unmistakably Tutankhamun's. I am somewhat unsteady myself as I read:

Beloved, I have charged a messenger to deliver this directly to you. It is the last official act I shall ever perform. By the time you read it, you must already know of my death. It is, as you have long feared, a result of my overreaching my own abilities on the battlefield. My one consolation is that I shall not hear you rage at me for not heeding your advice.

I choke back a laugh mixed with tears. Yes, my beloved, I dearly yearn for you to be here now so I might scold you for leaving me.

I wish for you to know that, though we have not always agreed, I could have asked for no better companion or helpmate in life. I also wish for you to live long and be content, knowing that I will be waiting for you with our daughters in the Field of Reeds. Though I will not be whole until we are reunited, I hope for your sake my wait will be many years long.

I die knowing Kemet is in capable hands and that you shall continue with the plan with which I have charged you and that you shall succeed.

Be well, my love.

The words waver before my eyes, and I wipe away the tears. There is no time for grieving, for I must fulfill his final wish. The scroll. The one acknowledging Kawit's child as the heir. I enter my bedchamber and check the hiding place. The scroll is undisturbed. I must collect the copy in the archive and present it to the court when I announce the death of the King. Horemheb also possesses a copy, but as the document removes all hope he has of attaining the throne, I cannot depend on him to safeguard it. Yet, Horemheb is some weeks away from returning to Waset, and none but he and I know of the scroll's existence. Making the contents of the scroll public is the only way to ensure its safety and to smooth the succession. I shall continue to rule, but as Regent to the Crown Prince until he comes of age. Please, gods, let Kawit's child (Tutankhamun's child, I correct myself, for I must always think of him as such) be a boy. If it is a girl, all is lost.

On my way to the archive, I am waylaid by one of the lesser wives. I brush her aside without listening to her inane chatter until two words catch my attention: royal perfumer.

"I beg your pardon?" I ask. "Please repeat that."

She lets out a sharp breath, not daring any more overt signs of impatience. "I sent my regular order for my special blend of kyphi perfume, and it was refused, along with a message that the royal perfumer has gone and, not only is there no more stock of the perfume, supplies on cinnamon and myrrh are exhausted, so it is unknown when they will be able to fill the order."

"What do you mean he has gone? Is he dead or merely missing?"

The woman's eyes widen. "The message did not say, only that he has gone." She wrings her hands. "Oh, I hope he is not dead. There are many feasts and celebrations to come. What should I do without my favorite perfume?"

"Do not concern yourself. I shall discover what has happened and, if necessary, find another perfumer."

She nods. "I do hope it will not take too long. I am almost out."

I turn and continue down the corridor.

"Oh, poor Kawit," says the woman.

I freeze. I arrange my face into a neutral expression before turning back. "Poor Kawit?" My heart is racing. Has Kawit been telling tales she should not be telling?

"The perfumer is her uncle, is he not?"

My heart rate slows. "Yes, he is, but best not to grieve her prematurely. Allow me to find the truth first."

She bows. "Yes, Highness."

On the way to the archive, I send a messenger to my spies in the Delta, but I am hopeful Wajmose's disappearance is exactly what it appears. That Tutankhamun eliminated him before he … before he left on campaign.

In the archive, it takes some searching before I locate the scroll in question. Somehow, it was filed in the "new" section instead of the "King's directives" section. Perhaps this was deliberate. Tutankhamun may have reasoned that if it were difficult to find, it would be difficult to destroy. As I pull it from the box, I notice another scroll marked simply, "Shedet."

This one is not sealed, so it must not be secret. I unroll it. As I read, I sink to my knees. The scroll contains plans for a villa in Shedet. Further on are plans for a provisional government, to be implemented for two months of the year, during the height of the inundation, when little happens. Tutankhamun and I are to be disturbed only in the case of emergency. This is for me. To fulfill the promise he made last year. I attempt to swallow the lump in my throat but cannot stop the tears streaming down my face. Did he mean to present this to me as a surprise when he returned home?

Ankhesenamun

Ay and the other ministers stand facing me as I sit behind Tutankhamun's writing table. Their hands are behind their backs and their heads are bowed, as is fitting upon hearing of the death of their King.

"There is one further matter to discuss." I close my eyes, briefly, to squeeze back the tears. "That of succession."

Ay glances up at me, his mouth a thin line. Though he has not been officially informed, there has been much talk amongst the ladies of Kawit carrying the King's child, so he must know what I am about to say. They all must.

I motion for the guard to allow in my special guest. "I am sure you are all acquainted with Dedu, head of the royal archive. He has in his possession, a document given him by the King prior to his departure that concerns the matter at hand."

Dedu bows his way into the King's chamber. My chamber now. "Dedu, did the King himself hand you the scroll you now carry in your hand?"

"Yes, Highness. More, I witnessed him write this scroll, plus two copies of it, and I witnessed him seal all three."

"Please tell us, were there any other witnesses?"

"Yes, General Horemheb."

"One copy was left in your care in the archive," I say. "Where are the other two?"

"General Horemheb took one with him. I believe the third is in your keeping. At least, that was his Highness's intention."

I nod. "I do indeed have the third copy. I invite you now to break the seal and read the scroll aloud to the assembled ministers."

Using a small mallet, Dedu taps the seal bearing Tutankhamun's name, shattering the clay. He unrolls the scroll and clears his throat. "I, Tutankhamun, the Strong Bull, Lord of the forms of Ra, Living Image of Amun, Ruler of Upper Iunu, do hereby declare the Lady Kawit to be my concubine and mine alone. I do hereby declare her child to be of my seed. Should the child be a boy, it is my intention to marry the Lady Kawit, giving her a rank second only to that of the Great Royal Wife, Ankhesenamun. Further, the boy shall be my designated heir, unless and until the Great Royal Wife bears a son, at which time that child shall be my designated heir."

Though I have read the document already, I tear up at Tutankhamun thinking to take care that none at court should know of my barrenness.

Dedu continues. "Should I pass to the West prior to the birth of the Lady Kawit's child, the child, should it be a boy, shall be my designated heir. In such case, the Great Royal Wife, Ankhesenamun, shall rule as Regent until the boy reaches the age of maturity, at which time he shall become King. Should the child be a girl, still the Great Royal Wife shall rule as Regent until the girl reaches the age of maturity and marries, at which point her husband shall become King."

It is well that Tutankhamun intended for the child to inherit, boy or girl, yet I pray fervently that it be a boy. For if it be a girl, Kemet shall remain in chaos until she marries, and she shall face the danger I now face and be just as uncertain of the outcome.

Dedu finishes and the room falls silent.

I take a breath. "Our King wished to make his intentions clear prior to leaving on campaign, in the event …" my voice breaks, "… in the event he does not return to Kemet. We shall all carry out his wishes as he has written them." I look at each minister in turn. Each nods to me. "We shall meet again later."

The ministers file out, save Ay, who remains. "You must start funeral arrangements. Distances being what they are, it has already been many days since the Wesir-King passed to the West."

I cringe at the epithet, "Wesir", for I am still unused to thinking of Tutankhamun as being gone. If only he had passed at home, in my presence, perhaps it would be more real to me. Then I remember that if he stayed home, he would not have passed. I sigh. "Yes, there are fewer than sixty-five days left to prepare."

"His tomb is not yet prepared, is it?" says Ay.

I shake my head. "Excavations are well underway, but, no, it is not ready." I have been thinking long on what to do for a tomb. The thought had occurred that I might eject my father from his tomb, and have it repainted for Tutankhamun, but I cannot abide placing my beloved in such a cursed place. The gods would surely turn from him and block him from entering the Field of Reeds were his body to lie in the tomb of a heretic.

"Mine is fully excavated. It can be made ready in time," says Ay.

I stare at him. His tomb is in close proximity to the cursed place. Facing it, in fact. However, it is also very near Mother's tomb, which would be fitting. Presumably, in exchange, Ay would want Tutankhamun's tomb, which is in the West Valley, near to that of our grandfather, the third Amenhotep. Tutankhamun chose the place so he would always be known to posterity as Grandfather's heir, in thought and deed if not in fact, the restorer of Ma'at after the heresy of our father. Ay would know the strength of that message and I shudder to think of him claiming credit for Tutankhamun's accomplishments. Yet, there are no royal tombs sitting vacant. Aside from ejecting an already established inhabitant, I see no other way.

"What would need to be done to prepare your tomb?" I ask.

"The walls and floors need to be smoothed, and the walls plastered," says Ay. "The interior artwork, of course."

It should be done in time if the work is hurried just a little. I nod. "Fine. Order the work to start immediately."

Ay bows.

"Thank you. For the gift." I am unsure if he deserves my gratitude, for I distrust his motives.

"Anything for my King and for my granddaughter." He moves around and half-sits on the side of the writing table near me. "I am concerned about the King's final wishes."

I lean back, hoping to appear casual. "What, specifically, concerns you?"

"That all of his plans for the future depend on a child who is not yet born."

"By the time of the funeral, it will be near enough being born." Due to the discrepancy in actual versus claimed time of conception, the child may well be born before the funeral. Gods grant the child be small.

"Until the child is here, there are no guarantees," says Ay. "You should know that better than anyone."

I feel my face flush. "I am assured that late losses are exceedingly rare." Indeed, I was assured of this, repeatedly, my second time with child, and yet it happened again. As well, many children who are born healthy do not survive the first year. But Kawit is not me, and this child will have the best of care. All will be well.

Ay swings a leg, affecting a casual air. "Still, one must be prepared for all contingencies. Have I not taught you that?"

I say nothing, waiting for him to speak his mind.

"If you were to marry me, succession would be assured."

I almost laugh, but realize he is serious. He is always serious. I now understand why he volunteered his tomb so readily. Marry me, become King, style himself the heir of the great Amenhotep, the third of that name, the last great King before the heretic and the boy Ay never believed worthy of the throne. I clasp my hands together to keep them from trembling. "You are my grandfather."

"What of it? The King is your brother. You and your older sisters married your father."

I suppress a shudder at the recollection.

"You are the only descendant of the royal line still living and I am the most capable ruler in all of Kemet," says Ay. "After all, I have been advising the King since he ascended the throne. I was chief advisor for your mother as well."

"As you yourself have pointed out, the people fear Kemet being overtaken by foreign rule," I say. "No matter that you were born here, your father is Naharin, and the royal bloodline has been already too much diluted by the blood of Naharin."

Ay sniffs. "The people will fear Kemet being ruled by the Hatti even more. This is precisely the wrong moment to leave a woman and a child on the throne."

He may be correct that the people fear the Hatti more than a few more drops of Naharin blood in the royal line, but he is wrong about the other. I am as capable as any man. As capable, perhaps, as my mother.

"With me as King, you need not worry any longer about succession. Even should you never bear a son, my daughter, sister to your mother, the great Neferneferuaten Nefertiti, shall bear children, or her husband may take other wives to perform that function when he is King. Ma'at shall be preserved. Kemet shall remain stable."

He is most likely correct. A marriage to Ay could preserve Kemet, but I dare not trust him. His detailed plan for succession merely emphasizes the fact that, once the crown is achieved, he will not need me. Then, what should my fate become? I suppress a shudder at the thought of my battered corpse lying parched and shriveled in some forgotten wadi deep in the Red Lands. Further, I believe the urgency of his offer comes from a need to settle the matter before Horemheb returns from Retenu and comes to me with a similar plea.

"As this matter is of utmost importance for Kemet, I shall take some time to consider it."

Ay nods. "Of course." He stands and turns to leave. Just as he approaches the door, he turns back, as if a thought has just occurred to him. "Do not take too much time, mind. The matter must be settled quickly, lest some misfortune befall the Lady Kawit and her child."

A chill courses through me. Immediately after Ay leaves, I summon the captain of the palace guard and order increased protection for Kawit.

Ankhesenamun

I nod to the guard to usher in Horemheb. As he bows his way into my outer chamber, I hold my breath. He has lately arrived back in Kemet with the bulk of his officers. I need to hear Kemet and Naharin have prevailed, though the lack of a parade through the streets of Waset bodes ill. I hope at least for a stalemate.

When Horemheb rises, he meets my eye and hesitates before speaking. "What news of the war in Retenu?" I ask.

"Naharin has fallen. It is no more."

I close my eyes. Naharin has fallen. We have lost our best defence against the Hatti. They can now march with little hindrance through Retenu right to our borders. When I open my eyes, Horemheb is staring at me, eyebrows raised.

"I am very sorry about the King, Highness," he says.

I nod. He is silent so long it becomes disconcerting. "Is there anything else?" I ask.

Horemheb takes a breath. "There is the matter of succession."

"That has been decided," I say. "You have in your possession a copy of the document left by the King naming his heir."

"A child as yet unborn," he says. "A child that may never be born or may not survive its first year. Such an uncertain plan may simply be postponing a plunge into chaos."

"What do you suggest?" I ask, though I fear I know.

"You must marry me," he says. "That will give Kemet stability, bring us back to Ma'at."

"You do not have a drop of royal blood. You cannot rule as King."

"When the King elevated me to the nobility, it was seen as the equivalent to naming me his heir," he says. "We will simply be fulfilling the King's wishes."

"If the King wished for you to inherit the throne, he would have said so in his final document."

"With all due respect, Highness, the King was young and believed himself invincible. If he had known he would not return, he would have acted differently."

I think if he had known he would not return, he would not have left, but I say, "It is presumptuous of you to claim to know the mind of the King."

Horemheb falls silent again.

"As this matter is of utmost importance for Kemet, I shall take some time to consider it."

"Of course, Highness." Horemheb nods and leaves.

Tutankhamun arrived back in Waset two days ago and still I have not seen him. Perhaps it is time I do so.

A faint scent of decay drifts across the temple courtyard. Outside the embalming tent, I am greeted by one of the embalmers. He bows. "Highness, I do not recommend you go inside. It is not fit for your eyes."

I lift open the flap of the embalming tent and am hit by a smell of rotting flesh that makes my stomach want to retch. He is there, on the table, swathed in loose linen bandages, turning black with decay in places.

Now I understand the embalmer was not concerned for my sensibilities, but for his own skin. "How could this happen?"

The man bows again, twice. "He arrived in this state, Highness. The initial embalming was done far from Kemet by those who are not experts."

I want to lash out, but it is not this man's fault. "Can you fix it?"

He bows. "Yes, Highness."

I do not know if he tells the truth or not. "It is imperative that the King be whole for his journey to the Duat."

"Of course, Highness. He will be."

A noise reaches my ears, as if from a great distance. Echoes of metal on metal, metal on stone. I lift the tent flap and peek out. All is quiet within the temple courtyard, but priests are rushing to the doors, their white linen kilts entwining around their ankles; their papyrus sandals swooshing on the flagstones. I join them.

At the doors, I am stopped by the high priest. "Highness, do not leave here. A fight has broken out between returning soldiers and some of the palace guards. The city guards have been summoned."

The clashing grows louder, as if coming nearer the temple. The great cedar door thumps and rattles.

"Highness, please come to my chambers," says the high priest.

I nod and follow, with my guards. "When the city guards have quelled the fight, I want the instigators brought to me."

"Yes, Highness," says the high priest.

Inside his chambers, I pace back and forth. This delay is costing time I can ill afford. I must arrange for the funeral. There must be flowers and mourners and live bulls for sacrifice. The Opening of the Mouth Ceremony – as Regent, that duty falls to me and I must have training, for I am not familiar with all of its intricacies. And the tomb – how goes the final preparations on the tomb? I fall into the high priest's chair. I have fifty-five yet days to prepare. These few hours will make no difference. I sigh and, if not for the presence of my guards would allow myself to cry. I consider ordering them to wait outside the door, but at that moment there is a knock, and my guards admit the head of the city guards and two very disreputable-looking characters in military garb.

The city guardsman bows. "Highness, I have determined that the fight started with these two in a tavern. I have brought them to you, as requested, but surely a drunken brawl does not interest you."

I sniff. "A drunken brawl between armed military men that nearly threatened the sanctity of the Temple of Amun and kept the Great Royal Wife from fulfilling her duties." I look at the two miserable specimens, dirty and bloody and still staggering drunk. "May I ask what prompted the elite of Kemet's army to behave like deranged madmen in the streets of Waset?"

The two culprits exchange glances. "It was a silly argument that got out of hand, Highness," says one of them.

I feel a sinking sensation in my gut. "What was the argument about?"

The two look at each other and then at the floor.

"It is of no import, Highness," says the city guard.

"I decide what is of import." I look to the soldiers and speak through clenched teeth. "What was the argument about?"

They shuffle their feet, but one speaks. "There was a disagreement about who should be the next King. The army men, we feel it should be Horemheb, but the palace guards are in favor of Ay."

The heat seeps out of my body and the room spins. "I see. And did the two candidates in question have a hand in starting this 'disagreement?'"

Together they answer, "No, Highness!" rather too quickly to be convincing.

I nod to the city guard. "Escort them back to their respective barracks. They shall endure the harshest punishment applicable for their offense."

"No, Highness, please."

"Please, no."

I am unsure what the maximum punishment is for street brawling, but I rather hope it involves a solid public flogging.

Once the three of them leave, the high priest pokes his head back in. "It is safe to travel now, Highness."

"Out. I must think." He pulls his head out, the door slams and I immediately regret my harsh manner, but only for a moment. I ask my guards to wait outside.

Alone at last, I let out a breath, but I fight back the tears that threaten to spill. I cannot give in to weakness. Whether or not Ay and Horemheb instigated the day's events is immaterial. The battle for the throne has begun and I am the only one who may stop it. Ay and Horemheb are right about one thing – only my marriage would bring stability back to Kemet. Yet, neither one of them is suitable. Neither is royalty and Ay is a commoner. They are my subjects, not my equals. Ay has considerable experience at statecraft – indeed, he trained both my mother and myself – yet he is ruthless, quite possibly a murderer, and I fear for anyone who would have to work under an Ay with unlimited power. Horemheb has the support of the army, which is necessary to stay in power, but no experience governing, and I fear chaos in the state with Horemheb at the helm. Supposing I did choose one of the two? Would the other simply walk away? Doubtful. And there is the question of the Hatti, who will surely test Kemet's might soon. With Ay and Horemheb fighting for supremacy, Kemet is vulnerable.

I sit up and gasp. There is a solution, though it is bold. And risky. Long have the Kings of Kemet taken foreign wives to cement alliances with foreign kings. My grandfather did so. My father did so. Tutankhamun surely would have had he lived longer, though he did inherit some of those wives from our father. Suppose I take a Hatti prince as my husband. Kemet and Hatti would thus be allies, not enemies. Why should Suppiluliumas, the Hatti King, send his son? It is a small matter to send a daughter, but a son? I must stress to him that his son would not simply languish in the Women's Quarters, as a daughter would do, but would be on the throne of Kemet and that his grandson would be king, and his great-grandson and so forth. Would Kemet accept a foreign king? Already there has been too much foreign blood on the throne. Yet, if I give the alternative as domination by the Hatti and the loss of Kemet forever… yes, it could work. It must work.

I leave the high priest's chambers and my guards follow in my wake. I am restless during the brief boat ride upriver from the temple and along the canal to the palace and head straight from the water steps to the archive and to Dedu.

"I must have a wet clay tablet and a stylus."

Dedu stands and bows. "I can send for a scribe for you, Highness."

"That will not be necessary. I shall write this letter and seal it myself."

Dedu claps his hands and sends the servant who answers to prepare the materials I requested.

"I also need a network of reliable, discreet messengers," I say.

"What is the final destination of the letter?" asks Dedu.

"The palace of Suppiluliumas at Hattusa."

I consider it a mark of his trustworthiness that he hesitates only a single heartbeat before nodding. "It shall be arranged immediately."

When the clay is ready to be inscribed, I retreat to an alcove and consider my approach before beginning. I spend as few words as protocol permits on the formal greeting and go right to the heart of the message:

My husband has died, and I have no son. They say about you that you have many grown up sons. You might give me one of your sons to become my husband. Never shall I pick out a subject of mine and make him my husband.

I read through the letter. My hand hovers over it, unsure if I should continue. At last, I add one final line: *I am afraid.* I stare at what I just wrote and turn the stylus over, meaning to erase the admission of weakness. At length, I put aside the stylus, leaving the message as is. If Suppiluliumas knows I am afraid, that may prompt him to act quickly. All is lost if he hesitates too long.

I seal up the letter and trust it to Dedu's network of messengers.

Ankhesnamun

I find Mutnedjmet seated in the courtyard with Kawit and Meryetre, enjoying a respite from the heat under the shade of a sycamore. Meryetre nods, seemingly satisfied. Mutnedjmet turns her head slightly, the hint of a smile on her face.

Kawit is now quite heavy, but I am not sure whether her lethargy is an indication that her time is near, or an affectation designed to elicit sympathy. I hope it is the latter, for it would not do for her child – Tutankhamun's child, I remind myself – to make its appearance so soon. Tongues would surely wag. Best if it waits until after the funeral.

I stand in front of Mutnedjmet. "Walk with me, aunt," I say.

Mutnedjmet looks around at the other ladies, shrugs her shoulders and rises. "Where shall we walk?"

I move down the path around the pond. When we are out of earshot of the others, I say, "I understand you have petitioned for divorce."

She nods. "Yes, well, I should have predicted a marriage to that oaf would not last."

"I believe you did predict such, yet you married him anyway," I say. "Is it coincidence that Horemheb has also petitioned for divorce?"

She smiles. "It is not."

At least she has the good grace not to deny it. "It is a dangerous game."

"What game?" Mutnedjmet shrugs. "Horemheb and I have been lovers for years. You have known of it almost since the beginning."

"Yet you married Nakhtmenu."

"At my father's insistence."

We both know this is a weak argument. Never in her life has she done as her father commanded. I glance at her but continue walking so that those watching will not think there is anything amiss. "You married Nakhtmenu when you believed he might become heir to the throne. Now that Horemheb appears more likely, you will marry him."

"I will not apologize for looking out for myself. Gods know no one else is."

"You legitimize him and, thus, betray me. With you as his wife, Horemheb will be seen as a true heir."

"Then marry him yourself," she says. "He asked you and you have yet to give him an answer. As Great Royal Wife, you are a far better catch than I. You need simply say the word and he will choose you over me."

She speaks with no sense of potential loss, only cold calculation in her eyes. She cares for him no more than he cares for her. They are simply a means to an end for each other.

"He is not fit to rule," I say.

"Who are you to decide who is fit to rule?"

"I have been ruling Kemet for years."

Mutnedjmet glances toward the ladies, now at the opposite end of the courtyard from us. "If you were capable of ruling, you would know enough to take the opportunity before you."

I decide to try another tack. "What if you're wrong? What if Ay wins the struggle? Would it not be best to see who the victor is before throwing in your lot with one of them?"

"Without me, Nakhtmenu no longer has a claim to the throne."

"True, and the loss of a male heir hurts Ay's chances, but he still has considerable support amongst the army. The outcome is not a certainty."

Mutnedjmet nods. "And that is why I will not marry Horemheb now."

I narrow my eyes. "Then why the divorce?"

"So, I may be ready to marry the winner." She cocks her head. "Or remarry him, if that be the case."

I am about to answer when Mutnedjmet points her chin toward a spot behind me and to the left. I turn to see Tuya holding her skirts to descend the portico steps and then head toward us.

"Highness," says Tuya, "we have just received word that a messenger has arrived for you. He waits in your chambers."

I nod to her and to Mutnedjmet and hurry at once to my chambers. When I enter, the messenger bows and stays down until I am seated.

"Do you bring word from Hattusa?" I ask.

146

He is dark, heavily bearded, and wears a mid-calf length straight robe of wool. "Yes, Highness. I am Hattu-Zittish, chamberlain for the great King, Suppiluliumas. He has charged me with bringing back information."

I sit up straight. "What? He has not answered my letter?"

"No, Highness," says Hattu-Zittish. "Since the most ancient times, such a thing has never happened before. At first, he said, 'they are trying to deceive me.' Never has a Queen of Kemet requested a son of the king of the Hatti. The King wishes to know if, indeed, there is a prince."

"He accuses me of lying?"

"Oh, no, Highness," says Hattu-Zittish. "You must understand relations between our two peoples are less than friendly." He swallows. "If one wished to deceive him, leave him vulnerable, one might invite his son and entourage into your lands in order to plan an attack."

I grip the sides of the writing table and take a deep breath before answering. "You shall dine with us tonight and you shall see there is no prince of Kemet and the future of the throne is uncertain."

He bows.

"But you shall remain quiet about your mission here. I shall put it forward that you bring a message of conciliation from King Suppiluliumas. Tomorrow, you shall send your report back by messenger, so that it shall reach Hattusa in haste. I shall send a message of my own." Thirty-five days remain until the funeral. I do the calculation. A letter sent by messenger relay may arrive in less than ten days, and a prince and his entourage in another twenty, give or take. There is yet enough time, but barely.

"Yes, Highness. Thank you, Highness."

The moment Hattu-Zittish vanishes down the corridor, I go to the archive to write another letter:

Why do you say, "They are trying to deceive me?" If I had a son, should I write to a foreign land in a manner humiliating to me and to Kemet? You do not believe me, and you even say so to me! He who was my husband is dead and I have no son. Should I then perhaps take one of my subjects and make of him my husband? I have written to no other land; I have written to you. They say that you have many sons. Give me one of your sons and he will be my husband and the Lord of the Land of Kemet.

Ankhesenamun

"Unhand her immediately." I arrive at a run, having started the moment Henutmire told me of the trouble. On arriving in the Women's Quarters, I find Kawit with her arms held behind her back by one soldier and faced by another, with sword pointed at her exposed neck. Gashes on the cheek of the swordsman tell me she did not submit meekly. "The Lady Kawit carries the King's child, and she will not be treated in this manner."

Ay steps from the shadows, accompanied by a hooded figure. "Sadly, she does not carry the King's child. She is a lying, treasonous wench," he says.

I face him. "You dare impugn the Lady's honor?"

"The Lady has no honor," says a voice from under the hood. A hand pushes the hood back.

I gasp before I am able to regain my composure. "Wajmose. I heard you left Iunu."

Ay orders the soldiers to take Kawit away.

"Stop," I say.

Ay raises an eyebrow. "I would consider carefully whether or not you wish for mere soldiers to know the business of the crown."

I nod and turn to the soldiers. "Take her to her chambers and guard her there. If she comes to any harm, you will answer for it."

Kawit looks to me as she is led out. I nod and smile, hoping to reassure her.

When we are alone, I decide to play the innocent, in the hopes that there is no proof beyond Wajmose's word, which is worthless. "Will someone tell me the purpose of this chicanery?"

"It was I who sired the bastard in her belly," says Wajmose.

"The Lady Kawit is the King's concubine. Any child she carries belongs to him," I say.

"Not if it can be proven the child is not of the King's seed," says Ay.

I cross my arms. "Can you prove it is not?"

"Ipu has confirmed the child is ready to be born," says Ay. "That places conception firmly during the first month of the season of emergence, when Kawit was in Iunu at the home of Wajmose."

"That proves nothing," I say. "Some babes are born early, some late. The date of conception cannot be determined by the date of birth with any certainty."

Wajmose sneers and I catch a whiff of onions on his breath, not quite concealed by the cloying scent of lily and myrrh in his perfume. "Kawit spent most of that month flat on her back. She is quite insatiable."

I look at the pale, flabby flesh spilling over the top of his kilt and doubt very much that even his wife frequents his bed by choice. I think she would surely never do so again if she knew of his activities with young girls. Before I can decide to use his wife's potential displeasure to force a retraction of his words, I remember Kawit's mother knowing and doing nothing to stop it. Would her aunt – her mother's sister – behave any differently? Has she known all along and welcomed the relief from her own marital duties? I deliberately rove my eye up and down his corpulent frame. "You mean to tell us this lovely young woman finds herself unable to resist you?" I assume an air of arrogant disgust on the last word.

Wajmose scowls. "The girl is wanton. Every year when her family visits, she flaunts herself. Shifts too short, dousing herself with my best perfumes, smiling at me with feigned shyness."

I seize my opportunity. "Every year? Kawit has but recently reached marriageable age. Precisely how many years has she spent 'flat on her back,' as you put it, during her visits?"

Wajmose sputters. "She seduced me. What was I to do?"

I want to knock all of the teeth out of his head. Instead, I turn to Ay. "You would take the word of a man who admits to fornicating with children?"

Ay spreads his hands. "I do not rely solely on Wajmose's word," he says. "Shortly before the King left on his final campaign, the two soldiers who are now with the Lady Kawit approached me. The King had assigned them to go to Iunu and, shall we say, abuse Wajmose, mutilate him most cruelly and then kill him. They were to plunder Wajmose's production house and warehouse, making it appear to be a robbery. Naturally, I wondered why the King should wish to eliminate a perfume maker, so I instructed the soldiers to bring Wajmose to me while making it appear they had carried out the King's instructions."

"So, you have the word of a defiler of children and two mercenaries?" I ask. I speak with an assurance I do not feel. Ay does not need to prove the child is not Tutankhamun's, he need only raise doubts, which he has already done. It is enough to undermine the child's claim to the throne and give way to other contenders.

At a quick glance of the room, I see nothing that may be used as a weapon. Ay was once a powerful and highly trained military man, but now stoops when he stands and the flesh on his arms hangs loose. I could, perhaps, overpower him without a weapon. Wajmose, never trained in military arts, and slow to move, would pose little challenge. Who else knows? The soldiers with Kawit, of course. A word of wrongdoing in the right ear would eliminate them in short order. Are there others who know? If Ay is as smart as I believe him to be, he will have confided in others who would reveal the truth should Ay come to any harm.

Before I can fully consider my plan, Ay gives me a slow, triumphant smile, as if he knows my thoughts. He asks Wajmose to leave us and then speaks. "Kawit must be charged with treason."

I shake my head. "There is no treason."

Ay raises both eyebrows. "She deceived the King into believing the bastard she carried was his."

"The story you tell suggests the King was not only not deceived but actively participated in the deception. It is not treason if it is the King's wish."

Ay's nostrils flare. "The actions of the King are always above reproach, but those of the Great Royal Wife are not."

My belly flutters. "I do not understand your meaning."

Ay takes a step closer. "Those soldiers are as willing to state you are the one who ordered Wajmose dead as they are willing to state it was the King. Now, if you and Kawit staged a conspiracy to betray the King, you are both guilty of treason."

I place a finger to my lips and take a deep breath to give myself time to think of a response. There are yet fifteen days remaining until the funeral. If Suppiluliuma sent a son upon receipt of my message, it should be yet another ten days, at the least, before he arrives. Plenty of time for me to be executed for my "crime." Plenty of time, also, for Ay to find a remote wadi in which to dump my mangled remains. Despite the heat of the day, I shiver and the sweat that erupts on my forehead and under my arms is cold. Without an heir in place, I dare not think what should happen if Suppiluliuma refuses my request. "Kawit will not be charged with treason. She shall, however, be banished from Waset. Once it is known that the child she carries is not the King's, there will be no reason to harm it, for it will be no threat for whomever attains the throne."

Ay nods. "That is acceptable. I shall tell the Lady Kawit of her fate." "No. She is my Lady. I shall tell her."

Ay accompanies me to Kawit's chambers and leaves with the soldiers. She is pacing the room and glances at me tearfully as I enter. I sit on a chair in her reception hall and motion for her to sit on the one beside me. Her eyes are red and swollen and she sniffles, though she is no longer crying. For now.

"Am I to be executed?" Her lower lip trembles.

I place a hand over hers. "No. No, you will live. And so shall your child."

"Thank you." Kawit leans against me and sobs.

"Do not thank me yet," I say. "The price for your life is banishment. You are to leave Waset and never return."

She sits up. "You send me away?"

"It is not my choice." I cannot meet her eye. It is to my shame that my actions are more to save my own skin than hers.

"You are the Great Royal Wife. You may do as you please."

I heave a sigh from the very depths of my being. "Would that it were so."

"But where shall I go? My family will not have me now."

I stroke her hair. "I shall make for you a good marriage. Perhaps in Shedet, perhaps in the south."

"Marriage? Who would have me?" she says.

I do not respond. She is quite correct – no nobleman will take as a wife a woman who is known for lying about who sired her offspring. I had hoped not to have to be so brutal about her prospects. "Perhaps we would have more luck finding you a place as concubine."

Kawit glares at me. "For anyone other than the King, a concubine is little more than a pretty, but useless, ornament."

"Forgive me," I say. "I speak plainly so you will be clear about your current position."

"The position you have put me in," she says.

I touch her shoulder, and she turns away. "If I could change the present, I would." A lump lodges itself firmly in my throat and my stomach lurches. I rise and start for the door.

A hand tugs at my dress. "Please don't do this." Tears stream down Kawit's cheeks. I want to wipe them away and hold her. Instead, I clench my teeth to stave off my own tears. "You are a noblewoman of Kemet. You will behave as such, no matter your circumstances."

Kawit nods and wipes her nose with the back of her hand.

Once in the corridor, I move toward my chambers with as much speed as dignity will allow. Nearing my destination, as my stomach reels, I decide haste is the only way to preserve my dignity and break into a run. Without waiting for guards to do so, I throw open doors myself and arrive at the toilets with no time to spare. When the retching stops, I collapse onto the tile floor and hug my knees to my chest, trembling.

Ankhesenamun

"This is where I take the calf's leg, correct?" I ask.

The high priest shakes his head. "No, Highness. The calf's leg was earlier. Now you need the adze."

I put down the carved calf's leg substitute and pick up the adze. "Calf's leg first, adze last," I repeat to myself.

"It would have been better to leave more time, Highness," says the high priest. "Haste makes for errors."

I glare at him. "I will have it memorized in time." I delayed learning the Opening of the Mouth in the hopes that a son of the Hatti would arrive in time for a wedding feast. As successor, he would be the rightful one to perform the ceremony at the funeral. But with a scant three days left, even should a prince be present for the funeral, he surely would not have time to learn any of the rituals.

I hold the adze high, as if to touch it to the mouth of the mummy when I hear a commotion from outside my chambers. My first thought is that there is another army brawl, once again threatening the sanctity of the temple, but this noise is less chaotic.

The high priest bows. "Excuse me, Highness. I will go investigate."

When the door opens again, I expect the priest but am confronted by Horemheb and two soldiers. One of the soldiers carries a large sack, mostly empty, yet with a weight in the bottom dragging on the floor.

Horemheb can barely contain his contempt. "My apologies, Highness," he says, "but the duty falls to me to arrest you on charges of treason."

"I beg your pardon?" I wonder if he has discovered the truth about Kawit. She left a few days ago on her way to Syene to await the birth before continuing on to Kush, where a local chieftain has agreed to take her as a concubine.

Horemheb gestures to the soldier with the sack. The soldier opens the sack and upends it. Out of the mouth rolls an object covered in curly dark hair.

I clamp a hand to my mouth as bile rises in my throat. No, not Kawit. The object rolls and comes to a stop half an arms-length from my feet. The face, most definitely masculine, is pale, with a prominent nose and clean-shaven chin. I have never before seen this man.

I speak through clenched teeth. "Why do you bring this to me?"

Horemheb rolls the severed head with his foot so that the dead eyes stare at the ceiling. "You do not recognize your betrothed?"

I do not understand, and then I do.

"This is Zannanza," Horemheb's tongue falters over the unfamiliar syllables, "prince of the Hatti. He was sent here by his father, the Hatti King, at your request, so that he might marry you and become King of Kemet."

With my plan known and discovered, there is no reason to deny it. I advance on Horemheb. "What have you done? By killing a son of the Hatti king, you have brought war to our very threshold."

"You have done it yourself, Highness," says Horemheb. "You invited the enemy into Kemet so that he might devour us from inside."

"I forged an alliance that would open the Hatti lands to Kemet."

Horemheb nods to the soldiers and they move toward me. When one is near enough, I drop into fighting stance and deliver a quick jab to the face. He staggers back, blood pouring from his nose. The second draws his dagger and points it at me. I am unarmed and both men are double my size. Only my speed allowed me the one hit I scored. There will not be another, now they are prepared.

I draw myself up, willing my breathing to slow. "You dare threaten the Great Royal Wife?"

"Without a King, there can be no Great Royal Wife," says Horemheb. "You are nothing but a common traitor." He pulls his own dagger and holds it to my throat while his henchmen tie my wrists behind my back.

"Get her ankles as well. Don't want to be forced to harm her if she takes a mind to run," says Horemheb.

Once my ankles are bound, one soldier holds me by the arms while the other picks up the bag that held Zannanza's head. He holds the top open and advances on me. I tense and squirm.

Horemheb sheathes his dagger. "Come now, do you wish for all the people to see their former sovereign paraded through the streets like the criminal you are?"

I hold still while the rough, oiled linen is thrown over my head. My stomach lurches at the fetid smell and I swallow the bile. The interior brushing against my face is smeared with a rank, slimy substance. I breathe through my mouth and sparingly.

Arms circle around my hips and I am hoisted into the air and over a shoulder like a sack of onions. My sandals are pulled from my feet, presumably because they would give me away as a noblewoman, at the very least. Inside, I struggle to breathe and the more I gulp at the little air available, the more I inhale the stench. I gag but fight it down. Should I vomit in here, I would surely choke and die.

Without warning, I am tossed through the air and land, shoulder first, on a hard surface. I wince but refuse to give Horemheb the satisfaction of hearing me cry out. The surface beneath me begins to rattle in time with the sound of hooves on hard-packed earth. I must be in a donkey cart. I wriggle, shifting my weight off my aching shoulder. I do not know for certain where I was dumped into this cart, but it could not have been too far from the temple. The sound of the hoofbeats change when the road surface changes to stone and the jolting lessens. We must be on the main thoroughfare of Waset, though in what direction we are traveling I cannot say. I am suddenly grateful for my covering. Being carried through my city bound and helpless would be far worse than any filth or stink.

Shortly, the cart leaves the main road and is again on packed earth. It grows hotter. We must be leaving Waset, away from buildings that cast shade. The way is rougher and my shoulder pains with each rut or bump in the road. After a time, the heat and the mostly regular rhythm conspire to make my eyes grow heavy. I roll back onto my shoulder and revel in the pain that keeps me alert. I must not drowse. I must not be taken by surprise. I test my bindings by attempting to prise apart my ankles and wrists. The ropes cut into my flesh.

When all motion ceases, I lie still and strain my ears. Muffled voices reach me, but I cannot make out the words. One set of hands grabs me, yanks me out of the cart and holds me erect while another set pulls the sack up and off. The first set of hands let go and I collapse on the sand, gasping, yet reveling in the fresh, clean air filling my lungs.

A pair of sandaled feet step before my eyes. Horembeb reaches down and pulls me up by the upper arms. I cannot stop myself from groaning as my shoulder twists and I pretend not to see the light of triumph in Horemheb's eye.

When I am upright, I scan my surroundings. We are at the edge of the desert. Red cliffs rise against the horizon, bordering golden sand. Near at hand there is a sharpened stake fixed into the ground. To one side of it is a fire pit ringed with stones; to the other, a large open pit. Improbably, in front of these sit the writing table and chair from my chambers. On the writing table my reeds and ink palette lie next to an unrolled sheet of blank papyrus. I attempt to swallow, but find my mouth is as arid as the red lands before me.

Horemheb tugs at my arm and hands me over to the soldiers. They drag me to the table and sit me down in the chair. Then they unbind my ankles and tie them to the legs of the chair while Horemheb holds his dagger to my throat. When the soldiers have completed their task, Horemheb brings the dagger around and under my hands. I close my eyes and brace myself for the thrust to my heart. Instead, he severs the bindings around my wrists. I open my eyes and rub at my flesh where the ropes chafed.

Horemheb pushes my chair in. "You will write a formal declaration of abdication and name me as the successor to the King."

I glance up at the stake and the neighboring firepit, now directly in my line of sight. If I refuse, will he impale me and leave me to die slowly or burn me alive and have it done quickly? I fold my hands on the writing table in front of me. "I shall do no such thing."

He flicks his eyes to the execution ground. "Then you shall die as a traitor."

"You cannot order my death. Only the King may do so."

"I will be King in any event," he says. "The only question is if I must fight a war first. You have the power to avoid complete destruction of Ma'at. If you love Kemet, you will not see her in chaos."

No, I shall not see her in chaos, for Horemheb will kill me whether I accede to his wishes or not. He has Mutnedjmet to wed, he need not marry me to legitimize his claim, nor will my declaring him Tutankhamun's heir prevent

Ay from warring over the throne. My actions no longer have any effect. I stare at the pit in which either my mutilated corpse or my ashes shall be dumped and forgotten, robbing me even of an afterlife. He may have won, but I will have my small victory. I push the papyrus away.

He clenches his teeth and pushes it back.

I sit straight in my chair, hands on the armrests, gazing out at the sands before me as if I am at court, presiding over some ceremony or other. I feign not hearing the swish of a dagger unsheathing.

Horemheb grabs my left hand and places it on the writing table, pressing it into the polished wood. He stretches out the little finger and raises his dagger. I narrow my eyes but make no other response. He may slice off every digit I possess, hack my body into small pieces and leave them all for jackals. I will not name him King.

As I watch, the dagger spins around. The hilt smashes into my finger. White light explodes behind my eyes. Someone is screaming. Only once I am able to breathe again do I realize it is me.

He leans in to whisper in my ear. "Now, Highness, will you write, or do you need more incentive?"

Resisting the urge to pull my wounded hand to my chest and weep, I push the papyrus off the writing table.

Horemheb stretches out my third finger. The dagger falls again. When I am done screaming, the papyrus is in front of me once more. I look away.

Horemheb pulls my middle finger. I yank back my hand. Horemheb grabs the hand and squeezes. I manage not to cry out again yet tears flow down my cheeks. My body shakes.

Horemheb clenches his jaw. "Write the declaration."

I shake my head.

He stretches out my middle finger and brings down the dagger a third time. I abandon any attempt to stifle my screams. Instead, I use the pain to embolden me. When Horemheb leans close and opens his mouth to speak, I spit in his face. It hits him in the corner of his eye and slides down his nose.

His fist hits my jaw hard enough to topple me – chair and all – into the dust. I taste sand and spit out blood and bits of tooth.

"Cut her loose," says Horemheb.

Daggers cut at my bindings and rough hands haul me up and over a shoulder. If crushing the small bones of the hand is this excruciating, I do not think I shall withstand either flames or a post through my midsection. Yet, I will not beg. If I am to die today, I shall do so with some measure of dignity.

We pass both the firepit and the stake.

"Gentle, but not too gentle," says Horemheb. "We want her alive. For now."

I am swung around and placed on my feet at the edge of the pit. A hand – I am not certain whose – pushes me and I fall into the void. I land hard on my front. For a moment I lie still. When I am certain I have incurred no further damage, I flip myself onto my back. I am in an empty hollow barely twice my body length in one direction, less than that in the other, and though not deep, still too tall to climb out of.

At the edge, clearly visible, is the stake, its rough, jagged point thrusting up into the sky.

Ankhesenamun

My fingernails are torn and bloody. They are the only tools I may use to scrabble out of my prison, and they are not adequate for the task. The walls are hard-packed. It is impossible to dig out hand- and footholds without proper tools.

In the corner directly under the stake, where I cannot see it if I turn my back on it, I add one more scratch next to the first two. It is my third morning of confinement. Tutankhamun's funeral is today. Surely, I must be released. I hear footsteps. It must be Horemheb, or at least his soldiers, come to free me.

I smile at the face that appears over the edge of the pit, but it is only one of the guards with a basket of food and drink, which he lowers down.

"I won't be needing this today," I say. "I shall be dining at the funeral feast."

"I don't know anything about that," says the guard as he turns to go.

"Where is General Horemheb? Summon him." When there is no response, I repeat myself, but the continued silence tells me the guard has either gone or chooses not to speak. I sit down on the ground to wait.

My stomach rumbles, yet I ignore the basket. I shall dine far better later. Goose and antelope, pomegranates and honeyed figs, perhaps even sweetmeats. When the sun peeks over the edge of my cell, I hold the damaged hand against my body and, with the other, flip the linen away from the top of the basket, out of pure curiosity. A disc of rough barley bread. I pick it up and knock it against the side of the basket and it makes a hollow sound. Two days old, at least. With the bread is a handful of dates, rather too soft and sprouting a fine white fuzz in places, and a clay cup filled with what smells like cheap, thin ale. Mean though this fare may be my mouth waters and my gut aches at the mere thought of it. My jailers feed me, but no more than enough to keep me from joining my husband in the Field of Reeds.

As the sun reaches the summit of the day's journey, it grows hot, and my mouth grows dry. I hoist the flagon, intending to sip, but one taste and I suck greedily, then wipe my mouth with the back of my hand. The entire ration fails to quench me. I think it is a good thing I shall be eating elsewhere today, for it will be difficult to chew the bread without liquid. I wonder at the late hour. The procession should have started by now and still I am here. Perhaps there is a delay of some sort. Yet, they must come soon for me, for I shall need time to bathe and dress. I cannot attend my husband's funeral in the state in which I find myself.

It is not until the sun sinks and twilight falls that I begin to shake and give in to the sobs I have been keeping back. I am not to be released. Not today. Not any day.

The cold of the desert night descends, and between the chattering of my teeth and the turmoil of my thoughts, I fear I shall not sleep at all. Yet, I must have done, for in the deepest part of the night I am wakened by the scent of lotus and myrrh and when I open my eyes, a faint glow fills my wretched pit. I look around to find the source of the light and startle when I see it emanated from a figure squatting by my feet. At first, I think I have surely passed to the West, but the clouds of my breath filling the air in front of my face tell me I still live.

"Mother?" I say to the apparition. I would think her a fever-dream, as before, save this time I am not ill.

She smiles at me, and I rush to her. She feels solid within my arms. She rocks me, as she used to do when I was small.

"I am sorry," I tell her.

"For what?" she asks.

I cannot tell if her words challenge me to tell her my true failings or if she is genuinely ignorant of them. "I have failed Tutankhamun. I have failed Ma'at, and I have failed Kemet." I struggle with whether or not to detail recent events, but when I try, my throat closes. "I have failed you," is all I manage to say.

She releases me and sits in the dust beside me, hands clasped around her knees. "You speak of failure while you yet live. There are still choices left to you."

I glance to the walls of my prison.

"Do not allow your present state to discourage you. It is only temporary."

"I shall be released?"

Mother nods. "Of course. Ay and Horemheb still have use for you. How you respond to their manipulations will determine your fate."

"Mine, perhaps," I say, "but I cannot see how to keep Kemet from utter chaos."

She regards me for a long moment before speaking again. "Perhaps it is time you relieved yourself of that responsibility."

At once, I feel the cold again. My body trembles. I long to ask her meaning, but dread hearing her answer. In the end, resignation overcomes fear. "Do you say this because I shall die soon and so my actions are of no consequence?"

"I say so because you are no longer in a position to dictate matters of state. That is not to say your actions will have no consequence, but never again will you rule. As to your death, the time and manner of it are up to you. Choose wisely."

I nod. My prospects are not rosy, but not so bad as I feared. "What of Tutankhamun? Is he with you and our daughters in the Field of Reeds?"

She shakes her head. "He yet awaits his entrance into the Duat and the subsequent battles."

"He will make it through, do you think?"

"What do you think?" she asks. "Do you have faith in him?"

I wipe away a tear. "Yes."

"As do I," she says. "I always did." She places one last kiss on my forehead before fading into the dark shadows of my prison.

I settle back to sleep, the turmoil within now calmed. Once I am released, I shall do what needs to be done. The cost is no longer of any import.

Some few days later I am startled by a loud clatter. I cannot be certain how many days, for once I knew I was to die here, I ceased marking the sunrises, but I believe it to be no more than five and no fewer than three. Voices follow the clatter, though I cannot make out the words. Footsteps approach and a ladder slides down to the floor and rests against the wall. I stand, unwilling to meet whoever approaches on my knees, and stare at the ladder, waiting.

At length, a face appears above me. "If you'd rather stay down there, that's fine with me, but I'm not waiting all day."

"I'm sorry? Am I to be released?"

The soldier shrugs. "I have orders to take you to the palace to be cleaned up. That's all I know."

I place fingers from my good hand on the ladder tentatively, as if it is an illusion to be shattered with a touch. When it remains solid, I lift one foot to the first rung, and then the second. Unable to grip the rungs with my left hand, I instead hook my elbow around the side rail. My head, light with lack of food or sleep, swims and I sway. After a deep breath I continue. The guards watch as I struggle to emerge onto high ground, but do not offer to help. They give me a hooded robe and I put it on for the cart ride.

Back in the palace, I am directed away from my own chambers and sent instead to the Women's Quarters. I enter the courtyard where several of the King's wives and concubines lounge, indulging in gossip, playing games of senet, or walking by the pond.

I descend the portico steps, assume my most commanding tone and request a body servant. Every head swivels in my direction and none attempts to disguise either shock or revulsion at my appearance. Nor do they respond to my command, which I take to be an indicator of my new, less exalted status. I nod and attempt a dignified retreat.

"Highness."

I turn to see a plump figure rushing toward me from under the sycamores. My knees threaten to buckle, and I lean on a column for support. "Tuya," I say.

As she approaches, she reaches for my hand. I pull it back and hold it against my chest.

She eyes the three crushed fingers, now swollen and purple. "Oh, Highness," she says.

The concern in her usually affable face brings a lump to my throat. "It will heal," I say.

Tuya nods. "Come with me to the bath chambers. I shall attend to you."

I blink back tears. I shall not give Horemheb or Ay the satisfaction of hearing I crumbled before my own lady.

In the bath chamber, Tuya gently removes my wig. I shudder to see how dusty and unkempt it has become. When I find it difficult to remove my dress one-handed, Tuya assists. She rubs my skin down with natron, rinses it off with water.

"What of Henutmire and Meryetre?" I ask.

Tuya pours oil into one of her palms, rubs her hands together and runs them through my hair, gently kneading out the tangles. "They now serve the …" she stumbles over her words, "… Lady Tey."

"I see."

"Do not think too harshly of them," she says. "We did not know whether you would return."

I turn my head as much as is possible with her fingers still combing my hair. "Do you now serve the Lady Tey?"

She lowers her eyes and nod.

I take a deep breath. "Will you be in trouble for tending to me now?"

She bites her lip. "I shouldn't think so." She opens her mouth, then closes it again.

"Tuya? What is it you have to say?"

She releases my hair and examines my torn, ragged fingernails. "There's no fix for these, but henna should conceal most of the damage."

When I am once again clad in fine linen and perfumed wig, I am taken to the King's council chamber, now occupied by both Horemheb and Ay, who stand when I enter.

"Sit please," says Ay.

I glance at the proffered chair but make no move toward it.

"As you wish," says Ay. "We thought you'd like to know what we have decided for the future of Kemet." He sits behind the writing table.

"What you have decided." I say. My voice is flat, without interest. I won't give them the satisfaction of any emotion.

Horemheb rests one hip on the writing table. "We have come to a compromise that will preserve the peace. I should think you would be pleased."

I look from one to the other. "I live; therefore, I presume your compromise involves me."

Ay smirks. "You always were a clever girl. The compromise is thus: I ascend to the throne as King and Horemheb shall be my heir."

"I shouldn't think this would please you," I say to Horemheb.

Horemheb shrugs. "Not entirely, but such is the nature of compromise. Ay is an old man. It seemed wiser to let him reign the few paltry years he has remaining and then inherit the crown by right than to empty the coffers and waste lives taking it by force."

Horemheb wears an air of humor, yet his body tenses as he speaks. For his part, Ay scowls at the mention of his name and gives Horemheb a sidelong glance. I wager neither man will sleep well until the other has become a Westerner.

I lift my chin. "And what is to become of me?"

"You legitimize my claim to the throne by becoming my wife," says Ay.

"Never," I say.

"It is already done. The contracts have been drawn and signed," says Ay.

"I have signed no contract," I say, "nor have I consented. You cannot force me to marry."

"Freedom in marriage is for the lower classes, you know that," says Horemheb. "Your belongings have been moved into the Women's Quarters, into rooms suitable for the secondary wife of the King."

I can't help my voice from rising in pitch. "Secondary wife?"

"You did not think you could continue as Great Royal Wife, did you?" says Ay. "That honor falls to Tey, who has been beside me these many years."

"You would leave me to languish in the Women's Quarters?" I feel foolish the moment the words leave my lips. I have no doubt they could do far worse and may yet.

Horemheb's face hardens. "It is more than you deserve."

I tense my legs and clench a fist to keep from shaking with rage. "Without my royal blood your claim is baseless."

"Agreed," says Ay. "But that is all we need from you, and we have it already. Consider yourself lucky we allow you the privilege of remaining an ornament to the court." He flicks his eyes toward the door. "You are dismissed."

An ornament? I am to spend festival and feast days sitting and smiling while peasants gawk at me and the times between festivals roaming the corridors. With the King as husband, I can never leave the palace without his permission. I can never so much as read incoming missives or continue my military training unless he chooses to indulge me. With a shudder, it occurs to me what services I might be required to provide in order for him to want to indulge me and I pray to whatever gods are listening that he has no intention of demanding such. For how long will I be permitted to continue this vacuous life? Once Ay is well established, I shall gradually be forgotten and then I shall be of no further use. I will wonder whether each sunrise shall be my last until the executioner comes to answer. I cannot prevent Ay from taking the throne, but I am not yet so powerless as to give myself over to his whims.

"Well?" says Ay. "Have your days in the pit robbed you of your wits or simply of your hearing? I said you are dismissed."

I nod and turn to go.

Before I reach the door, Horemheb calls out, "Ankhesenamun."

I seethe at the use of my name instead of my title. Former title, I admonish myself, though at the very least I still merit "Lady." It is enough to remind me that even the death of Ay would not free me, for Horemheb would enforce my confinement, and he would be considerably more difficult to kill than Ay. I turn back.

"You are expected at the procession for the Wesir-King in the morning."

I freeze. "The funeral has not been held yet? It is late."

"Only a matter of a few days," says Horemheb. "We thought it best to settle the matter of succession before sending him on his journey West."

I nod and leave. On my way through the corridors, I devise my plan. Before the sun sets tomorrow, as my beloved begins his trials in the Duat, I shall be free of both Ay and Horemheb forever.

Ankhesenamun

161

Tutankhamun's gilded coffin lies on the cart inside the embalmer's tent, ready for its trek across the desert to the Valley of the Kings. His image appears to be in repose, encircled by the feathered wings of the goddess Aset and her sister Nebt-het. His hands, holding the crook and flail of office, are covered in a paler gold than the rest of the coffin, giving the appearance of grey death. I have been granted a few moments with him before the procession so that I may leave one last gift of farewell, a wreath of flowers. If Mutnedjmet plays her part, I will not be alone for long.

On a table in the back, the tools of the trade are arranged in neat rows. I run a hand along the adzes and hooks and obsidian blades with their curved bronze handles. A glance at the tent flap tells me the guard is facing the other way, out of respect. I take a blade and slip it into my sash, out of sight. It is one of several and will not be missed until after the funeral. By then it will be too late.

Returning to Tutankhamun, I tie the wreath around the cobra and vulture at his brow. I bound the blue cornflowers, lotus petals and olive leaves myself. I even arranged the leaves so that the green fronts alternate with the silver backs. I lean my cheek against the cool metal of his. A few tears wend their way down my cheek, but these are tears of relief rather than sadness. It shall soon be over.

All the long trek through the desert, I am alert for the sight of white linen fluttering in my peripheral vision, hoping to catch a glimpse again of my mother, or to hear her voice, as I did at Nebetah's funeral. I worry when I do not, for what discomfited me then would lend me strength now.

I wait for the perfect moment. While Ay is performing the Opening of the Mouth, he is apart from any guards and it occurs to me that if I altered my plan ever so slightly, more than one person could die today. Yet, I do not wish to jeopardize Tutankhamun's passage, and so I remain still.

On the edge of my vision, I see that which I have been seeking and turn my head. As in the pit, this is no transitory glimpse. Mother stands to the side of the mourners, though they seem not to see her. Her smile emboldens me.

When the rite is complete and the Wesir-King drawn into the tomb, I leave the column of mourners. I take quick, deliberate steps, each one drawing me closer to my target. Ay, returning to his place among us, is the first to spot me. He points a finger and yells an order. The blood rushing in my ears drowns out his voice and I cannot hear the words. But soldiers emerge, moving in my direction.

I pick up my skirts and run. There will be no second chance. I reach Ay before the soldiers do and run full into him, knocking him down. He is unarmed and too weakened with age to fight back. I plant a foot on his neck and withdraw the blade from my sash.

He is shaking all over. From the smell of him, he has soiled himself.

"If you kill me, you will die, too. You cannot escape."

I glance to the soldiers, now closing in. I must choose. If I kill Ay, I will be taken, and my death will be long and slow.

"I shall suffer because of you no more." I jab the obsidian into the side of my neck and pull it across, under my throat. There is no pain. I have failed. I place a hand on my throat and feel a sticky warmth. I pull it away and examine the dripping redness. A river of red flows down the whiteness of my dress, pooling in the golden sand between my feet.

The world teeters. The soldiers are still coming toward me, though their movements slow down, as though time itself is running down. Voices echo, as if from afar. My knees buckle and I fall. The sun grows dim. Mutnedjmet will read the scroll and will grant my last wish. She must. If she does not, who will perform the ceremonies for a traitor? How shall I enter the Field of Reeds? Am I doomed to oblivion?

A sudden light eclipses the scene before me. Upon the river floats a wooden barge formed into the shape of a papyrus raft. On the deck stand four hooded figures. In front of the barge, on the shore, Mother waits, her arms outstretched.

Kemet (Egypt)

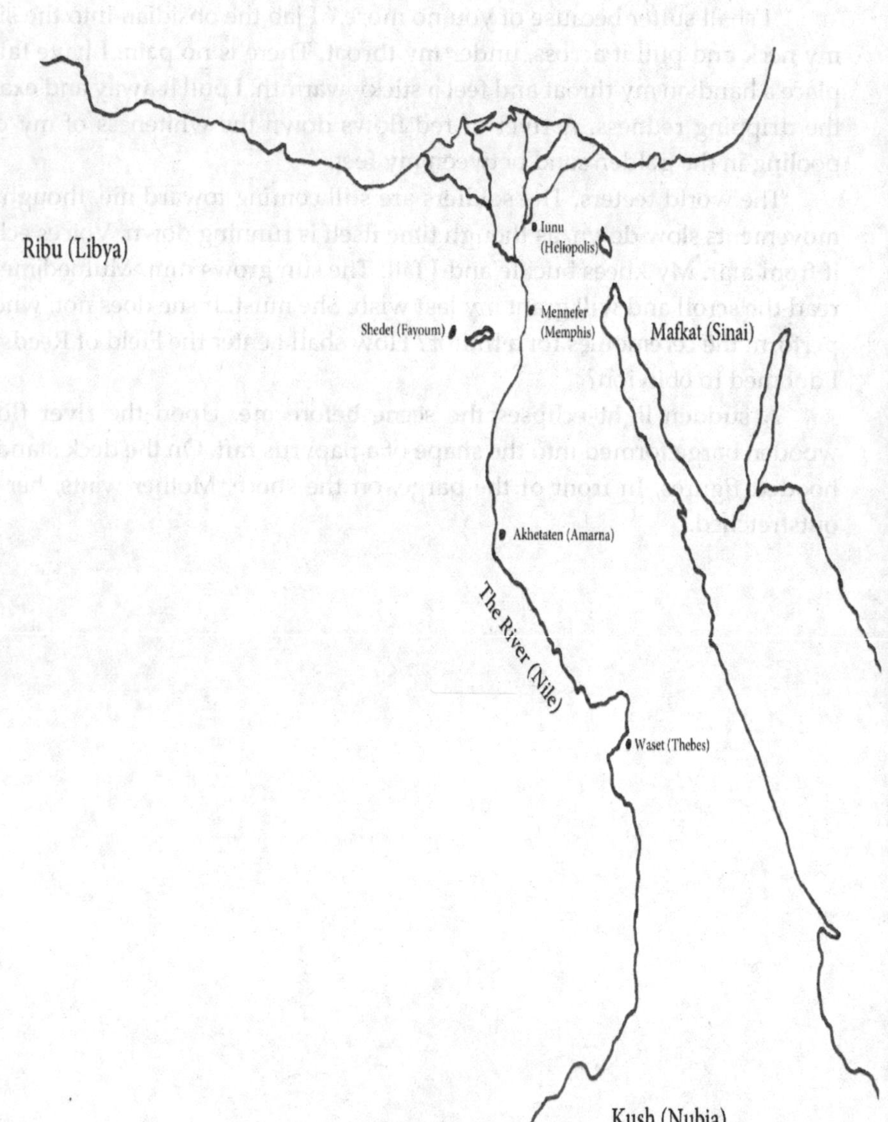

Ribu (Libya)
Iunu (Heliopolis)
Mennefer (Memphis)
Shedet (Fayoum)
Mafkat (Sinai)
Akhetaten (Amarna)
The River (Nile)
Waset (Thebes)
Kush (Nubia)

Characters

Royal Family

Ankhesenpaaten (an-kees-en-pa-AH-ten) – Great Royal Wife (original name)

Ankhesenamun (an-kees-en-a-MOON) – Great Royal Wife (new name)

Tutankhaten (too-tan-KAH-ten) – King (original name)

Tutankhamun (too-tan-kah-MOON) – King (new name)

Nebetah (ne-be-TA) – mother of the King

Mutnedjmet (moot-NEJ-met) – Ankhesenamun's aunt

Ay (eye) – Ankhesenamun's grandfather

Tey (tay) – Ay's wife

Neferneferuaten Nefertiti (nef-ur-nef-ur-oo-AH-ten nef-ur-TEE-tee) – Ankhesenamun's mother (deceased)

Meritaten (mur-ee-TAH-ten) – Ankhesenamun's sister (deceased)

Meketaten (me-ke-TAH-ten) – Ankhesenamun's sister (deceased)

Court Ladies

Henutmire (he-noot-mee-RAY)

Ast (ast)

Meryetre (mer-ee-ET-ray)

Tuya (TOO-yah)

Kawit (KAH-wit)

Officials/Others

Horemheb (HOR-em-heb) – army general

Nakhtmenu (nahkt-MEN-oo) – army general, nephew to Ay

Paramessu (pa-ra-MESS-you) – military man

Parannefer (pa-ra-NEF-er) – priest of Amun

Intef (IN-tef) – tutor

Menna (MEN-na) – sword master

Menwi (MEN-wee) – servant who aids with births

Kheruef (CARE-oo-ef) – Ast's paramour

Djehutymose (je-HOO-tee-mose) – former king

Ideally, historical fiction strikes a balance between telling a compelling story and historical accuracy. This balance can be tricky to achieve. When writing about such a distant past, there are few written records, and many of the sources we do have are, in effect, royal propaganda. That being said, I tried as much as possible to stick to valid archaeological theories when crafting this novel.

A Note on Terminology

Egypt's final royal dynasty, the Ptolemies (which culminated in Cleopatra VII) was actually Greek. While Egyptian culture continued undisturbed, the Greek rulers established sizable Greek populations within Egypt, most notably at Alexandria. This resulted in Hellenized names for many Egyptian gods and cities. Later Arab invasions further changed some of the geographical terms. It is largely these Greek and Arabic names that we are familiar with today.

For the sake of authenticity, I chose to use the Egyptian words for all proper nouns. In the accompanying maps I have given both the Egyptian name and the more familiar name.

You may be wondering why I used the term "King" instead of "Pharoah." The reason is that the term Pharoah did not originally mean King. In the beginning, it meant Royal House. Over the centuries, the meaning drifted until it came to refer to the ruler himself. This drift wasn't complete until the 19th dynasty, which began shortly after the events in this novel. The term was probably still in flux at the time of Tutankhamun.

Dates

Ancient Egyptians kept track of time by counting the regnal years of their kings, so that is what I have done. In order to give modern readers a sense of when events transpired, I have provided the equivalents in our calendar. These dates are approximate, so depending on which sources you consult, you will see variations.

The eagle-eyed among you who read the previous book in the series, The Feather of Ma'at, will notice that, although this book continues exactly where the previous one ended, there is a discrepancy of a few years. This is because, in reality, there was a king that reigned for a few years between Akhenaten and Tutankhamun. I left him out of the narrative for the sake of the plot of the previous novel. I have adjusted the dates in this book back to the accepted norm so that the dates in the next book will be accurate.

Nakhtmenu

Nakhtmenu was possibly a nephew of Ay, as I indicated in the novel. He was a high official during Ay's kingship and was promoted to heir, as Ay had no sons who might inherit the throne.

Paramessu

Paramessu was a general in the army under Tutankhamun and, later, under Horemheb, when he became king. After Horemheb died without an heir, Paramessu ascended to the throne, at which time he took the name Ramesses (no, he was not THE Ramesses, that was his grandson).

I can almost feel the ripples of shock caused by my description of Paramessu as a pale-skinned ginger. While we don't know what Paramessu looked like, we do know a great deal about his grandson, Ramesses II (quite possibly the Pharoah of the Exodus). The mummy of that Ramesses reveals that he had naturally red hair and carried genes that indicated pale skin.

At the time of Tutankhamun, Egypt was a superpower. As such, it had communities of foreigners throughout the country, many of whom had completely assimilated into Egyptian society. It is supposed the Ramesses originated in one of these communities, and were possibly of North African Berber origin (many of whom are still pale-skinned gingers today).

Horemheb

Horemheb was an army general and fulfilled other official roles during Tutankhamun's reign. He was not part of the royal family, nor was he born into the nobility. He probably came from Hutnesut, a smaller city in the north. Tutankhamun granted him the title of Hereditary Noble and possibly named him as his heir, though that is uncertain. What is certain is that Horemheb became king after the death of Ay and he may have legitimized his claim by marrying Ay's (possible) daughter, Mutnedjmet.

Depending on how your perspective, Horemheb was either the final king of the 18th Dynasty, due to his connection to Tutankhamun, or the first king of the 19th Dynasty, due to his elevation of the Ramesside family. But this is a strictly modern distinction. The Egyptians themselves viewed their history as one long, unbroken line of kings, whether they were related by blood or not.

Ay

Ay was quite probably related to the royal family through a sister, Tiye, who married Amenhotep III. He was possibly also the father of Nefertiti, though this is not certain.

He was incredibly ambitious. He must also have been incredibly patient. For decades, he served a succession of kings, rising a little more with each one. After the death of Tutankhamun, he finally grabbed his chance for the ultimate title by marrying his (possible) granddaughter, Ankkhesenamun, and becoming king himself.

It is likely there was some competition for the throne between Ay and Horemheb, but the transition after the death of Tutankhamun seems to have been peaceful. There may well have been an agreement between the two men that Ay would rule first, followed by Horemheb. Given Ay's advanced age at the time, Horemheb had little to lose by waiting a bit. Alas, if there were such an agreement, Ay later broke it by naming Nakhtmenu his heir.

Nebetah

A mummy found in a cache tomb in the Valley of the Kings, and known by archaeologists as the younger lady, has been genetically identified as the mother of Tutankhamun. She was likely a sister of his father (or possibly a first cousin after three generations of inbreeding). In the previous book, I identified Nebetah with this mummy and Tut's mother.

The younger lady has a nasty hole on the side of her face that occurred prior to death, but not long prior as it shows no signs of healing. It is consistent with a kick from a horse, though of course there are multiple other possible explanations (chariot accident or deliberate murder have been suggested).

Tutankhamun

"The boy king" is an epithet that has haunted Tutankhamun ever since his mummy was first examined in 1923. Yes, he was a child when he became king at around the age of ten. However, in Egyptian society, adulthood began by age fifteen. Therefore, when he died around the age of nineteen, he had been a full adult for some years and, therefore, was likely in full command of the country.

One of Tut's first, and most important, tasks was to restore the balance – the Ma'at – destroyed by his father, Akhenaten. To this end, he erected a stele which proclaimed this accomplishment. When I quote the stele in the novel, I am using Tutankhamun's own words.

CT scans of Tut's mummy show some physical challenges. He had a club foot, on the left, and also a cleft palate. There is also possible evidence of mild scoliosis. These results are not universally accepted. When Howard Carter attempted to remove the mummy from the sarcophagus, he found it quite stuck to it by ancient resins. He resorted to dismembering it in order to remove it. It's possible that some of the damage showing on CT scans is a result of this post-mortem damage and not any congenital deformity.

However, one hundred and thirty walking staffs were discovered in his tomb, most of which show signs of wear. As well, sandals were found that had an extra strap never seen on any other Egyptian sandals of the period. Archaeologists speculate this extra strap may have been needed to keep the sandals on Tut's feet. When you take the CT evidence together with the tomb evidence, it seems likely Tutankhamun had some degree of physical disability.

Also found in the tomb were six chariots. These may have been wholly symbolic – after all, the king was expected to defend the nation in war. Or, he may have found a way to use them.

His mummy also shows a thigh fracture that may have become infected and caused his death. One theory as to how this happened is a chariot accident. His mummy was also bathed in an unusually large amount of resins and his remains are in poor condition (even excluding damage done by Carter). One possible explanation is that he died far from home and his body had already begun to decompose before the mummification process could begin.

There is evidence that Tutankhamun's Egypt waged war in the Levant area. Whether or not he went there personally is up for debate, but I chose to put him there. The battle I depict at Qadesh was not THE battle of Qadesh – that happened about fifty years later under Ramesses II. But the area was disputed between the Egyptians and the Hittites well before then, and it is likely there were several battles of Qadesh.

Ankhesenamun

The third daughter of Akhenaten and Nefertiti, Ankhesenamun married her half-brother, Tutankhamun, to become queen of Egypt. She was about three or four years older than he was, so at the time of their rise to the throne, she was also still a child, though not too far from adulthood.

Little is known about the relationship of the two young monarchs with each other. There are numerous depictions of them as a happy couple, though images are not proof of anything. But given that, at the start of their reign at least, they would have been at the mercy of officials and advisors with their own agendas, I imagine the two of them becoming firm allies.

Tutankhamun died without an heir, but in his tomb the mummies of two stillborn infants were laid to rest with him. Both of these were born prematurely. DNA evidence shows Tutankhamun was their father. Since he had no other wives that we know of, it is likely Ankhesenamun was their mother. By this era, the royal family had endured about two hundred years of inbreeding and it is speculated this may be the reason Ankhesenamun and Tutankhamun were unable to produce a child (it may also be the reason for Tutankhamun's disability, if indeed he had one).

The letters from Ankhesenamun were found in the archives of the Hatti (known to us as the Hittites) and in the novel I use her words. An Egyptian queen wrote to the Hittite king asking him to send her one of his sons so she could marry him and make him king of Egypt. The king at first did not believe her. Eventually he sent his son, who was murdered on his way to Egypt. Traditionally, this queen has been thought to be Ankhesenamun, though some think it may have been her mother, Nefertiti. There is also speculation that this was propaganda invented by the Hittite king and the events never happened at all.

Neither Ankhesenamun's tomb nor her mummy have been found. After Tut's death, it seems she did marry her (possible) grandfather, Ay, thereby making him king. She disappears from the historic record immediately after and it is supposed that she died.

Acknowledgments

Writing is largely a solitary act, but a book is a collaboration.

To Sue Reynolds and James Dewar – thank you for continuing to do the work that keeps my procrastinating ass in the chair. Neither snow nor rain nor global pandemics kept you from your chosen vocation, which means I was able to push through with mine as well.

Thanks also to Ruth Walker, the first editor who took on my manuscript. Your comments were both constructive and thorough, and without your input my book would not have been ready to pitch to agents and publishers.

To my oldest daughter, Willow – thank you for so often herding the younger children so I can write undisturbed.

Last, but definitely not least, to all the staff at Liminal Books for persisting with me through a second book. Abby Macenka, cofounder, Siân Hyleg, author services coordinator, Penny Dowden, editor, Cherie Fox, graphic designer. THANK YOU!!

Lisa Llamrei was born and raised in the Toronto area. She studied languages at York University. At various times, she has been an actor, professional belly dancer, holistic nutritionist and entrepreneur. She currently lives north of Toronto with her family.